"You got a ... these days I'll ...

"Is that a threat, Sheriff? I understand you and your deputies shot down eleven men and one woman in the past four months."

"Line of duty. They were all low-class riffraff."

"Like the preacher, Fowler? That kind of riffraff?"

The sheriff quivered with rage.

"What's the matter, Sheriff? Isn't Pistol Pete here to back up your hand anymore?"

The sheriff roared in fury and charged McCoy. The big man waited until the last second, spun aside and slammed his fist down on the sheriff's neck as he careened past. Sheriff Johnson kept right on going, rammed into a bar chair, tipped over a table and rolled on his back.

"Johnson, you're all through in this town," Spur said. "Pull off that badge right now, and ride just as far and as fast as you can before the good people of this town rise up and shoot you so full of holes they'll use you for a drain gauge."

PORTLAND PUSSYCAT

Spur moved over to the edge of the wall. He removed his hat with his left hand, peered into the lobby and whipped back to safety.

The image crystallized in his brain. A gunman held a woman by her throat. She knelt, looking pleadingly up at the man as he aimed at her.

"Say good-bye, girl!"

Spur lunged past the wall and peeled off a shot, instantly lining up his first target. The second man turned as his partner reeled. Spur's hogleg sounded again.

Both men went down as he paused, staring at them. Blue smoke filled the air and the echoes of the twin explosions bounced around in the big building for several seonds. Neither gunman moved....

Other Spur Double Editions:

S P U R   D O U B L E :

WYOMING
WENCH

PORTLAND
PUSSYCAT

DIRK FLETCHER

LEISURE BOOKS NEW YORK CITY

A LEISURE BOOK®

September 2007

Published by

Dorchester Publishing Co., Inc.
200 Madison Avenue
New York, NY 10016

ISBN 10: 0-8439-3699-1
ISBN 13: 978-0-8439-3699-5

Visit us on the web at www.dorchesterpub.com.

CHAPTER ONE

May 14, 1872

(Yellowstone National Park was set aside as a national preserve by Congress in 1872. U. S. Grant was President and Hamilton Fish of New York was his Secretary of State. The adding machine which could print totals and subtotals was patented by E. D. Barbour in Boston. The U.S. census for 1870 showed 38,558,371 people in the nation. This was a seven million increase over 1860 or almost 18%. James Fisk and Jay Gould's corrupt Erie Ring collapsed. The United States Congress abolished the federal income tax. The Post Office Department became an executive

department of government. Popular Science Monthly *was published for the first time. The first Catholic Presidential candidate, Charles O'Connor, was nominated. Susan B. Anthony was arrested for attempting to vote in New York. On November 6, 1872 President Grant was reelected.)*

Spur McCoy was not putting up much of a fight. He gave a pair of half-hearted swings, then let a telegraph round house right clip his jaw and spin him around. He should get a medal for acting, he thought, as he fell into the dust of an alley next to the stagecoach station in the northern Wyoming crossroads cowtown called Elk Creek.

"Stay down, asshole!" the big man over Spur roared. "I'm bruising my knuckles and you're not worth it." The man talking was Tyler Johnson, Sheriff of River Bend County. Johnson stood over McCoy, fists still clenched.

"I run this county, asshole! I don't like your looks and want you out of here on the next stage. Problem is, it don't come for a week. So you peddle your knives and keep your big nose out of county business. Otherwise I'll drag you out of town behind my horse until you're skinned alive." He kicked Spur in the side. "You get the message?"

Spur looked up, he was shaking, his head bobbing. "Yes, sir. I am certain that I understand your directions. I will do my utmost, Mr. Sheriff, to handle myself with the required decorum."

"Christ, an *over-educated* asshole! I don't even know what he's saying." Sheriff Johnson took one long look at him, went back to the open knife sample case in the dirt and picked out a six-inch sheath knife. "I'll take this here blade as a gift from you, drummer. Any complaints?"

"Absolutely none, sir. It is my privilege to serve you and to be in your remarkable little town."

"Yeah, right. One week. Remember that." The sheriff turned and walked into the darkening street. Lights came on in buildings. Spur sat up in the dust. He had rolled with most of the punches, but one had taken a gash out of his cheek. He'd get that looked at as soon as he got a hotel room.

He started to rise when a door opened in the building behind him and two women rushed out. One knelt in the dust beside him and touched a handkerchief to his cheek.

"You're hurt. We'll help you. Come inside here and I'll fix up that cheek in no time, give you a drink and get you cleaned up."

Spur took his hat which the other woman had picked up. The beat-up hat didn't match his black suit. It was a low-crowned light brown, with a wide brim and a row of Mexican silver centavos pieces around the band.

"Not necessary, ma'am. I'm not hurt."

"You *are* hurt, and bleeding. Not a gracious way to greet a stranger. Our sheriff is crude and overbearing. I won't take no for an answer."

Spur looked closer at her through the shadows. She wore a calico print dress buttoned tight to her chin. Shoulder length blonde hair had been curled and framed a round face with high cheekbones and greenish eyes. He couldn't see much else before the women took his arms and walked him into the building. The smaller woman went back for his sample case and lugged it into the room, then brought in his carpetbag. The girl with green eyes turned up the lamp on a dresser. He saw at once that it was a bedroom, perhaps in one of the two hotels in town—he wasn't sure. The other girl was gone, the door closed.

In the light he saw the concern on the blonde woman's face as she washed his cheek and applied some ointment to the cut. It stung.

She sat beside him on the bed and began opening the buttons on the top of her dress.

"I'm terribly sorry the sheriff gave you such an unpleasant impression of our town. It really isn't that bad. We have some fine people here and they are interested in seeing that you stay around, and that you are treated right."

Spur looked at her, fascinated. The buttons were coming open, one by one, proving that she was a full-busted woman on the plump side. She smiled.

"Heard you tell the sheriff your name was Spur McCoy. That's a good name. Spur, this dress is just so tight I have to loosen it. I hope you don't mind."

"Don't mind at all, ma'am."

"Good," she said and leaned in and kissed his lips full and hard. Her tongue brushed at them until he opened them for her. Her tongue darted into his mouth and she gave a little sigh as her arms came around him.

She didn't let the kiss end as she pulled him down on top of her on the big bed. Her legs spread apart so he lay fully on her and could feel the heat of her body through the clothes. One of her hands worked between them and massaged the growing bulge at his crotch. Her other arm crooked around his neck, pinning his mouth to hers.

She moaned softly with anticipation and let go of his neck. He leaned up and looked at her smiling face.

"Oh yes! You feel so good lying on me this way. I can feel your big thing down there pushing against me! My name is Jodi, and I don't never like to see a big hunk of new man like you come to town and get run plumb out before I get a chance or two at him." She frowned. "Oh, lordy, I hope you don't mind!"

Spur kissed her soft lips twice, then quickly twice more and her nose once.

"Why the fuck should I mind, Jodi?"

"Great! If there is one thing I really love it is a quick one that you don't expect. You know what I mean? Just bumping into somebody, and liking him and trying to get my dress open and letting him look at my titties quick."

Spur helped her, undoing the rest of the buttons to her waist, then lifting the lacy chemise.

"My god! At last I've found the Rocky Mountains!"

She laughed. "You are so nice! But wait until I

sit up and let them hang down to you."

Spur had to use one hand to hold himself up. With the other he caressed her big breasts. The areolas were large and dark brownish red, and her nipples by now were extended and bloated with hot blood. He bent and kissed one and felt her hips pumping hard at him.

"Oh, damn!" She wailed. "I'm climaxing already! Oh, god. Oh, shit but that is good! Great. Great. Great!" Her voice rose in a wailing tribute to kisses and lying on your back and getting fondled. Her hips beat a steady tattoo on his crotch.

Her hands pushed him to one side and tore at his fly, pulling the buttons open, working her hand inside until she closed around his erection. She gasped and gave one final shudder and went limp.

Before he could move away she was alert again. She pulled his penis from his pants and crooned to it.

"So beautiful. So marvelous! The best part of any man! And he's so huge! I just can't imagine anything that big finding room inside me . . . anywhere!" She bent and kissed the purple head, saw it jerk and laughed. "There's going to be a lot more of that, big guy. Just wait until we both get our clothes off."

She sat back and began working out of her dress, then the chemise and at last her drawers of white cotton that extended to her knee. Spur undressed as she did, sliding out of his boots, then out of the cheap black suit he had bought to match his disguise as a salesman.

"You like big tits?" she asked Spur. "Big tits I got, maybe not a lot of brains, but in the tits department I win." She sat straighter and pushed her shoulders back, forcing her breasts forward until they hung like twin peaks, sagging only slightly from their size.

"This must be heaven," Spur said, bending to attend to them. He kissed each nipple, then worked a trail of kisses and tongue licks around each mount back to the peak. He was leaning in to reach her when her hand found his crotch.

"Christ, what a fucking fence post!" Jodi whispered. "No way that is going to fit either one of my hot holes."

"We can always try him for size," Spur suggested.

She pumped him six times. "If you don't, I'll chew him right down to the roots!"

Spur suddenly froze. He pulled her face up to look at him.

"Where is that other girl?"

"Why, ain't I enough for you? You need *two* cunts?"

"Who is she?"

"My sister. She's the shy one. We live here together. Why you worried about her?"

"She's not going to get the sheriff and bring him back and give him an excuse for hanging me?"

Jodi laughed. "Christ, no! She's out in the other room wondering what we're doing. And in another ten minutes she'll find her favorite candle and push it up her twat and candle fuck herself to death. Don't worry about her. She's a little weird but harmless. Me, I'm just a clerk at the town's only good store. Hey, don't worry. This is the last place Sheriff Johnson would come looking for you. Believe me. Little sister Rebecca ain't going to the sheriff. We gonna talk about her all night?''

Spur showed her that they weren't. He lay on his back and pulled her on top of him. She dangled one breast after the other into his mouth. She fastened one hand on his crotch, massaging his balls tenderly, pumping him a half dozen times to keep on the edge.

She began trembling again. She wailed softly, got on her knees over him and lifted his sword straight up and lowered her scabbard around him until they were locked together.

"Oh, Christ, that *is* fine!" she crooned. "Damn, I've never been touched that deep before. You come half way out of my throat, I swear."

She shivered and then fell forward and rode him like a bucking bronco, bouncing and twisting, churning and turning him, putting more pressure and action on his lance than he had known for months.

He was gasping after the first twenty seconds. He saw sweat pop out on her forehead as she provided the motion, bucking and fucking him like a talented artist. He knew he was moving quickly down the path now. She was moaning and gasping with each lunge and twist.

Her hands were planted on his shoulders, then she dropped them to the bed beside him and the added thrust into her brought a soft scream of

14

need, a demand for the ultimate fulfillment. She wailed again and her motions increased in speed and depth until they slammed together at the bottom of her stroke, sending shivers through their bodies.

Again and again and again they crushed their pelvic bones together until she was trembling and shrieking so violently that she couldn't maintain the riding motion.

She climaxed again and again, and Spur found himself over the edge, riding down the trail with only one ending. He was pounding upward now, unable to lie still when she ceased her motion, needing the surge of the pumping action to reach his glory land.

Sweat drenched both their bodies, their mouths hung open, gasping for air as Spur exploded and blasted his seed upward into her throbbing cavity.

She collapsed on top of him and they lay panting, sweat streaming off her body onto his. Neither could move. He heard the door open and wished he had the gun from his carpetbag. He didn't.

In the soft light of the lamp he saw the girl come in the door. She was the same one he had seen before, but now she wore a cotton flannel nightgown. She stared at the two bodies, moved on hand under the gown to her crotch and walked up beside the bed. She didn't look Spur in the eye. She watched for several minutes and he could see her hand moving. She gasped once, turned and went out of the room and closed the door.

Jodi sighed and pushed up so she could focus on Spur's face.

"That was my little sister, Rebecca. She's just curious."

"She's what twenty, twenty-one?"

"She twenty-two and I'm twenty-four and I'm still a virgin."

They both laughed.

"Rebecca has never been with a man?"

"True. No fucky-Becky. That's why she's curious. You'll have to show her what it's all about one of these nights, but not tonight. You're all mine."

She snuggled against him and Spur realized he had found a good information source. He could get started on his assignment tonight, after they settled down a little.

Spur McCoy was a U.S. Secret Service Agent. He stood 6-2, weighed 200 pounds, was 32 years old and had a full moustache, medium mutton chop sideburns that almost met his moustache, and a full head of brownish red hair.

He was an excellent horseman, a crack shot with derringer, six-gun and rifle, and kept in top physical shape at all times. He was an expert at hand to hand fighting as well as with knives and the staff.

He had come to this small Wyoming town in response to a Territorial representative to Congress who had complained about a sheriff in a northern county who had gone wild and set up his own little kingdom. Spur received the report through his boss, General William D. Halleck.

His job was to investigate the problem, and if practical, put an end to it. If that was not possible he was to call on troops from the nearest military post and settle the matter.

Usually he worked undercover, but this was so far away from the mainstream of western life, he figured that no one would have heard of Spur McCoy.

There was only one stage through town a week. He wanted to come in as low key as possible, and it was well he had. Anything else would have meant a shootout in the main street when he arrived. He figured he should be able to get a lot of good local information about the sheriff and his activities from Jodi. At least he had all night to work on it.

"You hungry?" Jodi said, sitting up, letting her fine breasts swing from side to side. She laughed. "Not these goodies, real food. Becky will be getting supper for us. She knows you will be hungry after your workout."

"Hungry—yes. First tell me about this sheriff. How does he expect anyone to stay in town when he meets them the way he did me?"

"You was big and looked able. So you was a threat to him. Little guys he don't work over so hard. He had a mean eye for you minute you lit from the rig."

"Does he own the whole town?"

"Mostly. We got a newspaper that tries to get the town to move, to get better. Little guy runs it. His name is Les Van Dyke. Been here three or four months. Bought the place sight unseen from the other publisher who Sheriff Johnson ran out of town."

She jumped up, found her clothes and began dressing.

"Supper gonna be ready soon. You better get your pants on. Not that I'd mind you eating bare-assed. But Becky would be embarrassed."

He dressed. "The sheriff have everyone in town under his thumb? Isn't there anyone fighting him?"

"Yeah, a few, but they don't advertise. Biggest one right out in the open I guess is the Circle K. Big spread outside of town north called the Circle K run by Hans Klanhouser. He usually runs about ten thousand head and has from twenty to thirty hands, most of the time. Old Hans has more guns than the sheriff does if it comes to a range war."

"You're just full of good news."

She paused as she smoothed the chemise down over her breasts. "Why you so interested?"

"How can I sell my knives if this sheriff won't let me stay in town more than a week? I need more time than that to cover every business, every ranch, and every house in town. That's how I make my living."

"Oh, well, we'll buy something, you can bet on that. If the other samples are as good as the ones I saw in the case. I won't make any order though until morning, when I can figure out if the samples are good enough."

He swatted her on the bottom. She grinned and pushed her round cheeks out for him to swat again. He did and she nodded and started to lift her skirts.

"Supper's ready." Becky called from the other side of the door.

Spur relaxed. He had a start on the assignment. He had found a playmate and now he was going to get supper. He opened the door for Jodi and they walked into the living room and kitchen of the small flat. A girl stood near the wood stove on the cooking side of the room. When she turned she glared at Spur and in her hand was a deadly little Adams pocket revolver with its ugly .32 caliber muzzle aimed directly at his chest!

CHAPTER TWO

Jodi froze for a second when she saw the gun, then she smiled.

"Well, Princess Rebecca, what have you fixed us for dinner, something just fine, I bet."

Spur took Jodi's lead. He grinned, nodded.

"Hi, Princess. Jodi tells me you're the best cook this side of the Mississippi! I'm Spur, you helped me out there in the alley when Sheriff Johnson bashed me. I just want to thank you a lot for helping me, Rebecca. Not everyone would come out there and help a stranger that way. I appreciate it."

The wild look in her eyes faded. The angry, dangerous expression melted from her face and her right hand slowly lowered the Adams. She was dressed the same way she had been in the alley, simple print, high around the throat, full skirt sweeping the floor.

Rebecca cocked her head to the side, blinked, and the start of a smile flickered across her face. It was gone, then came back and she put the pistol in a pocket somewhere in the big skirt. She smiled, bobbed in a try at a curtsy. She was prettier than her sister. Rebecca laughed and pointed at the big kettle on the stove.

"Stew, with a lot of vegetables and potatoes but not much meat, mostly left over rabbit from when I went hunting."

Jodi unfroze from her position and went to the stove.

"I'll help. You talk with our guest," Jodi said.

A few moments later they sat at the table. The stew was good and the bread thick and light. There was coffee and crabapple jelly. For dessert they had deep dish apple pie.

Spur sat back and reached for Rebecca's hand. She pulled it back.

"Princess, that was the best meal I've had in a long time. You should be cooking at the hotel or open a restaurant of your own somewhere."

"Oh, Mr. McCoy!" She turned, not able to hide her blush.

"Really, Rebecca," Jodi said. "It was a fine dinner. Thank you. Now, Mr. McCoy and I have to talk business. You understand, don't you,

Princess?"

"Yes." She didn't turn back.

Spur and Jodi went to the bedroom where she kissed him passionately.

"Eating always makes me feel sexy," she said.

"First, business," Spur said.

"Business?"

"Business. Who told you to watch for me at the stage? I saw you there when I got off."

She sighed, shook her head. "He said I wasn't supposed to tell anyone." Then she grinned. "But I guess that doesn't include you. His name is Lester Van Dyke. He runs the newspaper here. But you already knew that."

Spur relaxed. "Good. Now we're getting somewhere. What do you know about all this?"

"Only that Les complained to somebody and they told someone else and here you are. Federal lawman of some kind."

"And Sheriff Johnson always brings his new arrivals down this alley to beat them up?"

"Something like that." She unbuttoned the top of her dress, and he saw that she had nothing under it.

"That's a great pose, Jodi, but later. I have to see this Van Dyke as soon as possible. Where does he live?"

"Over the newspaper print shop."

"I'll find it." Spur reached for his hat, then cupped one of her big breasts through the open dress, bent and kissed it. "Delicious." He straightened and kissed her lips. "Now, what about Princess Rebecca?"

"Well . . . she has a few problems. But as far as I know she's been good as can be lately. I take care of her. She doesn't go out much, and never without me."

"How did it happen, her problem?"

"Our father was over-protective, over everything. Our mother died when Princess was born, and by the time she was ten, Pa was messing around with us. He'd get horny and need some and try, but I was twelve or thirteen and I'd tell him how bad he was and talk him out of it. I never had no idea he was messing with Rebecca.

"She never told me. I found out about that afterward. For three months he was having intercourse with her almost every night. She just kind of died inside. Then one night I caught them, and I hit Pa with a chair and ran him out of the house. I told Becky how ugly and evil it was and I guess I scared her. The next day she was sick and couldn't go to school and Pa came home early.

"I found them when I got back from school. We wasn't in this town then. The sheriff said Princess had been raped, so he knew. He didn't tell no one else but me. She killed Pa with a butcher knife when he was in her they figured. Then she pushed him off and kept stabbing and cutting and slashing. It was the most terrible thing I've ever seen. Blood all over the room, and it was hard to tell who he was. Wasn't nothing left between his legs at all.

"She's never been right since then. I wanted you to know."

"Thanks. Now, I better get a hotel room so the

sheriff can see me, and then I'll look up Van Dyke."

"You can stay here!"

"Then the sheriff would get curious. I better be more public." He bent and kissed one breast that peeked out of her dress. "I can't stay here, but I can spend some interesting nights here. Is there another entrance besides the alley?"

"No, I thought it would be safer this way for Princess."

He kissed her and took his gear out the alley door.

A half hour later he had registered in the Hotel Hartford, a rundown two-storey affair with twenty rooms and only six of them full. This was not a big tourist town.

He had little to unpack. For a moment he wasn't sure what to do with the six-gun and gun-belt, then he lifted the mattress and put them at the foot on top of the springs. A good search would find them, but he doubted if the sheriff was that interested in him just yet. Later he would be sleeping somewhere else. McCoy put a hideout derringer in his pocket. He left his suit on and walked into the crisp Wyoming night. The two saloons and gambling palaces in town were open and roaring.

He found the print shop and home of the *Wyoming Courier* in a small two-storey frame building that still had lights on. Spur tried the front door and found it unlocked. Inside he smelled that unique perfume of printers' ink mixed with newsprint that has a flavor like no other. To one side sat a desk and in front of it there was a long counter with banded sheafs of back issues of the paper. A man with a green eye-shade looked up, nodded, and waved Spur into the back room.

A press squatted in the middle of the floor with the printer's trade essentials grouped around it: boxes of flat paper, cases of type, cans of ink, and stacks of back records and old issues.

"Van Dyke?" Spur asked.

"Yes, did anyone see you come in?"

"I don't know. The sheriff didn't seem overly interested in me."

"Not after knocking you down. I saw you get off the stage."

"Like my performance?"

"Good enough so far. Do you know a general by the name of William D.?"

"Halleck is the last name of my boss. Was that the agreed on code and countersign?"

"Yes. Johnson will kill you if he knows who you are."

"How have you lasted so long here, Van Dyke?"

"I pretend to be a coward too. I print what he wants me to, but I'm about to change all that now that you're here."

"Don't be in a rush. Who can help us besides the Circle K?"

"Nobody. The banker in town is Otto Toller. He's weak, soft, and has his life's work and savings invested in this town. He wants to help us but he won't, he's too afraid."

Van Dyke sat down on a box of paper. "Hell, McCoy. I'm afraid too. Every dime I own is tied up in this paper. I paid fifteen hundred dollars for it, sight unseen, and without knowing a thing about the political situation. Now I'm in the middle of a county where the sheriff has just elevated himself to King and we all bow and scrape. That goes against my nature."

Van Dyke was five feet four inches tall, and slender. He had quick hands, a fertile and facile mind, and an enormous amount of drive and energy. He took off his spectacles and pinched his nose, then rubbed his forehead.

"Damned headache again." He looked up, small dark eyes evaluating McCoy. Van Dyke had a lean, whisker darkened jaw, a full moustache and dark hair that needed cutting. "What is your plan to put Sheriff Johnson in jail where he belongs?"

"I don't have one. I'm just trying to get my feet on the ground and find out what is going on. In jail? You have evidence that can convict him of a felony?"

"I can get it, plenty of it, when we have a safe situation for witnesses in this town. That won't be until after the sheriff is in jail or dead and his gunslinging deputies are jailed, shot or run out of town."

"He has it that tight?"

"He does. The only other man I would say just might help us is Nehemiah Hardy. Runs Hardy's Emporium. Biggest store in town and a damn fine man. He's level headed, a square shooter, and a man I'd bank on if I needed help in a rush. But remember, he has a big investment here, too."

"I'll have a talk with him. Now, specifics. Is there one wide open case that we can work on to build up evidence of wrongdoing and hang it on Johnson? We'll need signed affidavits, hard evidence that can be backed up in court."

"Christ, there are so many."

"Evidence, we need hard, irrefutable evidence. Have there been any killings?"

Van Dyke laughed. "I've been here three months, and I have records showing that twelve men and one woman have been shot down in the streets. All by the sheriff or his deputies, and all 'in the line of duty'. How can you fight that?"

"We need just one flagrant case, one with witnesses that can prove the dead man was not armed, did not make any threatening moves, and show that the sheriff had serious, substantial and monetary ulterior motives for the killing."

"Like the county commissioner who tried to get Johnson recalled as sheriff. It would have worked, because women have the vote here, have ever since we became a territory back in sixty-eight. But the county commissioner wound up 'accidentally' dying in a fire that burned down his blacksmith and saddle shop. Happened late at night and nobody found him until the next morning. The sheriff certified it as an accidental death."

"This Sheriff Johnson covers his tracks?"

"Damn good. And he has three gunslingers he calls his deputies. I swear I had a wanted poster on one of them. But somehow it turned up missing from my stack."

"Hey, anybody home?" A booming voice came from the front of the office.

"I know that voice. Stay back here out of sight." Van Dyke went through the draped door into the office. Spur edged up to the fabric and looked through a crack along one side.

"Saw your lights on, thought I would check," the big man leaning over the counter said. He wore a leather vest with a silver star pinned to it.

Spur stared at the face. He had seen it before. Where?

"Just closing up. Need anything special?"

"Matter of fact, the sheriff gave me something for you. A guest editorial. Wants you to run it on the front page in your next issue. He's sure you'll cooperate. This is an important issue that affects the public safety." He put a sheaf of papers on the counter. "Here is it, not too long, but important. You take good care of it now, y'hear?" The man turned and headed out the door.

That was when Spur saw the scar down the deputy's right cheek. A three-inch curved scar. Spur tensed. He knew the man and he was positive the guy would recognize him. The deputy was Pete, Pistol Pete Bovert. Spur had helped put him away for ten years not too long ago in Arizona on a charge of multiple murder and rape.

Van Dyke went into the back. He made sure the deputy had left before he waved the pages of paper in an angry gesture.

"See what I mean? The man is smart, he

doesn't want to close me down, he wants to use me to cement his position. I'll be damned if I'm going to do it anymore!"

CHAPTER THREE

"Easy," Spur McCoy said. "I know you've been wanting to throw it in their faces, but not all at once. Fact is I know that deputy. Last time I saw him I was testifying against him in Yuma. He got five to ten at the Yuma Territorial prison. I'm going to have to work slow and careful on this and I want you with me, not dead in a gully somewhere."

"Goddamnit!" Les Van Dyke said, slapping his hand down on the box of newsprint. "I'm dying a little every day I have to knuckle under to these vermin. What was this guy's name when he went to prison?''

"Pete Bovert. The gang called him Pistol Pete because he always wore two of them and used them at the slightest excuse."

"Sounds familiar. Here they call him Pistol Pete, too, but his last name is Cody. Trying to sound Western I guess. He must have been the one I saw on the wanted poster."

"Where does this guy Hardy live? I need to talk to him, see what he knows, what he can do."

"I'll close up here and walk you over there and introduce you. He's a good man, but a little cautious. Hell, I'd be cautious too. He must have a twenty thousand dollar investment in this town."

Ten minutes later the men stood in the shadows in back of the Hardy house. Spur hadn't been inside, there was no way he could be tied to Hardy.

Nehemiah Hardy was a tall, slender man, with a gaunt, stubbled face, deep set eyes and a hawk nose. Fringes of black hair showed over his ears and around the back of his head. His eyes were quick and brown, and his handshake firm.

"Mr. McCoy, pleased to meet you."

"I'm glad. You might not be so happy once Les and I have had this little talk. I hope we can be friends, and work closely together. This is a problem for the whole county, and the leaders of the community must help."

"Well now, this sounds serious. Let me get a pint of cheer from the cellar and we can talk this over."

A half hour later Hardy shook his head. "Men, I appreciate you coming over, but it just won't work. Johnson has got everybody so tied in knots they don't know how to spit 'cept up wind. Nope, I'd say the only way to take care of the situation is like we used to in the army. When you got a sergeant who kept getting troops killed without cause, you just took care of him in the next little skirmish. Killed in the line of duty and that was it.

"Way I look at it, gents, the only way we can solve this here probelm is to put a bullet in fancy Mr. Sheriff Johnson and then run his riff-raff deputies out of the state."

"The West is coming of age, Mr. Hardy," Spur said. "We must uphold the law, use the law to take care of people like Sheriff Johnson. Which is precisely what we are going to do."

"Good luck. Hope it works." He paused. "Course now, you need a good rifle, I got some in stock, plenty of rounds. You just let me know. Got me some new Spencer seven shot repeaters, .52 caliber rim fire. Nice piece."

"I'll certainly keep that in mind, Mr. Hardy. Thanks for talking to us. This is all confidential, you understand."

They shook hands and Spur and Van Dyke headed back toward the newspaper office.

Rebecca sat in the main room of their small quarters and stared at the cross stitch design she worked on. Jodi was over at a "friend's" house. Rebecca was sure what Jodi was doing, but she would not think about that. Things like that should not be thought of by a good girl!

She needed to take a walk. It had been almost a month since she had taken a walk. This was a good time to do it since Jodi said she would not be home before midnight and told Rebecca not to wait up for her.

Rebecca told her that the book, the magazine and the cross stitch would be quite enough to keep her busy all evening. She smiled. Jodi didn't know everything.

She stood in front of the mirror by the door and studied her face. Yes, pretty, and her hair would be better when she combed it. Quickly she put on her best dress, and one with red and white figures on it. It was a little tight for her, but she managed to get the buttons over her breasts fastened. Yes, she looked nice.

She filled the pocket she had sewn in the long skirt of the dress as she usually did. Then she stood at the door leading into the alley until she saw someone stumble in and walk her way. Quickly she left the door and closed it. She walked slowly toward the figure who had lurched and stumbled forward. It was dark in the alley, but the moon had grown to half a round and smiled down on the hard packed earth.

Rebecca moved to the other side of the alley so she would meet the man who came toward her. She had never sen him before, and she knew he had been drinking. Fine, it didn't matter. He was a man, like the one she had seen today with his clothes all off lying under her sister who also was naked.

Naked! A dirty word! She smiled. Dirty word!

The man stopped when he saw her coming. He looked up and she smiled. He was about thirty, maybe thirty-five, half drunk, taking a short-cut home. He didn't wear a gun, which was better. His brown hair spilled down over his forehead, and he brushed it back showing a two-day beard stubble and curious eyes.

"Well now, lookee here!"

"Hello, are you lonely?" Rebecca asked. She walked up until she could touch him and brushed her hand along his cheek. "You look lonely. Would you like me to be nice to you?"

"Keeereist, I must be drunk. I'm imagining you."

She caught his hand and put it on her breast. "No, you're not imagining it. I'm here. Let's sit down on those boxes over there and talk. I like your hand there. Does it feel good?"

"Oh, man, so pretty, and me drunk. Never too drunk for a good woman."

"Over here, and sit down. It's easier that way."

She led him to a place in the alley where one store was shorter than the rest and there was a twenty foot jog to its back door. A big packing crate lay there and she sat on it and waited for him to sit beside her.

Rebecca took his hand and put in on her breasts again, then she began unbuttoning the fasteners at her throat. A minute later he kissed her cheek, and he helped undo the buttons. He chuckled softly.

"Goddamn you are pretty! And you got big tits! My woman got little nubs. I'm feeling good. Gonna get it hard and everything! Damn, what a lucky night. Won twenty dollars at poker and now a beautiful fucking girl!"

The buttons were open to her breasts. He reached inside and caught her big orb. She wore no undergarments. Her breast popped out of the dress and he moaned in delight and bent to kiss it.

Rebecca had taken the butcher knife from the pocket she had made in her skirt. Using her right hand and gripping the knife like a club, with the point upward, she swung her right hand with all her might, aiming the tip of the twelve-inch blade for his stomach. The power of her swing drove the sharp blade through the man's thin shirt. The anger created the drive that plunged the knife into his belly just under the rib cage and sliced upward, penetrating his lung, then stabbing into his heart.

He rolled his eyes up at her in deadly surprise, before he collapsed away from her and rolled off the box. He lay on his back. He didn't move. Just like Pa. Good! He wouldn't hurt any more young girls. For a moment the man's face became that of her father.

Calmly she bent and pulled the knife from his chest, wiped the blood on his shirt until she was sure the knife was clean, then she put it safely in her skirt pocket and walked back to the unlocked door of her rooms, and slipped inside.

Rebecca washed the butcher knife carefully, dried it, and replaced it in the rack in the kitchen.

She was still awake and reading a book of poems by Edgar Allen Poe when Jodi came in. Her sister was used to Rebecca staying up until she got home, and she thought nothing of it. They talked about the poems and stories. Rebecca was not sure if she liked the *Cask of Amontillado* best of *The Tell Tale Heart.*

Jodi shrugged. Both of them were strange, vengeance-filled and bloodthirsty. But then Rebecca could be a little strange at times.

Back in the hotel room, Spur worked on his next course of action. He decided to give up on the knife selling guise. The deputy who knew him had ruined that plan. The first time Pistol Pete saw Spur he would reach for his gun. So Spur could get out of his city clothes and back to his jeans, shirt and brown vest.

He hadn't thought about the rancher yet. He could be a valuable ally if it came to a shootout. But Spur figured he should be able to handle this one without that kind of backing. His first project was to select one of the killings the sheriff himself had done, and start getting background on the man killed, and try to find some evidence of gain by the sheriff from the death.

He had to keep it as legal as he could and for as long as he could. Of course, if the other guys started shooting, he was more than ready to trade hot lead with them.

Spur got out his .44, a Remington New Model army six-gun he had picked up recently and found it balanced well for his kind of shooting. It had an eight inch barrel, five rifling grooves, an iron blade front sight and rear groove. It was blued, but worn some now and the varnished walnut grips were smooth. He cleaned the Remington, oiled it and loaded in five rounds, leaving the chamber under the hammer empty for safety's sake.

It was just after eight o'clock that Spur heard a knock on his door. He wasn't expecting company. In one fluid motion he picked up the .44, cocked the hammer with his thumb and flattened himself against the wall beside the knob side of the door.

"Yes, who is it?"

"A friend," a woman's voice said softly. Jodi? She wouldn't take that kind of chance. Curious, he unlocked the door and opened it slowly. No one came in.

He edged his eye around the door jamb and saw a girl of about seventeen standing in the hall. She wore a white blouse, long blue skirt and had black hair and dark eyes. She grinned at him and her eyes locked on his.

"Spur McCoy?" she asked, her voice teen-age thin.

"Yes."

"You must remember me from Denver."

He frowned, stepped out so he could get a better look at her. He saw her eyes appraising him from head to toe.

"Denver? No, I'm afraid not."

She darted into his room and closed the door, leaning against it.

"Of course you remember me. I'm the one with

a brown mole on my right breast. See." She opened her blouse, flapping it back to show her right breast where there was a mole.

"Miss, I've never been to Denver." He lied easily, worried what she might be a part of. She grinned, shrugged out of the blouse and laughed.

"So it was a way to get into your room. I was downstairs when you registered. I like you, like the tough smile, your moustache, the way you carry yourself. I've decided you are the man I want to . . . to deflower me, to take my virginity."

"That's flattering, Miss. But right now I have more important business. I have to. . . ."

"What's more important than taking a girl to bed, you know, fucking her?"

Spur laughed, picked up her blouse and handed it to her.

"What is more important is staying out of jail. Men get thrown into prison for just touching an underage girl like you. It's called statutory rape and it comes with a twenty year ticket. You should be worried about saving your virginity, not trying to get rid of it."

She ran to him, grabbed him around his back with her arms and pushed herself hard against his chest. She hung on, her head pressed into his shoulder.

She was crying when she looked up.

"You don't want me, you think I'm ugly. Even an ugly virgin should be a prize. Why won't you make love to me?"

She stepped back and began working at buttons on her skirt. He grabbed her hands.

"What's your name?"

"Violet."

He brushed the tears away from her face.

"Violet, you are a pretty girl. In another year or two you'll be a beautiful woman. Then you'll be glad that you still have your innocence. Some man will come along and be knocked out by you, and you by him. Hell, I haven't thrown a pretty girl out of my room for a long time, but I'm going to tonight. Now you put your blouse back on and button it, or you're going into the hall bare breasted. Do you want that?"

She pulled his hand up to her breasts but he moved it away.

"No tricks. Out you go."

He held one wrist, pulled her to the door and then pushed her into the hall. He threw her blouse after her and closed and locked the door quickly. He had seen no one in the hall. He listened for a minute, heard her sigh and then footsteps down the hall going away. He shook his head. That was one problem he really didn't need.

When Spur decided she had left, he put the room's only wooden chair under the door handle, bracing it so anyone coming into the room would have to break the chair first. Then he looked at the bed and tested it. Hard, lumpy, but softer than the floor.

Spur took out his carpetbag and checked the contents, then found the badge he had been sent. It was a shield with the U.S. seal on it and the words: U. S. Secret Service. It was new. Each officer was supposed to carry one. In undercover work, Spur was relieved of that duty. He took his badge and the thin leather folder they had made for it, and opened the false bottom section of his carpetbag. It came unhinged on the side of the bag when he pressed a small trigger set into the outside of the base of the bag. In the small compartment, a half inch deep and six inches square, he put the badge and a card that could also identify him. Already in the compartment were five one-hundred dollar bills. He had forty dollars in his wallet, and one hundred dollar bill in a hard to find section.

Spur had just put everything away and stretched out on the bed wondering what he could do that night. For a moment he froze thinking about Pistol Pete. Then he relaxed. He had been using a cover name on that Arizona operation. Pete would not recognize his real name. So all he had to do was stay out of sight when the deputy was around.

Five minutes later, as Spur was deciding if he wanted to go to bed, someone pounded on the door.

"Open up, McCoy. This is the sheriff."

Spur caught up his six-gun and held it behind his hip as he moved the chair.

"Yes, just a minute, I'm coming."

He unlocked the door and as he did it was kicked forward.

Spur stared into the angry face of Deputy Sheriff Pistol Pete Bovert who had both hand guns aimed at Spur's chest.

"Sure as hell! When Sheriff Johnson described

you, I was sure as shit that it was you. Welcome to Wyoming, Spur McCoy, or Sam Martin as we called you in Yuma. As the Indians say, this is a good day for you to die!"

CHAPTER FOUR

Spur looked at the twin deathbringer .44 muzzles and chuckled.

"Yes, I can see we have an efficient sheriff's department in this county. I was wondering when you might come by looking for your free knife. It is my extreme pleasure to facilitate such a small benevolent contribution to the law enforcement personnel of the county. If, my good man, you will step this way I'll be glad to show you the latest in fine cutlery, and you may make the selection of your choice. Oh, of course, with no charge to a lawman. I didn't quite catch what you said about Yuma or that other name, but no matter. Would you like to see something in a skinning knife, or perhaps a matched set of steak knives?"

Spur hoped to catch Pete completely off guard. He did with his spiel. He ignored the guns and managed to hide his own Remington behind his hip as he led Pistol Pete to the bed where the sample case still lay open.

Pistol Pete never had been long on brains. He turned and looked at Spur again.

"Goddamn! Swear you was the same hombre that fried my ass in Yuma and put me in the Territorial. Hell, I busted out after six months. Got me a couple of them fucking guards in the break!" He stared at Spur. "You sure you ain't been in Yuma? You was some kind of federal marshal or special agent or some damn thing back then."

"My good man. I came here directly from Boston and the Boston Knife Works, probably the best cutlery makers in all of the nation. We have excellent knives for commerce, for the house, and even for fighting."

Spur watched as Pistol Pete shoved both hog legs into leather and looked at the knives. Spur picked up a six-inch bladed hunting knife and began talking about it. Then he gave a small demonstration how it could be used for slashing, stabbing, skinning or almost any frontier use.

"Notice how the tip is Bowie sharpened. Cuts both ways." Spur flicked the blade and sliced a two-inch wound on Pistol Pete's right arm.

"What the hell?"

Spur pulled up his left hand which held his own .44.

"Bovert, you filth! You could have at least had the brains to change all of your name."

The Deputy backed to the door, his hands poised over his six-guns.

"Right, get rid of them before I have to shoot you in the balls and watch you cry. You want to cry, Bovert? You want to cry and beg for mercy the way you made that Indian girl do before you raped and then multilated her?"

"God, you *are* McCoy!" His hands twitched over his guns. "I should have shot first and then talked. Damn it!"

"Take the right hand six-gun out by your thumb and finger, easy, and put it on the floor. Then do the same thing with the other one."

"No. I don't give up my guns."

"Then you die where you stand. Take your choice. You have five seconds. One . . . Two . . . Three . . ."

Pistol Pete lifted the weapons and put them on the floor.

"Man to man, McCoy. You and me, each with one of them knives right here! I'll take you on."

"Yes, you probably would, if I gave you the chance. Too many men have given you that chance. How many men and women have you killed now, Pete? Twenty, thirty? And most of them when they were unarmed. Remember the rancher and his wife? They just got in your way. But you raped the woman and made her husband

45

watch. Then you sliced them into pieces with your knife. You're a dead man, Pete. The law will get you one way or the other. If prison didn't work, the equalizer will. A .44 slug judiciously applied works wonders.''

Pistol Pete charged. Spur had hoped he would. The Secret Service man slashed with the knife, laying open a wound across Pete's chest to draw his attention. Then Spur clubbed the big man with the butt of his pistol just hard enough to put him down and unconscious.

McCoy rolled over the big form, stopped the flow of blood and tied him hand and foot, then he waited. By midnight there would be fewer people around the hotel and on the streets.

Spur dozed off on the bed, woke up when Pistol Pete began kicking his boot heels against the wooden floor. Spur hit him with a pillow and he stopped. It was 2:00 A.M. when Spur pulled on his boots and strapped on his six-gun. He checked the hall and saw no one there.

McCoy knelt beside Pistol Pete. "See this derringer? It's a .45 and it will be buried in your gut. I'm going to untie your hands and feet and help you walk out to the street. You so much as blink crooked or make a sound, and I'll blow your belly full of lead, you understand?''

"Yeah, McCoy. And I understand that you're a dead man. No way I'm not coming after you.''

"There's one way, dead. And you remember that.''

They met no one going down the back stairs to the alley. Once there Spur marched the deputy to

46

the next street and through the next block to the edge of town.

"Keep walking, killer," Spur told Pete. "You and me are going to have a little talk out here away from town."

"I'll take you on anywhere, McCoy."

They walked for twenty minutes, through a shelf of land and down toward the Greybull River. The farther they walked the more nervous Pete became.

"What the hell you looking for?" Pete screamed. "Nothing out here but some cattle and some worked out mines."

"Sounds good," Spur said. He had out his six-gun now as he had for the past mile.

Without warning Pete began to run. He sprinted for a ledge and dove over it. By the time Spur got to the top, Pete was still rolling toward the water at the bottom of the wash.

Spur shot twice. He saw the first slug tear into Pete's legs. The second took him just below his navel and plowed a bloody, dirty track through his intestines and slammed out his back not far from his backbone.

Spur walked down the slope easily, watching in the half moonlight, the figure on the dry grass near the edge of the water.

"Oh, goddamn!" Pistol Pete said. He repeated the phrase a dozen times, then saw Spur standing over him.

"Gut shot me, you bastard!"

"Seems I remember hearing how you gut shot a woman and two kids in a store in California. Sat

47

there and watched all three die."

"Bastard!"

"It's different when you're on the other end of the hot lead, isn't it, Pete?"

"Dirty bastard!"

"What can you tell me about Johnson? I came after him, you're just a bonus. You might as well even out the score a little. Where is Johnson weak? Where should I attack him?"

"Go fuck yourself!"

"Figure you have another half hour to live, Pete. Maybe an hour if you're unlucky. Hurts like hell, doesn't it? Just try to think about all those people you slaughtered. About that old Breed woman you tied to her rocking chair and then burned her shack down around her. You didn't leave until she stopped screaming. Think about that, Pete."

"McCoy! Don't make it happen this way. End it for me now! I can't stand it any more!"

"Where is Johnson weak?"

"Women, damnit! He's a cockhound. Tease him with a good woman and he'll jump through a hoop. Now do it! I can't stand the pain! Do it right . . ."

Spur's .44 blasted a hollow hole in the northern Wyoming wilderness. Society had been relieved of one of its failures. The sound echoed and echoed again and again down the sleek flow of the Greybull River, rolled up the banks and washed out over the plateau until it was ground into dusty sound particles which scattered into the winds of Wyoming's night.

Pete Bovert slammed forward, a small hole in the base of his skull. He flopped on his face inches from the water. Spur rolled him over and pushed him into the fast flow of the water which moved away from the town of Elk Creek. It would be better if the body were not found for a few days. After that it shouldn't make any difference.

Spur held the Remington for a minute, then pushed it into his holster and watched the body sliding away downstream. He had been an executioner tonight. He didn't mind. It had been a miscarriage of justice when Bovert had been given a jail sentence in Yuma. He should have been hung. Spur was only carrying out the just intent of the law. No animal like Bovert should be allowed to grow up, let alone carry a lawman's badge.

Women! So the high and mighty sheriff was a glutton for women. Maybe Jodi could help him out some way—but not if she would be in any danger. He would work on the idea, keep it as a last resort.

Spur walked back to town, slipped into the hotel when no one was watching the back door, and got into bed. He locked the door and braced a chair under the handle, then went to sleep. His .44 was beside his right hand. He lay on his back, fully clothed and with his boots on. He would sleep on his back, and be alert at the slightest sound. After tonight he would not be able to sleep in the hotel, because he was sure the sheriff would be looking for him.

* * *

Spur came awake at dawn. He stretched, got up and changed clothes, putting on his jeans and shirt, brown vest and his brown hat. Then he packed his belongings, took the bag and his knife sample case and slipped out of the hotel. He had to knock twice on the door in the alley behind Main Street before Jodi came to open it. She grinned when she saw him.

"One hell of a time to come calling. Want some breakfast?" She was still half asleep. He put her back in bed, kissed her forehead and she was sleeping again.

Spur left his bags in the big living room-kitchen, and when he turned around he found Rebecca dressed and alert, eyes sparkling as she nodded a shy good morning. Spur watched her light a fire in the small wood range and make breakfast. He tried to talk to her, but she would only smile, answering questions with a shake or nod.

In ten minutes she had breakfast for him: scrambled eggs, hash browns, three strips of thick bacon, toast and coffee. She ate as he did. He noticed that she wore an old, faded dress that was slightly large for her, conveniently hiding almost all signs of her breasts or her waist.

"Thank you, Rebecca. I have to do some things this morning. The sheriff will be looking for me today. Would it be all right if I stayed here tonight? I can sleep on the floor somewhere."

"That would be fine, Mr. McCoy," she said. "I'll tell Jodi so she'll know too."

"Thanks, Rebecca. That was a fine breakfast."

He reached out to touch her hand, but she pulled it back quickly.

She nodded, mumbled something and her hand snaked into the pocket she had sewn into the full skirt.

Spur went to the door, checked the position of his six-gun, waved at Rebecca and went into the alley. He walked quickly to the alley in back of the newspaper office, found the right door and stepped inside.

The rear door was unlocked. Spur almost called out so he wouldn't get shot as a prowler. But he heard voices coming from the front. Without a sound, Spur made his way past the press toward the draped doorway. The voices came stronger now.

"Look, you little shit head! I don't care if you disagree with what I have to say or not. You goddamn well better run it on the front page with my name on it, or I'm gonna run your skinny little ass right out of town. Do I make myself clear?"

Spur didn't recognize the voice. The next one he knew at once: it was Les Van Dyke.

"Sheriff, I've been pressured to run stories before, but nobody in his right mind ever threatened me like that. I'd say you are in one hell of a lot of trouble. We do have a territorial government, you know. And laws. And right now I could charge you with three or four different felonies. I'm sure you know all this. You just don't quite understand that you aren't the king of Elk Creek anymore."

"I'm not, huh? We'll see. You run the goddamn story or we'll fucking well see!"

"You kill me, who is going to set the type and run the press? You think about that for a while."

The shot came almost at once. Spur drew his gun and pulled back the drape so he could see into the office.

CHAPTER FIVE

When Spur McCoy heard the shot he peered through the curtained door into the front of the newspaper office. Sheriff Johnson lowered his gun. A few pieces of the big window in front of the office had fallen to the floor from the shot the lawman had sent into it. Johnson laughed, stepped through the jagged glass onto the boardwalk and walked down the street.

"Damnit! I'm going to send a bill to the county!" Van Dyke yelled through the window toward the retreating lawman. "Christ, what a mess!"

"Van Dyke, it's McCoy in the back room," Spur called. "The door was open. I heard. This seems like a bad time to come calling."

Van Dyke didn't reply. Two people came to stare in the window. "Yes, I know it's broken," he said to them, and picked up a broom and a cardboard box and went outside to clean up the glass. "Talk to you when I get back inside," he said as he went past the draped doorway of the printing plant.

Spur waited. He thought at first that he could glean important facts from back issues of the newspaper about some of the killings, or just one target murder. But he quickly discounted that. Johnson would reveal nothing important about any of the deaths, and if Van Dyke found out any incriminating evidence, he wouldn't be able to print it anyway.

But Van Dyke would know which of the killings would be the easiest to prove as murder against the sheriff and his deputies. The hired deputies undoubtedly pulled the trigger. When they did it was on orders of the sheriff, so he had conspiracy, as well as a murder charge against the sheriff.

Ten minutes later Van Dyke came back inside for some boards to cover the broken window. It measured six feet square and he said it would take him three months to get another piece of glass that big from Cheyenne.

"I've been thinking about the best murder to pin on the sheriff," Van Dyke said when he had the boards in place. "Have to be Adam Fowler. He got shot from ambush about three weeks ago.

The word was that his wife had been friendly, shall we say, with the sheriff, and Adam went to settle up with him. Adam Fowler was the only preacher we had in town."

"Interesting. Fowler wound up shot in the back?"

"How did you know?"

"A specialty of Pistol Pete. What else do we have?"

"Not much. The widow is still in town. Staying at the parsonage, being supported by the community church. She's been carrying on, crying and weeping, but nobody believes much of it. From what I hear, the lady still sees the sheriff."

"Tell me where I can find the widow," Spur said. "I should pay my respects."

"I also hear that she is the best spy the sheriff has to the goings on around town. So be careful of Kate Fowler."

A half hour later Spur knocked on the back door of the Community Church parsonage at the north end of the little town. At first there was no reaction. After a second knock he heard a sound, then a voice asking him to wait a minute. Two minutes later heels clicked on hardwood floors as someone came to the door. It opened.

The woman who stood looking at him was tall, five eight at least. She wore high heels and a black dress that clung tightly to her upper body, nearly bursting at the bodice and pinched in at her tiny waist, then flaring over hips into flounces of four different colors. It was a dance hall girl's dress.

"Hello. Who are you? You're not from the church committee. You're staring, did you want something?"

Spur laughed. "Yes, I'm Spur McCoy, are you Kate Fowler?"

She nodded. Her clear brown eyes were unblinking. She had her dark hair piled on top of her head and the dress was cut low showing half of each white mound of breast.

"I'd like to talk to you a few minutes."

She smiled, and Spur enjoyed the picture. "You're the new man in town, on the stage yesterday and already our sheriff doesn't like you. Come in, come in. I was trying on costumes that someone left. This is a snazzy one, don't you think?"

"It looks perfect on you, if you're working a saloon."

"You don't think I could?"

"Kate, I expect that you may have. You certainly have a full, provocative body."

She glowed at the praise. "Well, thank you. I like you. I can tell you're a man with a lot of potential. I like my men big. I mean most men are proportionally large all over. It's a kind of hobby of mine."

"Interesting hobby."

"True. You said you had some questions?"

"Yes. I'm here to find out who killed your husband and why."

They were in the kitchen of the small house, and she waved him into the living room, then on to her bedroom. The bed had not been made, and clothes lay scattered around the room. She didn't apologize, just reached to the dresser where she picked up a hand rolled cigarette, and lit it with a stinker match.

"The why is the easy part. He thought I was stepping out on him, making love with another man."

"Were you?"

She laughed. "In four months you're the first person who has ever had enough guts to come right out and ask me. The answer is yes. But not who he thought."

"Did your lover kill your husband?"

"Hardly. We were in bed with each other at the time."

It was Spur's turn to chuckle. "You seem to be an extremely honest, straightforward person, Kate."

"I know what I like." She smiled and looked Spur up and down. "The more I see and hear of you, Mr. McCoy, the more I like."

"I was about to say the same thing."

"You haven't seen much of me yet."

"I can always hope." He moved toward her. She waited. He leaned in and kissed her cheek, then her lips. She backed off and shook her head.

"Not right. I'd need a dozen or more that way to decide. Let's sit down and figure out if we enjoy that or not."

She sat on the edge of the bed and Spur dropped beside her.

"First, undo some of those buttons up the back of this dress. It's so damn tight it hurts."

Spur unfastened all the buttons and she held the dress on with her arms as he leaned in to kiss her again. This time they both had their lips parted and their tongues wandered lazily in and out of each other's mouths.

"I think I like that," she said as they came apart.

"I know I like it," Spur said. He nibbled at her lips then kissed her again and eased her backward onto the bed.

"Now you're getting serious. I'm a girl who can't think well lying on her back."

"You don't have to do any thinking," he said.

She kissed him again. Spur took the top of the dress and pulled it down. Her breasts tumbled out like two ripe melons.

He teased them with feather touches until she moaned in delight.

"How did you know I love it that way?" she asked. "Yes, sweetheart, yes!"

He touched them more and then massaged them delicately before he bent down and kissed each straining nipple.

"Oh nice, nice. Love that almost as much as fucking."

Spur spread her legs with his knee and lay directly on top of her, his body pressing down hard on her crotch. He kissed her breasts again, then her lips.

"So you were fucking the sheriff's brains out when he had your husband gunned down?"

"Christ, don't ask now!"

"Now is when I'm asking. You were with him?"

"Yes, yes!"

"And the sheriff told one of his men to blow your husband into heaven or hell. Which man did he tell?"

"Somebody in the hall."

"And you'll testify in court you heard him say the words."

"No. Tyler would cut my tits off if I did that! You know he would."

"Not if Tyler Johnson was in a jail cell."

"He ain't."

Spur pulled up her long skirt and his hand worked between her legs.

"Oh, lordy but that feels good! You've got a gentle way with a woman, Spur. Most men would have pumped off and had their pants back on by now."

"The second time will be fast and hard."

"Just keep it hard!" She found his penis and rubbed it through his pants. "Get him out for me."

"You're not ready yet," he said. Spur sat up, stripped out of his vest and shirt, then pulled off her skirt and her drawers. They were made of soft silky material, the same knee length as most women wore. As he pulled them down over her little belly, she moaned. Then he began kissing them down to her crotch, kissing around the hairy pubis and on down her inner thigh.

Kate Fowler jerked and moaned and writhed all the way.

"Hurry, lover! I want you inside of me right now. Please hurry. I'm all wet and swollen and

59

ready. Please get in me right now, Spur! I need you in me."

"Which deputy was it Johnson told to kill your husband?"

"Christ! What difference does it make? He's dead. But I'm alive. I won't be if I keep talking about the sheriff. Christ, Spur come on, fuck me!"

His finger found her secret place and he rubbed. She jolted with one spasma of joy and then he withdrew. "Which one was it, Kate?"

"Hell, what does it matter? It was Pistol Pete. And that's all I know. I was busy, after that. Now, Spur, let's make it one to remember."

Spur stripped off his pants and underdrawers, then moved between her legs and worked into her slowly. She climaxed before he was settled, and then again. He knew he had a problem with Pete being dead. Still he could prove conspiracy to murder, and also a charge of murder. If the woman's testimony would hold up. It wouldn't. A defense attorney would have a circus with her on the stand. And he had no witnesses to prove that Pete pulled the trigger on the Reverend Mr. Adam Fowler. It had been a good try, a close miss. However, in any court action he could call on the woman as a witness to show general, if not specific, misconduct. That would help.

Spur was thinking more about the girl under him now than the job. She was an exciting combination of good looks, good body and absolute wanton desire. How could she miss? He came away from her suddenly. She had already climaxed four times.

60

"Get up on your hands and knees," he told her.

"Oh, no!"

"Oh, yes!"

Spur mounted her from behind, driving into her still pulsating vagina with one solid thrust and she looked over her shoulder at him.

"Oh, there!"

But Spur was too busy to notice. He had slid over the last ridge and began the long ride down through the chute, around the corners and slamming into the open with the speed of a runaway railway locomotive. He was pounding and shaking and shouting. He felt and heard her doing the same as they climaxed together and fell on the bed in a tangle.

Five minutes later after they had recovered enough to talk, she grinned and played with the hair on his chest.

"Not bad for a preacher's widow, right?"

"You weren't always a preacher's woman."

"True. Adam 'saved' me from my life of sin. He pulled me out of a whorehouse in Arizona and brought me up here to reform, reeducate, and religionize me. He called them my own kind of the three R's. It didn't work. But then he only had a little under a year to work on me. Hell, I just like to fuck. I don't see what's so wrong doing it. Who gets hurt? Did I hurt you? Hell no! Made you feel damn fine there for a few minutes. How can that be bad?"

"There are other considerations," Spur said.

"Not for me. I got sick when I was thirteen. German measles or something like that. Anyway, it killed me as a mother. No kid is ever gonna stick his head out of my crotch and scream. My insides are all sick. Doctor didn't tell me why, just said I couldn't never have none."

"At least you aren't bitter."

"How can I get mad at the measles?"

"But you can get mad at Tyler Johnson. He's had as many as a dozen men killed in this county. Does that mean anything to you, Kate?"

"Yeah, sure, it's wrong. And one woman he killed I know of. I don't want Kate Fowler to be the second one."

"When it gets that far, when we have enough evidence to arrest him, we'll shut down his deputies too, and he won't have a chance to hurt anyone."

"Then you got yourself a witness."

"It won't be long."

She reached for his crotch and found him limp.

"Hey, what about that second fast and furious one you promised me?"

"Give me a minute to catch my breath. I need to know who else in this town can help me nail Sheriff Johnson inside his own jail house."

She talked about half the people in town, but none of them seemed right. Spur was stalling. In college once he had made love to three different girls in an hour on a bet.

He won the bet and spent his winnings sending the loser to a bawdy house for the night. Now he needed a half hour between go-rounds.

Kate stopped talking and bent to his crotch. In a moment she had him in her mouth coaxing him until her ministrations resulted in his total firmness. She looked up and smiled.

"Do you mind? I haven't tasted any in so long."

He growled at her as she went down on him and Spur lay there delighted and fascinated. Somehow he never had any staying power when a beautiful woman began sucking on him. He didn't this time. It was less than two minutes until he was shouting and moaning and clawing the air as he climaxed in a bursting surge of powerful feelings that left him at once drained, and curiously, hungry.

She slid away from him and grinned. "You just don't know all the talents I have. What's for number three?"

Spur began pulling on his clothes. "Number three is for me to get back to work."

Spur turned. "Someone is knocking on your front door."

She jumped up, pulled on a robe and looked through the hallway at the glassed front door.

"God, get your clothes on fast, it's Sheriff Johnson and he looks madder than all hell!"

CHAPTER SIX

Nehemiah Hardy gave Jodi her week's wages. Jodi was the best retail person he had ever hired for the store, man or woman. She had taken over the housewares and house supplies sections and done the ordering and most of the selling. That left him time to take care of the rest of the store, the hardware, fencing, barbed wire and the rest of the man-related items. Now he wasn't sure he could run the store without her.

"Thanks, Jodi, for another week of good work. I'm glad you're here."

"So am I Mr. Hardy. I don't know what

Rebecca and I would do without you." She touched his hand. "We appreciate it."

Something flared deep in his loins but he swept it away.

"Goodnight, Jodi," he said firmly.

She smiled and went out the door locking it behind her.

Nehamiah turned down the last lamp and went into the back room to work on the books. He was making money, not a lot but enough to live on comfortably. That word reminded him of the ranch. He should go out and check on everything. He tried to get out there once a month, but it was hard. He knew it would be tough sometimes, but he had gone ahead. At times he told himself he had no choice. He had been young and not as smart as he was now.

So long ago. Nehemiah Hardy let the years wind back to the day he arrived in the county fresh from Boston. He had ridden a horse in from Casper so he could see some of the country. That last night outside of town he had camped by the Greybull River and early in the morning had gone for a walk. He wasn't the only one up. Two women were bathing and splashing in the cool waters of the river. One dressed and left hurriedly, but the other, the younger one stayed.

Hardy had grinned and slipped up as close as he could. Then he could see that she was an Indian. He had no idea what tribe, but he figured she was about sixteen. She had a slender young body, full hips and small breasts that kept him in a constant state of excitement.

She washed herself again, then sat in the sun to dry and made no attempt to cover her young and tempting body. At last he could stand it no longer and rose and walked toward her. She was not surprised. She had known he was watching and had waited for him. She stood and turned slowly so he could see her, then cupped her breasts in her hands and walked slowly toward him.

He had no idea what it meant, but when she pulled him down in the grass, he knew what she wanted. They made love in the grass all morning until he was absolutely limp beyond recall. Hardy was mesmerized. Never had he made love so long, or so gloriously. She did anything he wanted her to.

She knew two words of English: *You stay.* He did, for a week, making love every morning until he was exhausted, then they worked together at a small lean-to she had fashioned in a bend of the river where a blush of green trees came down to the water. She had only the most primitive clay pots and no metal tools or utensils at all.

He stayed another week, watching her hunt rabbits, and pheasant. He was curiously contented. Then he remembered his business waiting for him in Elk Creek. It had been a family business that one of his uncles began years ago. Now the man wanted out, and offered it to Hardy at a pittance but enough for the old man to live on back in Boston.

Hardy had started calling the slender Indian, *Girl,* and the name stuck. He explained to her with signs that he would return, that he had to go to

Elk Creek. She had communicated to him that it was a half day's ride to the town.

Hardy promised he would come back with pots and cooking things. She wept and wailed, tore off her fringed buckskin dress and beat her fists on the ground. At last he rode away.

The store had been everything his uncle promised. The older man stayed two weeks, getting Hardy familiar with the business, the merchandise, his set of books, and the various wholesale houses he ordered goods from. It was another two weeks before Hardy thought of Girl. He closed the store late Saturday night, loaded up a pack horse with two big sacks of kitchen and cooking gear, blankets, and some ready to wear clothes he thought might fit her, and rode for the camp.

That Saturday night he had missed the bend in the river, and by morning was lost. He came back down the river and at last found the bend, and where her camp had been, but she wasn't there. He searched until almost dark before he found her in another cope of woods back from the stream. She did not believe that he had returned.

To greet him she at once made love with him in the grass, then she looked at all the things he had brought to her. She wept with joy. Never had she had a metal pot to cook in. She was so delighted he couldn't stop her tears.

That night, and all day Monday he stayed. He taught her the first words of English, *Go, come back, Girl, Hardy*. He told her to stay at that spot, he would build her a log house. Then at midnight he left again, promising that he would come back and this time she believed him.

Gently Hardy probed the locals how they felt about squaw men, and got quick and hostile reactions. Then he knew he had to keep his Indian woman a secret.

The first four months he managed to get out to see her every other Sunday. He told people who asked that he went fishing and hunting up the Greybull. They believed him. What else was there to do in the wilderness?

On the first visit he made in August of that year he saw that she was pregnant. Girl was pleased. She jabbered at him excitedly. He slowed her down and they used English and some words of Sioux. She belonged to a split off tribe of the Teton Sioux, but few of her people remained.

On each visit he learned more Sioux words and she learned more English. Two trips later he found an older woman living there and Girl said she was her mother. She stayed. Before winter he had built a twelve foot square log house. He had it roofed by the time the snows fell, and with the snows came a one-eyed brave. Girl said he was One-Eye, her brother. He had a squaw and built a lodge in the deepest part of the woods. During the heavy snows that winter One-Eye and his squaw lived in the cabin.

In February, Hardy's son was born, and he brought a small wood stove to the cabin, and a month later a wood burning range with eight lids.

With the coming of spring Hardy bought six calves, five heifers and one good bull for his ranch. Now most of the town knew he had a ranch out there, and that he used Indians to run it for him, and if the people thought that strange, they didn't say so.

He found out the land was available and homesteaded his 160 acres. A year later he had a daughter with blue eyes like her brother. The herd had grown to twelve due to some strays One-Eye had collected. None of them had brands. Hardy made up his own brand, Bar H, but never registered it.

A year later Hardy met Wendy, who played the pump organ for the church services. She had long blonde hair and fair skin and the bluest eyes he had ever seen. She was only five feet tall, and so pretty it made his chest burst just thinking about her. He was so much in love he dreamed about her day and night. He wanted to be around her constantly. He went places he knew she would be so he could see her, listen to her talk, let her look at him and sometimes talk with her. Nothing like this had happened with Girl. He had simply made love to her and lived with her.

With Wendy it was different.

Wendy would not permit him to touch her except hold her hand on special occasions. He asked her father permission to court her and at last won his approval. It was a nine month courtship. Nehemiah was seven years older than the seventeen year old Wendy.

She was the perfect lady, allowing him to touch her, to put his arm around her, and at last, after they had decided that they would get married and

70

he had her father's blessing, she let him kiss her
. . . once.

Wendy had been a perfect wife and mother.
They had four strong, happy children, and he
never breathed a thought about his Indian family
to her. His visits became less frequent to his
ranch. He herd grew and at last the railroad went
through and they could take some of the cattle to
the railroad at Rawlins.

Hardy hired two out-of-work cowhands to help,
and he got on a horse with them and with One-
Eye they drove a hundred head to the pens. That
year they got twenty dollars a head for the cattle,
and after Hardy paid off the drovers he still had
$1,800. He set up a bank account for One-Eye,
bought him a new saddle, a dozen blankets, and a
rifle he had been wanting. He split the profit in
the middle, and told Girl the rest of the money
was for her and the children. She wept. She didn't
know what to do with it. Hardy said to keep it for
the children.

Now his Indian children, Adam and Beth, were
13 and 14 years old. He wanted them to come to
the town school, but he knew that was not possible. Maybe in fifty years it would be. He took
them books and primers and taught them to
speak English, but it was hard at long range.

Now, Nehemiah Hardy looked at his ledger
books. He would clear more than three thousand
dollars again this year. He could live on six·
hundred a year. The profit went into his cousin's
bank in Boston where he now had a balance of
over $65,000. It was truly a fortune. His local

71

bank account was for the day to day running of the business. He didn't trust Otto Toller with a lot of money—and there were no guarantees.

His account for Adam and Beth had soared to nearly ten thousand dollars. The ranch was flourishing. He had hired a white manager, with the understanding that the Indians be left alone, and be provided for. They had built a new ranch house, and barns and outbuildings. It was a real ranch. Yearly they drove cattle to the railyards, sometimes as many as three hundred.

Hardy closed the books and turned out the last lamp. He walked to the front door in the dark, unlocked it and stepped out.

"Hold it right there!" A voice snapped. Hardy heard a six-gun cock.

"It's all right, Sheriff. I own the place. Hardy."

"Good," Sheriff Johnson said. "Just the man I want to see. Feeling is running high against the Injuns again. You hear the talk. I figure we better clear all the Sioux out of the county. You got four or five savages on your little ranch. You better get rid of them for their own safety."

"No, Sheriff. I don't think that's necessary. People around here know the Indians on my ranch. They seldom leave it, and I see no problem."

"Didn't ask you if you saw a problem, Hardy. I said move them savages out of there before I have to go out there with a posse and shoot them out."

"Sheriff. You don't have that kind of authority. Your job is to uphold and enforce the law. There

72

is no law against Indians living in this county. There couldn't be, it would be unconstitutional."

"That's what I figured."

"What did you figure?"

"That you're nothing but a goddamn squaw man. I done me some inquiries of my own. Them savages been on that land for fifteen years now. Lived there before you homesteaded. And you built that first little cabin on that place fourteen years ago. Just in time for the first brat that young squaw dropped. To me that makes you a squaw man, Hardy."

"Sheriff, you are entitled to any personal opinion you want. Personally I think you're a poor sheriff, but until I bring you up on some kind of specific charges, it's just my opinion. My advice to you, sheriff, is to stick to law, not opinion, it's a lot safer."

Sheriff Johnson bristled when Hardy began, then he burned silently until the store keeper was through.

"Hardy, you interest me. I'm going to dig a little deeper, find out more about your nest of savages out there. And when I do, I'll be paying you a visit, a damn interesting visit. Because then I'll have facts and witnesses and evidence that you're not going to like at all!"

The sheriff spun on his boot heel and marched away. Hardy took a deep breath. he didn't want to hurt Wendy. If she knew about Girl and the two kids out there it would break her heart. She had been a perfect wife. He couldn't let her down now. He thought of the new Winchester in his store. He could sit on a roof around town and pick off the sheriff as he made his nightly rounds. The town would be rid of an outrage, and society would be better off.

But he had never shot anyone, let alone set out to kill in cold, deliberate fashion. No, he couldn't do it. In a fit of rage, perhaps, but not this way. He hoped that the new man, Spur McCoy, might do the job for him. If Sheriff Johnson threatened to make it public that he was a squaw man, or if he tried to tell Wendy, Nehemiah Hardy swore a silent oath that he would kill the sheriff and be glad that he did!

CHAPTER SEVEN

Spur made it out of Kate Fowler's bedroom and away from the widow's house before the sheriff stormed into the front room. The lawman was hunting his deputy, and Spur could hear him as Spur went down the alley and headed for the hotel.

He'd had a good lunch and then watched the business firms close up. He went to the Red Eye Saloon and lifted a beer. By that time it was nearly eight o'clock and Spur was totaling up his assets on this assignment. He had a rogue sheriff, a sexy widow who might testify for him; Jodi, who was good in bed but not much help on the project, and the newsman Les Van Dyke. The publisher was getting mad enough to blow his top in print and earn himself an early pine box.

Spur didn't think the emporium owner Nehemiah Hardy would be much help. There did seem to be some deep seated anger just below the surface, but McCoy had no way of knowing how to trigger that. He would see Van Dyke later tonight. The fewer people the sheriff saw Spur talking to the better.

The sheriff himself of River Bend county pushed through the bat wing doors and scanned the drinkers. His gaze stopped at Spur and he marched up to him.

"Those don't look like knife selling clothes, mister."

"I'm off work, so I wear what I like. And I talk to whoever I want to." Spur turned his back on the sheriff.

"Turn around, asshole, or get your back sliced open!"

Spur turned suddenly, powering a backhand left fist that slammed against the sheriff's jaw and drove him sideways and to his knees. The lawman shook his head and reached for one of his two pistols.

"Hold it!" Spur barked at him. "Touch that iron and you earn yourself a pine box. You want to stand up nice and easy like and talk like a gentleman, I'll listen. Otherwise take your wise mouth and your convict deputies and get the hell out of here!"

Sheriff Johnson glared at Spur, his hand itching to draw, his brain telling him not to. He got to his feet slowly. Hatred seeped out of every pore in his body. Spur could feel the heat of his anger. With a great deal of control, the sheriff at last could talk.

"What was that crack about convict deputies?"

"Pistol Pete Cody Bovert, for one. He's wanted in at least four states I've been in lately. He has more wanted posters on him than Wes Hardin."

"Wanted? I don't believe it."

"Ask him. He was so stupid he didn't even change his first two names. Pistol Pete—how could anybody be dumb enough not to change that name?"

"I'm looking for him right now. He didn't come to work today. You seen Pistol Pete?"

"Sure, twice, that's why I knew it was him, crescent scar and all. Saw him when I got off the stage and again last night on the street."

"Nobody's seen him today. You seen him, McCoy?"

"Nope, have you?"

"You got a smart mouth, McCoy. One of these days I'll shut it for you, permanently."

"Is that a threat, Sheriff? I understand you and your deputies shot down eleven men and one woman in the past four months."

"Line of duty. They were all low class riff-raff."

"Like the preacher, Fowler? That kind of riff-raff?"

The sheriff quivered with rage. His eyes bulged, his hands hovered over his gun butts again.

"What's the matter, Sheriff? Isn't Pete here to back up your hand anymore?"

The sheriff roared in fury and charged McCoy. The big man waited until the last second, spun aside and slammed his fist down on the sheriff's neck as he careened past. Sheriff Johnson kept right on going, rammed into a bar chair, tipped over a table and rolled on his back.

Spur watched him a moment, then swept a half-filled glass of beer off a table and poured the contents on the sheriff's face. The lawman came up sputtering and swearing. He grabbed one gun but Spur kicked it out of his hand.

"Johnson, you're all through in this town. As of today nobody is going to be afraid of you. Nobody is going to take you seriously. I'd bet you'll be losing some more of your bully boy deputies in the next few days. They just aren't made for honest lawkeeping. Take my advice, Johnson. Pull off that badge right now, grab your money out of the bank and ride just as far and as fast as you can before the good people of this town rise up and shoot you so full of holes they'll use you for a drain gauge."

Spur heard some brief cheers from the thirty odd men in the saloon.

Sheriff Johnson got to his feet slowly.

"You're under arrest, McCoy, for the murder of Pistol Pete, and for assault on a law officer." He slowly drew his second pistol and pointed to two men in the crowd. "You, and you, I'm appointing you special deputies. Move over there and get his gun, and take him to the jail."

One of the men he pointed at shook his head and dove into the crowd. The other one shivered, but moved forward. He made the mistake of getting between Spur and the sheriff. The moment he crossed, Spur pushed the man into the sheriff who was trying to stand. Both tumbled to the floor. Spur sprinted for the door and was through the batwings before the sheriff could find the gun he had dropped. There were roars of laughter inside the saloon, then a shot and the bar mirror showered into hundreds of pieces.

Spur dashed down the street and around the corner. He stormed down the alley to the door where the girls lived and hoped it was not locked. Quickly he pulled the door, it came open and he was inside.

Rebecca stood at the kitchen sink peeling potatoes. She turned, the knife still in her hand, and glared at him.

"Hello, Rebecca. Sorry I had to burst in this way, but the sheriff was chasing me. I'll leave just as soon as I can. Is there another way out of here?"

Her eyes flared angrily for a moment. Then she touched her forehead with her empty hand and when she turned back she was smiling. The knife was in the pan of potatoes.

"Hello, Mr. McCoy. Nice to see you again. Jodi is still taking her bath. I'll tell her you're here."

"No, no, that's all right. I thought you smiled when I asked if there was another way out of here. I didn't necessarily mean a door. Some other way?"

She grinned. "We're not supposed to know it's there. But there is another way. Somebody built a walkway over the top of the gambling hall. I think they cheated that way with the cards. Anyway, it's in here."

In Rebecca's bedroom there was a panel that slid to one side. Beyond it a long corridor, narrow and low, led away into the darkness. Rebecca gave him a candle and a match to light it. He went ahead with the flickering light. Here and there were peek holes into the rooms below. The first part of the corridor led over bedrooms. One was occupied by two people in an age-old wrestling match. Beyond them came the cardrooms—three small ones, then the casino-like main room, with the dance hall girls and small tables for poker and faro.

A cool draft flowed through the corridor and ahead he could see lights. Soon he came to a partition that opened on the second floor balcony leading to the stairway to the third floor. Spur pushed the panel back, stepped out leaving the candle at the end of the corridor. He pushed the panel back in place and ran quickly down the stairs, around two blocks and in to the back door of the newspaper office.

Lights were on. Les Van Dyke wore a paper hat made out of a sheet of newspaper and swore as he worked on the small flat bed press. It was an old model that had to be hand cranked and pressure put on each page to make the impression. He looked up and laughed.

"You don't waste any time making enemies

80

when you get started. The sheriff was already in here looking for you. He was so mad he was even nice to me. Hear you burned his ears off with some true words over in the saloon."

"Something like that."

"Just in time. Some cowboy riding the grub line found your buddy Pistol Pete in the Greybull about ten miles downstream. Figured he was a lawman by his tin badge, so he carted the bloated corpse back up here. Your friend the sheriff has really got a wild hair up his ass."

"So now we take the kid gloves off and the real fight begins. What can you help me get done?"

"What needs doing?"

"Who else know anything about the Fowler shooting? I may have one circumstantial witness, but I need somebody who actually saw the man gunned down. Got any names?"

"None alive. Word was that Pete pulled the trigger on orders from on up the line, Johnson."

"But did anyone *see* Pete pull the trigger?"

"Not that I've heard of. You talk to the widow?"

"Yes. But I'd hate to put her on the witness stand."

"Don't worry about that. She's fucked half the grown men and boys in town. No local jury would believe anything she said. She thinks with her crotch."

"Maybe now that there's some opposition, our friend the sheriff will do something stupid that we can pin on him," Spur said. "Do we have an honest district attorney in this county?"

"Yep, but his assistant is bought and paid for by the sheriff so he knows everything that happens."

"Who is the assistant?"

"Kid by the name of Yale Crowningshield. He's reading for the law and thinks he's hot piss."

"I'll have to have a talk with the lad."

"Somebody left a message for you today. I don't know why or who but it was on the door when I got back from lunch." Les handed the envelope to Spur who tore it open. Inside was a small sheet of paper with printing on it. It read:

I have something valuable for you. It is vital that you get it today. Come to livery stable in midnight.

There was no signature.

Spur showed it to Les, who read it and shrugged. "I always ignore anonymous messages. The person who wrote this printed it so it wouldn't point to any kind of type of person, young, old, literate, etc. Could be almost anyone."

"But probably not the sheriff," Spur said. "He's the only one I really won't go out of my way to see. The letter said something valuable. That could be a witness or something to tie up the sheriff."

"How many people know that's what you're looking for?"

"Not many, true." Spur helped Les rip open a new package of paper. "Well, I'll have to decide whether to go or not. At least I have a couple of hours. You going to work all night?"

"Only until I get this week's issue printed."

"Want some help? I can fold and stuff."

Les looked at him. "Sounds like you've been around a newspaper plant before."

"Now and then. Which ones are dry? Show me what to insert and then fold. Let's get this organized!"

Two hours later the paper was done, folded and ready to deliver to the four places in town in the morning. Spur left by the back way and went into the livery stable by the corral gate. He climbed to the loft without a sound and sat by the hay feed door near the front where they put down hay for the stock. He could see the front door and the small office to one side. There was a light on low, and he could see a wrangler sleeping in a bunk. Who had said he would meet Spur here at midnight? The agent settled down. He would give the guy a half hour, then he was going to go to sleep in the hay.

CHAPTER EIGHT

Spur McCoy waited fifteen minutes, growing more impatient all the time. He had moved once to the other side of the hay feed hole, then settled down.

Without warning someone jumped into the hay beside him. He pawed for his gun as he turned hoping he wasn't too late. He came up with the six-gun and stared, almost nose to nose with the impish grin of Violet, the dark-haired, black-eyed, seventeen-year-old who had darted into his room at the hotel that first night he was in town.

She laughed softly when she saw his weapon.

"I promise I won't hurt you, Spur. You can put away that gun."

McCoy relaxed. "The little girl with the mole on her breast. I remember you."

"You forgot to say I have big tits and that I want you to make love to me." She shrugged out of her blouse, and Spur couldn't help but look at her full breasts.

"Come on, kiss me or something so I won't feel foolish. Here you've got me in the hay and my blouse is off. You're the one who is supposed to know what to do."

Spur sighed, bent and kissed her pouting lips and changed her frown to a glorious smile.

"Oh, yes! That was heaven! I knew you would steal my cherry. I just knew it! Let's move back from here a ways so we don't get all excited and fall through."

Spur cupped one of her breasts in his hand. "Violet, I'm not going to make love to you."

"Oh shit. Why the fuck not?"

"Don't swear and talk dirty, it isn't ladylike."

"I don't want to be a lady!" She hissed at him, her voice rising. "I just want to know what it feels like to be caressed and seduced and fucked by a real man like you!"

"You have lots of time for that, the rest of your life. That comes after you get a husband. That's your first big task."

"Oh, *that*. I can get married anytime I want to. Been asked four times already. Two of them were older men. One was a foreman at the mines!"

"Good, pick out one and get married before you

make a mistake like this."

She touched his crotch and he moved her hand. "Come on Spur, give me a chance. You're touching me. Let me mess around a little."

He was tempted. She was delicious, new and unused, unspoiled, trainable. He bent and kissed her breasts, then chewed lightly on both nipples.

Violet tensed, then she went rigid and fell on top of him, her body quivering with a climax. He held her so they wouldn't fall through the hole and she moaned softly as the tremors shot through her sleek young body again and again. His hand found her breasts and he massaged them tenderly until she gave a soft little cry and went limp against him.

A minute later she lifted her head, then moved his hand back to her breasts and sighed.

"Spur, that was glorious! Absolutely fantastic. Now let me get my skirt off and you can poke my little pussy."

"No." He looked at her in the dimness of the hayloft. "Violet, did you leave that note for me at the newspaper office?"

"Yes, and you came."

"I didn't know who it was. I have other important things I have to do."

"I only want another half hour so you can make love to me."

"NO. Now put back on your blouse."

"You don't like me. You think I'm ugly."

"You're ugly, yes, if that's what it takes to get rid of you. I'm going out the back door. If you really want to become a tramp, a prostitute, a

87

slut, you'll find lots of men to help you. But I don't think you want that. I've given you a little thrill. Now go home and finish growing up. Then send me a note in about three years."

Spur moved away from her, walking through the packed down hay to the back door where he went down a ladder, through the corral and over the fence.

Violet again. He had forgotten how sweet and delicious a seventeen-year-old girl could be. When he had been young he'd never properly appreciated them. He shook his head. That was one type in which he could not afford to become interested. Furious fathers had a way of shooting first and charging a man with rape second—if the victim lived.

Spur knew that he could not go back to either of the hotels for a night's sleep. Instead he tried the alley door where the girls lived. It was locked. Too late to wake them. He went to the stairway, climbed to the second storey and found the panel in front. He slid it back far enough to enter and closed it. The candle was where he had left it. Spur lit it with a stinker match and soon slid the panel to one side in Rebecca's room.

She had left a lamp burning low. Rebecca slept soundly, one arm thrown out and her nightgown in a pile on the floor. She moved and her breasts showed above the sheet. He moved on quietly, went out her door toward the other bedroom. He could see a light burning under the door. Spur blew out the candle and edged the panel open.

Jodi sat up in bed reading a book. She glanced

up expectantly as she heard the door open.

"Spur?" she asked. Her green eyes probed the darkness around the door.

"Yes. I need a place to sleep tonight. The sheriff has the hotels covered."

"I have a warm bed for you," Jodi said. She pulled a thin nightgown over her head and sat there watching him, her big breasts swaying gently from her body motion.

"Don't undress," she said. "Come here, with your boots on and your pants, everything. I want you just the way you are. Your clothes will feel rough on me."

Jodi kicked off the sheet and lifted her spread legs high in the air.

"I've been sitting here thinking about you. I've had about two hours of getting warmed up Please get up here and slam it right into me!"

Spur did. He realized he had been more excited by the nubile teenager than he wanted to admit. She had been damn tempting, but Jodi was much more practical. They plunged together into a crashing, shouting, exhausting climax and then lay side by side talking. Spur undressed.

"I hear you knocked down our sheriff today, and then tongue-lashed him to a fare-thee-well. Our Sheriff Johnson does not like that. He may have some misgivings about you now."

Spur laughed. "Afraid you're right. Sometimes my mouth gets me in trouble."

"There's some talk around town that you were the one who shot Deputy Pistol Pete."

"Just speculation. They want to blame it on me

so nobody else in town will be suspect."

"Are you any closer to tying the sheriff to the Rev. Fowler's shooting?"

"Is the word around town that I'm working on that, too?"

"I hear most everything at the Emporium. I know for certain that my boss, Mr. Hardy, would like to see the sheriff jailed and convicted."

"The more people who feel that way, the quicker we'll get the job done."

"Another fun playtime?" she asked.

"No, let's talk."

"Fine. It's nice, you know? Nice just lying here beside you and feeling all warm and soft inside. Knowing that you'll be there in the morning when I wake up. Kind of great. Maybe that's what it's like to be married."

"Probably. I wouldn't know."

"Now, don't get skitterish. I wasn't hinting."

"How is Rebecca?"

"Fine, usually. Once in a while she gets frightened. You know she carried knives in her skirts. She's got a knife sewn in a pocket in the folds of each one. Probably just a fear of men. One of these days maybe . . ." Jodi stopped and shook her head. "No, I probably shouldn't mess with that idea at all."

"What idea?"

She turned to him, green eyes worried, unsure. "You know she was molested when she was young, and raped, and then she killed our father. It left scars and troubles her deeply. But I was wondering, maybe . . . No, forget it."

"What are you suggesting?"

"Maybe if someone could show her that sex between a man and woman was natural, not terrible, she would get over her terror of men."

"Possibly. I had a doctor friend in Washington who specialized in crazy people. He said some of them could regain their sanity, but it would take a long time, a lot of work and care. Might be the same with Rebecca."

"Probably. I shouldn't have talked about it. As long as she doesn't get in trouble, or hurt anyone, I guess we can go on this way."

"Wasn't there something yesterday about a man being killed with a knife back here in the alley?"

"I heard that. But men get in knife fights all the time. Somebody is bound to get hurt."

"Yeah, you're right." He kissed her gently, then said goodnight and was asleep quickly.

Jodi thought about the dead man in the alley. No, it couldn't be. Rebecca never went out of their rooms unless Jodi went with her.

But Jodi thought about it until she went to sleep. There was a chance that Rebecca had been in the alley that night, but there was no way to find out for sure. Jodi pondered it again as she dropped off to sleep, one hand on Spur McCoy's shoulder.

CHAPTER NINE

Rebecca sat across the table from Spur and Jodi, watching them as they ate.

"You two going to get married?" Rebecca asked. "You been sleeping together, so I wondered."

"No, we're not getting married, Rebecca," Jodi said before Spur could react. "Although I wouldn't mind at all. You see, good friends sometimes do that, sleep together, even though they are not getting married. Rebecca, making love is the most wonderful thing anyone can experience. It's beautiful, tender, marvelous. You will find out about that someday."

For a moment Rebecca's eyes burned with a strange, savage glow, then she shrugged.

"Maybe. I don't much like men."

"That will change, Rebecca," Spur said. "One of these days you'll meet a fine young man and learn to like him a lot."

"Not if he tries to touch me!" Her eyes blazed again.

"Touching isn't that bad, Rebecca," Spur said. "Here, touch my hand. You touch me."

"That's different." She reached out and touched his hand, then his arm. When he started to hold her hand she jerked it back.

"No!"

"It may take a while," Jodi sighed. "Now, what are we going to do today, Becky? Is that new chair cover done yet, the cross-stitch you were working on?"

Rebecca recovered at once. "No, not yet. I'll get busy on it today."

Spur finished his breakfast of eggs and bacon and reached for his hat.

"Going to talk to the district attorney this morning. See what kind of law enforcement you have in this county. I don't expect any results, but I could get lucky. Does the courthouse open at eight?"

"Usually. It's not a big courthouse. In fact it's two rooms in the Bayless building just down from the hotel. This isn't a rich county."

"I noticed. Can I walk you to work?"

She said he could, and a few minutes later they

paused in front of the store. She touched his shoulder.

"You be careful. Don't do anything to give the sheriff a clean shot at you, legally or with his bully boys. I want you back in my bed tonight."

"You're trying to wear me out."

"I'd love to try." She smiled and went into the Emporium general store.

Spur walked another block to the Bayless building and went through the door marked "River Bend County Offices."

It *was* a poor county. From what Spur could see there were only four employees for the county, besides the sheriff, and they were all on the premises.

A small gray-haired lady with spectacles looked up from a big ledger as he stepped to the elbow high counter that ran across the twenty-foot wide room.

"I'd like to see the district attorney," Spur said.

"Yes sir. He'll be right here." She went to one of two other desks in the room and a moment later a man in a black suit and string tie came to the counter.

"Clyde Oberholtzer. How can I help you?"

"Where can we talk in private?"

The man's glance darted toward Spur. "Private?"

"Extremely private."

"Over by the window. We don't have separate offices yet. It's in the new building plans."

They sat by the window in straight backed

chairs and the man watched Spur expectantly.

"You're the new man in town who has been arguing with our sheriff?"

"Yes, and you're the district attorney?"

"Right."

"Good. I want to swear out a citizen's complaint against the sheriff and his three deputies, charging them with murder, with conspiracy to murder, with malfeasance in office, and grand theft. I want them arrested and no bail set due to the extreme seriousness of the cases and the fact that they would then have the power to bring illegal duress against the complainant masquerading it as their legal law enforcement duty. I think you'll find this action justified and with precedent."

Oberholtzer sat back, surprised. "Those are serious charges. Before I swore out a complaint, I would need some evidence, some legal testimony that would stand up in court."

"I have such evidence. A sworn statement by a witness who heard Sheriff Johnson order one of his deputies, Pete Bovert, to kill the Rev. Mr. Fowler."

"Yes, that is evidence, I must say," he smiled. "The people of the county would cheer roundly if this could work. But, I don't see how I can do it. Who would be our law enforcement?"

"You have the legal right to appoint an acting sheriff and allow him to deputize as many men as he needs."

"If only it would work! You don't know how the honest people in this county have been praying for something like this. But what if it doesn't hold? What if a judge throws it out of court?"

"Then we would have a start. We could hold a recall election and throw the sheriff out of office. With no power, he would cause a little hell here and then move on."

"Probably, but only after killing you and me. Do you want to risk that?"

"Yes. Where are the papers so I can fill them out and get this started?"

It was almost two hours later before Spur had the papers completed, his complaint written out in triplicate and filed with the district attorney. He had read them as Spur was writing, nodding and exclaiming. When Spur finished and he read the last page, Oberholtzer nodded.

"It could work, and it could stick. We're going to need more evidence for a jury, but this should get it started. Once we get him in jail, I think more people will come forward with evidence."

"Now, one more thing. I'm told Yale Crowningshield is on the sheriff's payroll. Can you keep these charges from him until you arrest the sheriff?"

"Yale is being bribed by the sheriff? That's another charge if we can prove it. Something like this is hard to keep quiet in a small town. I'll try."

Spur left the courthouse and walked to a side street. He had just turned the corner leading to the alley where they girls lived when he heard a six-gun cock behind him.

"Hold it right here, asshole!"

Before he turned around, Spur knew it was the sheriff. He made sure his hands were not moving and nowhere near his weapon. He turned slowly.

"Good morning, Johnson. From what I hear around town you've got a death wish."

"A what?" Johnson said, not understanding. It took the initiative away from him.

"You keep doing all these wild, dangerous things just hoping that one of them will kill you. A death wish. You're too yellow to shoot yourself so you keep hoping somebody else will."

The sheriff waved his gun at Spur. "If anybody dies around here, it's gonna be you. I'm arresting you for the murder of Pistol Pete. He told one of my deputies the night before he vanished that he was dead certain he knew you from somewhere before. Dead certain, he said. I think you killed him."

"I takes proof to arrest somebody. Where's yours?"

"I'll get it, somehow." He frowned. "Or maybe I should just save the county the cost of the trial."

"You've been doing that a lot lately."

"So what does one more hurt?"

"Not a thing," Spur said. "Except for those six people behind you watching. Be hard to convince them that it was a case of self defense, or my resisting arrest or trying to escape."

He looked over his shoulder for just a second. That was all Spur needed. He drew his six-gun as he dove for the ground and brought the weapon up firing a shot into the lawman's gun hand shoulder before he could get off a shot. There were people behind them. Nehemiah Hardy, Jodi, and three others Spur didn't know.

The sheriff dropped his weapon, roared with pain and anger and started to draw his second six-gun with his left hand.

"Touch it, Sheriff, and you're a dead man. Would save the county a trial, come to think of it."

Johnson started twice to take the gun out of the holster, but each time he stopped. Then he grabbed his shoulder with his left hand and glared at Spur.

"Gunning a peace officer. I got you good now, McCoy."

"Not so, ex-Sheriff. I'm placing you under citizen's arrest for attempted murder and extortion. My own murder. Just stand steady and I'll relieve you of that weapon."

Spur took the Colt from its leather, picked up the other one from the ground and shoved both inside his belt. Then he marched Johnson up the street.

"First we go see the doctor to get you patched up. Then you go into one of your own jail cells."

Sheriff Johnson's face was so red Spur thought he was going to explode. Blood seeped down his shirt sleeve. His fringed leather vest had spots of blood on it. His eyes went wild with hatred and fury.

"You'll not get half way to the jail, bastard! My men will cut you down like the asshole you are!" They walked to Main Street and Johnson looked around frantically. At last he saw one of his men.

"Take him, Winslow! Blow him into hell!"

Spur saw the man lift his six-gun. In the split second left him, Spur jumped behind Johnson, using him as a shield.

"Go ahead, Winslow," Spur called. "Put a couple of bullets right through the sheriff. Did Johnson tell you that he's under arrest for attempted murder, for murder, for conspiracy, and about a dozen other charges?"

Spur wasn't paying enough attention to the sheriff. He swung his good left hand, slapping Spur's weapon out of his hand and powering the agent away from his protection. Two shots thundered from forty feet away. Spur hit the ground rolling, came on his feet running and got behind a buckboard at the boardwalk. He dodged again, into a store, and bolted through to the back door where he got out and into the alley.

A minute later he banged on the door where Rebecca let him inside. He was panting, he was dirt smeared and dusty.

Rebecca looked different. She had on a tight dress that made her good breasts surge forward. A thin line of cleavage showed at the low neckline. She smiled a strange smile, and he nodded.

"Somebody chasing me again. Don't tell anyone I was here."

He had to go past her. As he did to get to her bedroom door, he bent and kissed her lips gently, then ran on. He failed to see an expression of anger on her face that quickly changed to delight.

She lifted her fingers to touch her lips, and stared after him.

Spur was through the hidden panel and into the passageway. He didn't bother with a candle this time, simply moving quietly and quickly toward the front of the building. He had tied it this time. He couldn't stay in town, at least not anywhere he could be seen. The sheriff would be after him now with every weapon and every man he had. He had to know he was fighting for his life.

When Spur came to the front of the passageway, he looked through a crack at the balcony and the street. A good place to bide his time. Twice in the next half hour he saw a deputy with a badge pinned on his vest work slowly up the street, looking at everyone, checking in each store along the way. The deputy even came up the stairs and looked into the second storey building. Spur could have reached out and touched him.

When the deputy left, Spur made his decision. It was time he checked out the last element in this equation, the rancher, Hans Klanhouser. His place was north of town and just across the Greybull River. He should be able to find it. He would wait there in the passageway until dark, then he would get down to the livery, rent a horse and saddle and strike out for the ranch. Somebody said it was ten miles out of town. He would be there in a couple of hours.

Then Spur heard movement behind him in the passage. He drew his revolver and cocked the hammer muffling the sound. Whoever was coming would get a hot lead reception.

CHAPTER TEN

Spur McCoy realized he was silhouetted against the light coming in from the secret opening behind him. He moved cautiously toward the sounds for ten feet then stopped. He held his breath and listened. Yes, the sounds were still coming, someone moving slowly. There was no lighted candle.

He waited another three or four minutes and he could hear the other person breathing.

"Ouch! Oh, dear!"

Spur heard the words and the woman's voice. A woman? Jodi or Rebecca? It could be no one else.

He let the hammer down soundlessly on his weapon, but still held it. Someone might be forcing her to come, to show him the passage.

Two minutes more and he could see a form ahead of him in the blackness. One form. He caught the flash of the same dress. It was Rebecca.

"Rebecca?" Spur whispered.

There was silence for a while. Her movement stopped.

"Yes. Spur?"

"Right, what are you doing in here?"

"I . . . I just wanted to see what was at the other end. I've never been through it."

He told her where it came out. They both walked hunched over toward the opening. He showed her the street and she giggled.

"Strange, it seemed so far."

"I have to stay here until it's dark outside. The sheriff wants to shoot me."

"Oh, no!" she said surprising him with her reaction. "He can't do that. I'll tell him not to."

"Right now he's real mad at me. He wouldn't listen to you."

He saw now that the dress seemed even tighter. One of the buttons on the bodice had come undone, letting more of her breasts show.

Spur sat down in the narrow passage. "I have to stay until dark so I'm going to be comfortable. Do you want to wait with me?"

"Oh yes. That would be nice."

She sat beside him, so close their thighs touched.

"How long have you been here in Elk Creek?" he asked.

"Long, two or three years." She turned toward him. "Spur, would you touch me?" Her face took on a frown and he saw just a glint of the anger building in her eyes, then it faded. "I want . . . I want to be able to stand it when you touch me."

"Yes. Of course." He put his hand over hers where it lay on her leg. For a moment she tensed, then she took a deep breath and let it out slowly.

"I like the feeling. Yes, I like it. Touch my shoulder."

He did and she took another breath.

"Would you . . . would you put your arm around my shoulders?"

Spur did, watching her reaction. This time the anger surged stronger in her face, but she beat it down with a new found strength.

"Yes! Yes!" She turned her face toward him, which was close now, and he saw her beaming in relief and joy. "Yes, I can do it! I can let a man touch me!" For just a moment she relaxed and leaned against him, then sat up straighter.

"Spur, I appreciate this. I really do. I . . . I have been having some bad days lately. It all seems so useless. I . . . I had some terrible experiences when I was younger."

"Don't think about them, just think about now," Spur said. "About how it feels good when I hug you. It's going to take some time. But you have made a good start."

She leaned against him and shivered, then turned her face toward his.

"One more thing. Would you . . . would you kiss me the way you did in my room?"

He bent and brushed her lips with his, then came away. Her eyes were closed, and she sighed, then smiled. He did the same thing again, then when her hand reached out and touched him, he kissed her again, firmly on her mouth, and pulled away.

She sat there with her eyes closed, a smile on her face.

"That felt so good, Spur. It was wonderful. Now, just one more touch, then I have to leave." She picked up his hand and brought it to her breasts. They felt hot to his touch where they surged halfway out of her dress. She kept her hand on top of his and pressed it firmly on her bosom. She held it there for a full minute, then pulled his hand away, and smiled softly.

"Thank you, Spur. Thanks a lot!" She leaned in, kissed his lips quickly and stood. She bent over and walked down the narrow passageway. She never looked back.

Spur sat there a moment smiling after her. She just might make it into the human race yet. He worked quietly back to the passage opening and watched through the cracks. It wouldn't be dark for a long time.

Spur lay down on the bare boards and went to sleep. He would need the rest before this was over.

He woke up just before midnight, surprised that he had slept so long. No matter. He slipped out the opening, closed it and headed for the closest alley and to the livery stable.

Spur spent the two hours before dawn taking a nap less than half a mile from the buildings of the Circle K ranch. He had ridden here easily from town and waited for the sun to come up. When he heard the breakfast bell ring at the big mess hall, he rode in.

A rifle toting guard picked him up a quarter of a mile out and talked to him. Just a precaution, the guard said and told Spur to go on in and have breakfast.

He tied his horse to a hitching rail in front of the building and opened the door. Heads turned. An older man stood up and watched him.

"Mr. Klanhouser?" Spur asked.

The man nodded. "Sit down and eat, then we'll talk. I ain't hiring but a man is always welcome to breakfast."

Spur had forgotten about chuck wagon cooking. There were ten men at the long plank table, and a dozen trays filled with fried eggs, flapjacks, pitchers of coffee, bacon and sausage, stacks of toast, pitchers of milk and a big bowl of applesauce.

He was hungry and ate all he wanted, then took his cup of coffee and sat across from the ranch owner.

"Not looking for work," Spur said. "But I would like to talk to you for a few minutes."

Klanhouser nodded. He was a thickset man, with black hair that needed cutting, heavy eyebrows that shadowed gray eyes, and a nose that dominated his face. He wore a full beard and moustache.

"Got to ride up north about three miles to check out two dead steers. Welcome to ride along."

It took Spur two miles of easy riding to tell the ranch owner exactly why he was in Elk Creek and what he hoped to get done here.

"Do you have any hard evidence that I can use against the sheriff? It has to be proof that will stand up in court and convince a jury."

Hans Klanhouser stopped his bay and took off his low-crowned hat, wiped sweat off his forehead with his arm and nodded.

"Might have. The sheriff gunned down one of my riders in town about two months ago. Claimed he was wild drunk and shooting up the saloon. Said Jason drew down on the sheriff and he had to fire to save his own life."

"Any of your men witness the shooting?"

"Saw the whole thing. Jason won two hundred dollars off the sheriff at a poker game in the Long Trail Saloon. Two of my riders was in the same game. Sheriff arrested Jason on the spot and took him out the front door. By the time my other men got out there the sheriff had out his gun and Jason was trying to get his. He wasn't no shooter. Jason almost got himself killed cause he tried to shoot a rattler one day. Missed it five times from three feet.

"Anyways, the sheriff shot him twice from about ten feet. Late at night, nobody else on the street. Jason never got his iron out of leather."

"Now we're getting something solid," Spur

said. "I want the dead man's name, and the exact date when this happened. Are the riders still with you who saw all this?"

"Yep. One of them is my son. I'll give you the names. Now let's see what killed them steers. I just lost another eighty dollars. Steer worth forty dollars on the hoof down at the rail yards in Rawlins."

"The sheriff ever get out this way?"

"Never has. I talked to him one day in town. He told me what went on at the Circle K was my problem. The town situation was all his, and I was to keep my nose out of it. I don't let the men go in more than once a month. I don't want any more of them getting killed."

Spur spent the rest of the day there. He wrote down everything he could find out about the killing of Jason Roberts. He talked with both the witnesses, and took down the exact words they used in describing the card game, the loss, then the arrest and subsequent unprovoked killing.

Any district attorney would drool over an open and shut case like this one. But the sheriff being the killer made it a tough case to prosecute.

Spur stayed over in the bunk house that night and headed back for Elk Creek just after breakfast. He would be in town about ten, and would try to get to the courthouse without the sheriff spotting him.

But Spur didn't make it to town. He had just crossed the river at the ford a half mile out of town when somebody with a rifle opened up on him. The first round missed him but he could hear the whistle of the bullet. He dove off the back of his mount and the next round caught the mare in the head, knocking her down. She screamed for two minutes before Spur put a mercy round into her head, ending her misery.

He crawled away from the dead mare and the rifleman fired again. Spur sprinted ten yards to a pile of boulders and slid behind them as a round whined off the rocks. He crawled the next ten yards to the side of the river and rolled over into the twenty foot deep gully the Spring rains had gouged. Now the river was low allowing plenty of room along the dry bank.

Spur charged forward toward the spot he figured the rounds had come from. He had to get close to do any good with his six-gun. Somehow he figured the bushwhacker would sit in place, knowing Spur had no long gun. He would wait for a chance at Spur as he ran for town aross the flat lands.

The agent crawled up the bank to check his progress. The clump of cottonwoods was still fifty yards from him. He watched but could see no motion at the fringe of the green leaves. Another three minute run and he spotted the cottonwood tops. He went past them, when he came up to the lip of the bank and looked over.

He saw through the trees, and a pair of blue pants and tan shirt where the sniper lay behind a long fallen log.

Spur wished he had brought along a rifle. A Spencer would come in handy. Without it he was too far away to trust the six-gun. It was a new one to him. He bought it from the stable hand when he rented the horse. So he would have to be closer.

Spur worked up the side of the wash, crawled behind some brush and stood. The sniper was moving around. He peered over the log, then stood behind a tree, but was still looking to the front. McCoy needed another twenty feet to get in practical range.

There was no cover between him and the sniper. Spur stepped from the last cottonwood tree and walked quietly forward. He was still sixty feet away. He moved cautiously, without breaking a twig.

Fifty feet.

The man turned. Spur screamed and charged straight ahead, his weapon up and held with both hands as he aimed as he ran.

Forty feet.

The sniper's surprise cost him a second's hesitation, and that was what killed him. By the time he got the long gun swung around and up to aim, Spur was thirty feet from him and the Colt in his hand barked four times.

Three of the big slugs caught the sniper in the chest and bowled him over backwards. Two of the rounds roared through the victim's heart dumping him into the quiet blackness of never ending death.

Spur walked up and looked down at the man's face. He had not seen the bushwhacker around town. A new hire perhaps.

The agent went through the man's pockets. He

found four dollars in cash, a cheap watch and a folded piece of paper. Spur unfolded it and found a good description of himself, as well as the exact color of his horse and saddle type that he had rented.

The sheriff was covering all bases. The Secret Service agent checked the rifle, a Spencer seven shot repeater. The kind he liked. He found half a dozen rounds in the sniper's pockets, then looked for his horse. Seemed like a fair trade, one chance to bushwhack him for his rifle and horse. The six-gun the man carried was a relic, a .32. Spur would rather throw rocks at someone than try to hit them with the old .32.

He found the horse in the next smattering of trees upstream two hundred yards. Spur changed his mind about the mount when he saw it. She was almost as worn out as the six-gun. The saddle was a duplicate of his own. Evidently both horse and saddle had been rented from the livery in Elk Creek. He unsaddled the animal, took off the halter and whacked her on the rump. Let her have a year of freedom before she died of old age. She might join some wandering herd of wild horses.

Spur walked toward town. He circled off the trail and came in behind some houses not far from the livery.

He shook his head in sudden memory and realization as he walked along. His college friends would laugh at him if they could see him today. He had not started out as a cowboy. He was born and grew up in New York City where his father was a big time retailer and importer. Spur graduated from Harvard in the class of 1858 and went into business with his father for two years. Then the war began and he enlisted as a second lieutenant in the infantry. He advanced to a captain's rank. After two years in the army he went to Washington, D.C. to serve as an aide to Senator Arthur B. Walton, a long-time family friend.

In 1865, soon after the act was passed, Charles Spur McCoy was appointed one of the first twelve U.S. Secret Service Agents. Since the Secret Service was the only federal law enforcement agency at that time, it handled a wide range of problems. Most of these jobs were far removed from the group's original task of preventing currency counterfeiting.

Spur served six months in the Washington office, then was transferred to head the base in St. Louis and handled all cases west of the Mississippi. He had been chosen from ten applicants because he was the only one who could ride a horse well, and because he had won the service marksmanship contest. His boss, William Wood, figured Spur would need both skills in the wild west.

And he had.

As he came into town he pulled his hat down low over his face and watched for the sheriff or any of his deputies.

He came in the back door of the livery and grabbed the same stable man he had rented his horse from.

"Pardner, did the sheriff talk to you last night after I rented that horse? You lie about it and I'll pound the truth out of you."

The man spit a stream of tobaco juice into the dust, and nodded.

"Sure he did. You didn't tell me nothing about secrets. So I described you and the horse."

"You almost got me killed. Somebody tried to bushwhack me outside of town. Instead he killed your horse. You can bill the sheriff for the nag and pick up the saddle a half mile out anytime you want to. Now I am asking you to keep a secret. I'm trying to get rid of this sheriff and do it all legal. You want to help me, you just don't tell him or his deputies that I got back in one chunk. You understand?"

"Yes sir. I don't like our sheriff either."

Spur McCoy changed his mind, paid for the dead horse, shouldered the Spencer and looked out the livery door into the street. Now all he had to do was figure out how to stay alive until he could check with the district attorney, and see if he could arrest the sheriff.

CHAPTER ELEVEN

Sheriff Tyler Johnson paused beside a cell in his jail and grinned.

"What's the matter, old timer? Can't you hold your booze no more? We rolled you out of a saloon last night. You sober now?"

"Yeah, Sheriff. Cold, stone sober."

"Good. You want out of jail?"

"Christ yes!"

"Good, I'll tell you what I want you to do. I don't have me no 'representative' in that swill-bag saloon you was in. You keep your eyes and ears open in there and tell me what's going on, and you get out of jail without paying twenty dollars bail."

"Twenty dollars? Hell, Sheriff, you know I ain't had that kind of money in years. Be glad to tell you what I hear."

The sheriff unlocked the jail and gave the man his hat and jacket.

"I'll be in touch with you, old timer, every day."

The sheriff watched him out the door. Things were moving along better. For a while he was jittery, with that new man in town raising hell. But he wouldn't bother him any more, not with a .52 caliber slug in his chest. The district attorney said something about some charges had been filed against the sheriff and Johnson knocked the bastard down and tromped him. He wouldn't be saying anything for a week at least until he healed.

Yeah, and now for some fun. He'd been six months finding out what he needed to know about Nehemiah Hardy. But now he had the information he needed. It was going to be sweet revenge to cut that big shot down to size. And to bring that Wendy Hardy off her high horse. Shit! This was going to be a bucket of belly laughs!

This was the morning that Wendy worked at the store, helping out with the books. Damn! Sheriff Tyler Johnson scratched his balls as he stood there, then rubbed the growing bulge behind his fly. Goddamn, he better get on over there.

When the sheriff came in the front door of the

emporium, Jodi saw him and moved behind a display of crockery tubs. She didn't want to speak to him if she didn't have to. He always tried to undress her with his eyes. Once he had asked her out to dinner, but she turned him down politely.

He went directly to the office and closed the door. A moment later Hardy came out looking pale. He searched for Jodi and found her.

"Can you hold down the place for a while? Something has come up that I have to take care of in the office."

"Sure, just so nobody wants ten rolls of barbed wire."

He nodded but she knew he didn't hear her. He went back into the office. All he could think of was what the sheriff wanted to talk about. They never had any business. He did order ammunition for the county, but that went through the courthouse. Hardy sat in his chair behind the small desk with Wendy on the other side. Sheriff Johnson stood near the door. He was pleased to see there was no window in the door. They had a private place.

"Glad you could talk so quick, Hardy. You may not know about it but we've been having a lot of break-ins and robberies lately. That's why we're starting a new service for merchants. We have a special policing service we offer for you. For a hundred dollars a month we'll check your doors and windows twice a night just to make sure nobody is robbing your place.

"Yeah, I know, it seems like a lot of money. But

think how much it would cost to replace your front windows if a smash and run criminal came and stole a wagon load of goods."

"That's ridiculous!" Wendy Hardy said. "Our taxes pay for our police protection, and that's you and your men. What you're suggesting is a tribute, a forced contribution, the crudest form of graft and corruption. I'm going right this minute to the county courthouse and tell everyone what you're trying to do."

Hardy stood up and motioned for his wife to sit down. He turned and faced the larger man. "Sheriff, I've heard of this kind of highway robbery in other places. I never thought we would be faced with a payoff like this here. Maybe I misunderstood what you said."

"Hardy, you got it all straight. A hundred U.S. dollars a month or we can't guarantee your safety, or the safety of your store."

"I won't call you Sheriff again, Johnson. You're an insult to the badge and the office. You're nothing but a tin horn hoodlum, an outlaw masquerading behind a badge."

For a big man Johnson moved fast. He hit Hardy with his right fist on the cheek, tearing a flap of skin free. His left hand slammed into Hardy's nose smashing it so the blood ran freely. He slumped back into his chair. Wendy rushed around the desk and put her handkerchief over his nose to stop the blood.

"Lesson one, Hardy. This is my county. Whatever I say here goes. Nobody is going to stand up to me. Not with you and that sneaky newspaper out of the way. And this is just the start, Hardy. You are a special case. I know your family has money in the east, and you have a lot back there too in two separate bank accounts. Didn't you know it's against the law to take money out of the county?

"Your fine is five thousand dollars. Payable this afternoon in cash. If Otto doesn't have it, you tell him to get it as soon as he can, paper or gold, don't matter."

"I won't give you a copper!" Hardy shouted.

"Oh, I think you will. Maybe you want me to tell your wife about that friend you have outside town."

Hardy looked up quickly. "I have friends all around in the mines and the ranches."

"Yeah, especially one ranch. So I'll ᴜell her. Wendy, did you know you're living with a squaw man? True. He met the little Sioux about sixteen years ago, before he met you. They have two little breed bastards out at that ranch he owns. She's his live-in squaw, you're wife number two."

Johnson looked up just in time to see Hardy come at him with a hunting knife. Johnson knocked it out of his hand, slammed him to the floor with a roundhouse right fist and picked up the knife.

Wendy had slumped in the chair shaking her head. Hardy had not denied his squaw! That was what shocked her the most. She had known about the ranch, and that there were a few Indians there, but there had been no hint, no suggestion . . . Or had there? His frequent trips out there.

119

The goods he took out from the store. Yes, fabrics, clothes. She turned her head. Tears seeped from her eyes. How could he!

Johnson stood before them. "So now she knows. But, of course, we're going to have to keep this our little secret. If anyone in town heard about it . . ."

"You wouldn't!" Hardy said from where he sat on the floor. "If that got out it would ruin me. Nobody would buy a thing from me. I'd be bankrupt within a month."

"True, Hardy. Absolutely true. That's why the three of us are going to be very good friends. Wendy, stand up and come here."

There was a ring of authority in his voice. She looked at her husband, but he had hung his head. She stiffened. At least she could show some backbone. She stood in front of him and without warning flashed out her right hand, fingers bent into claws as she raked her nails down his cheek digging four deep furrows there four inches long. Blood oozed from the marks, and one drop dripped to the floor. He caught her hand.

"That was not a smart thing to do, Wendy." He forced her to kneel in front of him. "Wendy, I've got this bad itch. I want you to scratch it for me, gently now." He took her wrist and moved her hand to his crotch.

"Scratch it for me."

She burst into tears. He held her hand on his genitals.

"Now a few tears ain't gonna help. Need that itch scratched."

120

She wiped the wetness away from her other hand. "You're crude and evil and terrible!"

"That sure ain't taking care of my itch."

She sighed. "I scratch the itch and then you'll go away and leave us alone?"

"Course! I'm a man of my word."

She looked up at him, then slowly her fingers rubbed the bulge she found there. He chuckled.

"Yeah, now that is good. Lower down."

Her fingers curved around the bulge of his scrotum.

"Say, I think you've got the idea." He opened the buttons of his fly and she pulled her hand back. He caught it and when he put it back to his crotch his pants were open and his penis and scrotum both hung in front of her, his long tool half erect.

"You are good, Wendy. Look, Hardy don't mind. Go ahead and help junior down there get all hard. You can do that."

"You promised just some scratching then you would go."

"Shit, I lied, Wendy. I do that a lot. Get me hard, any fucking way you can!"

Hardy screamed and got up, his fists tight, an ugly distorted mask on his face as he surged toward Johnson. The street fighter felt no pressure. He simply kicked out with his boot slamming it into Hardy's face, smashing off three teeth, pulping his lips between teeth and boot, and hammering his nose so it bled again. Hardy fell to the side and rolled on the floor in agony.

"Sweet little cunt, Wendy," Johnson went on

as if nothing had happened. "Only way you gonna get junior hard down there is to use your mouth. You know how, suck it!"

She shook her head.

Johnson caught her hair with both hands and forced her face into his crotch, then pulled it back and flipped his penis up so she could take it.

"Eat it, slut, or I tell everyone about Girl, the little Sioux squaw and her bastard halfbreeds fucked up by your dear husband!"

Tears welled from her eyes. She shivered. Never had she felt so frightened, so alone, so in danger. This gone bad lawman could do anything he wanted, to the town, to her husband, to their business, to her . . . Slowly she opened her mouth and took his rod inside. She gagged, then made the adjustment and Johnson laughed.

"Damn, I think the little cunt has learned how to suck cock. Look at that! Best suck job I ever had. You're a most talented mouth, little bitch." He began to pump his hips back and forth, then slowed and stopped. "This isn't fun anymore."

He looked down at Hardy. The merchant had rolled around to see what was happening. His bloody, mashed-up face managed a furious glare.

Johnson lifted Wendy to her feet. She stood in front of him without moving, her eyes staring down but not at her husband.

"Yeah, now that's more like the proper respect. Let's see what's wrapped up in the package."

Before she could move he had caught the front of her dress in each hand and pulled sideways, popping the twenty buttons down the front from neck to navel. The dress tore apart showing her chemise.

"No!" she shrieked. "Stop that!" She tried to kick him, but missed. He laughed, pulled the dress down over her shoulders so it pinned her arms at her side. Then he took the thin, cotton chemise and ripped it off and let her breasts swing into view.

He had seen bigger, but these were here now.

Johnson felt the pain in his right shoulder where the bullet had gone in, but he was having too much fun to let it pain him that much. He grinned at her and bent and sucked on one of her breasts.

Just then Hardy swung his unloaded rifle by the barrel. He had aimed it at Johnson's head but when he bent to kiss her, it swooshed harmlessly over his back. Johnson saw it from his left eye, leaped back, grabbed the weapon, tore it from Hardy's hand and drove the butt hard into Hardy's stomach. The merchant doubled over and vomited on the floor, then curled up against the wall as spasms coursed through his aching body.

Johnson turned back to Wendy.

"Don't hurt him any more. He's my husband! Don't kill him. We'll do what you want!" She pushed the dress down off her arms, over her hips and stepped out of it, then unhooked the drawers and as he watched, she pushed them down a little at a time, teasing him.

Johnson stood there surprised, the rape aspect of his conquest was gone. She was giving it to him. Christ! He would still take it, make the old man watch him fucking his wife. Yeah!

"Just keep that cloth moving, sweet pussy," Johnson said. "You're going to get reamed out like the little guy there never did. You're gonna get yourself fucked by a real man." He bent and jerked the drawers off one of her legs, left them hanging on the other and grabbed her, sitting her on the top of the desk. He spread her legs and stepped between them, bent a little and nosed his shaft into her warm moist hole. He stopped.

"Hardy, you bastard. Stand up here and watch how a real man fucks your wife. Stand up, or so help me I'll blow your balls off with a .44 round!"

Dazed and unsure of what he was doing, Hardy stood and stared with unseeing eyes at the man in front of him. Then Johnson roared with laughter as he rammed hard into Wendy and heard her yelp in pain. She had to hold her arms around his neck to keep upright. Her legs trailed off the desk and he thundered into her body again and again, grunting like a bull, pulling her back to the front of the desk after he had pounded her away from him.

He lunged twice more into her, belched and pulled out of Wendy and pushed himself inside his pants.

"Now, little lady, you been fucked by the best, and don't you never forget it." He took a pair of deep breaths. "Back to business. Little lady, you listen to me good. If you don't want everybody in town to know about your husband's squaw and his two bastard breeds, you get that five thousand dollars for me by Tuesday. Then every week I come over here, you drop your drawers for me and give me five thousand. A simple, neat arrangement. You understand."

"Yes."

He turned to look at Hardy. She pulled the six-gun out of his holster and forgot to cock the trigger with her thumb. By the time she had pulled hard enough to cock the trigger so it would fire, Johnson had felt the gun move, and spun around, slamming the weapon just as it fired. The round roared downward, missed Johnson, and bored through Hardy's left leg.

"Fucking woman!" Johnson shouted as he backhanded her, hitting the side of her head and slamming her off the desk to the floor. He grabbed the gun and jammed it back in his holster, then stared at them both for a moment before he strode out the door and out of the building.

Jodi had stood frozen near the door to the office since she heard the first big argument. The shot had brought her back to life and she hurried into the room as soon as the sheriff stormed out. She found Mrs. Hardy rushing back into her clothes, and Mr. Hardy on the floor bleeding. She didn't say a word, she ran for Doc Paulson. He was in and just finishing with a patient. He rushed to the Emporium behind her and shook his head when he saw all the damage done to his friend.

"Looks like a locomotive ran over you, Hardy," he said. "Now don't talk. First let me get the bleeding stopped on that leg. Then we'll start patching you up—the worst parts first. Not a damn thing we can do about the teeth. Maybe someday we'll get a dentist in town. I don't even want to know who did all this to you."

"Sheriff Johnson did it," Wendy said. "He raped me and almost killed Hardy. When is somebody going to have enough courage to go up against him?" She paused a minute. "Maybe it's going to be up to me. Would you teach me to shoot a rifle, Doc?"

CHAPTER TWELVE

Spur moved like a shadow from the livery after paying for the dead horse. It was three blocks to the alley where the girls lived and he hoped the sheriff wasn't watching their door. It took him ten minutes to cover the distance, walking normally when he could, hiding in an alley mouth and behind a house as people went by. He wanted no one to see him knock on the door.

When he did, Rebecca opened it at once. She smiled at him and he saw she wore a print dress that buttoned high around her throat and had long sleeves and swept the floor. Good.

"You've been gone overnight," Rebecca said. "We missed you."

He looked quickly for that flash of anger in her eyes but saw none of it.

Spur touched her shoulder and she shivered. "Has Jodi said anything about the district attorney?"

"No."

It had been less than twenty-four hours. Spur left the rifle, got some more .44 rounds from his gear and smiled at Rebecca.

"I have to go out again, but I'll be back. You watch things for me." He touched her shoulder and checked the alley out the door. Clear. He closed the door after him and ran down the alley, crossed the street and walked casually along the far side of the street to the next alley and turned into it. This should be the alley in back of the Emporium. He hoped there was a sign on the back door.

It was almost noon when he slipped through the back door of the Emporium and looked around. A storage room. He went through it and checked a door on the far side. It opened into the main store. He saw Jodi behind the counter and whistled softly at her. She saw him and motioned him back, then came into the storage room.

Her face was strained, and he could tell she had been crying.

"Terrible! Just terrible. That damn sheriff came in here and had a fight with Hardy and mashed him up. He got shot in the leg and I think the sheriff raped Mrs. Hardy, and there was lots

128

of screaming and yelling. I don't know what it was all about, but I do know the sheriff is demanding five thousand dollars a week from Hardy."

"Slow down, take it easy. Now tell me again what happened."

She did, as much as she knew.

"I sent them both home. I'm running the store the rest of the day. Lordy, I never seen a face so beat up as Hardy's was. Teeth broken off, ripped skin, smashed nose, just terrible."

"So, we have another nail in the sheriff's coffin. What about the district attorney. Do you know if he did anything about filing charges against the sheriff?"

Jodi frowned. "Strange. Clyde Oberholtzer was in the doctor's office when I went in with Hardy. Seems he had some cuts on his face and a loose tooth and a hurt side. He looked like he had been beat up too."

"Figures," Spur said. "So much for our big legal action charges to get rid of the sheriff."

"Oh, oh. Customer. Don't go away, I'll be right back." She went through the door and into the store.

When Jodi came back five minutes later she was white with shock. She showed Spur a flyer she carried. Spur read it:

WANTED DEAD OR ALIVE! REWARD $1,000. SPUR McCOY. LAST SEEN IN ELK CREEK, WYO. WANTED FOR ASSAULT ON SHERIFF'S DEPUTY AND THE MURDER OF A LAW ENFORCEMENT OFFICER. ARMED AND DANGEROUS.

There followed an accurate description of Spur. He read it, folded it neatly and put it in his shirt pocket.

"I'm making a collection of these. It's been tried before. It simply means I'm going to have to be more careful. So don't worry."

"But a thousand dollars! Spur, that's four year's wages for most men! There will be gunmen from all over looking for you."

"Probably, but I'll be watching for them. Why did Johnson get so violent with Hardy?"

"I don't know for sure. All I heard was something about the ranch he owns. I knew something terrible was going on in there but I didn't want to get caught up in it."

"Right, nobody can help anyone else when she's dead. Now, where does the district attorney live?"

She told him. "You be careful. With those wanted posters and all . . . Well, I want you at my place again, not splattered all over the street somewhere."

"You're terrific at descriptions," Spur said and laughed. "Don't worry, I'll watch my hindside. I don't want to wind up in boot hill out there either. I'll see you for supper, all right? I'm starved."

She held her face up to be kissed and he drew her tightly against him and kissed her three times, and left her gasping. Someone came in the front and she had to go out and clerk. Spur went to the back door, checked the alley, waited for a merchant to go back in his store. Spur headed down the alley heading toward the house where the D.A. lived. It was a half block from the Hardy place.

Oberholtzer answered the knock on his back door himself. He had a bandage around his jaw, another on his forehead and he walked with deliberate caution. When he saw Spur he tried to close the door. Spur pushed it open slowly yet firmly.

"Sure it hurts to fight him," Spur said before Oberholtzer had a chance to say a word. "It's hurt me and this isn't even my town. Your job says you've got to expect a little hurt. At least you're still alive. Do you have a dead or alive wanted poster out on you?"

Oberholtzer shook his head.

Spur pulled the poster from his pocket. Oberholtzer shook his head in surprise. "I never thought he would go that far. The man is out of his mind."

"Now, tell me what happened with you and Johnson?"

"He came into the courthouse this morning and I served the papers on him. He laughed and tore them up. Then he punched me around until I fell down. When I was on the floor he began kicking me with his boots. If the two women hadn't come back from lunch right then I think he would have killed me."

"You're lucky, you have more charges to file against him. Assault and battery against a public official, attempted murder, conspiracy to murder. Write them up, and file them, but you don't have to give them to the sheriff. It's called piling up evidence. When we get enough I can take it to the

Territorial Governor and get some action from that level."

"If any of us are alive by then," Oberholtzer said. "I'm not going to work for a week. A vacation, I'm taking a vacation."

The man was scared. Spur had seen it before. There would be no more help from the district attorney. He cautioned Oberholtzer against going out of the house and faded out the back door.

Spur moved slowly, watching for tin stars on the chests of anyone on the street and worked his way to the back door of the newspaper office. It was unlocked. Spur stepped inside. He heard nothing, then someone began whistling near the front. Spur walked up and saw Les Van Dyke setting type at a type case. He had the eight point drawer out and was gathering body type for the next edition.

"I want three pages of advertising space every week for a year," Spur said.

Van Dyke jumped, surprised at the closeness of the voice, then he snorted.

"That's got to be McCoy. Nobody else in town has a wanted poster out on him, and nobody could be that cheerful when everything else around here is going to hell in a handbasket."

"You're still in business."

"Right, until this issue comes out. I've about decided to shoot it all in one big play and hope I can win."

"Don't do anything dumb, yet. We'll have our day, and it should be coming up fast. I think Johnson is getting worried. You know he beat up

Oberholtzer and then clobbered Hardy, making him look like a mummy."

"Hardy too? Why for god's sake?"

"Who knows? Something about blackmail. We've got enough to hang Johnson six times over if he wasn't the sheriff. We're so far off the beaten track up here, it would take us two weeks to get a company of militia up here. By then half the people in town would be dead. Looks like this is one we're going to have to take care of ourselves."

"We, meaning you," Van Dyke said. "The only thing I know about a .44 or a rifle is that they go bang. I'm a city boy. Don't count on me in your army. It sounds like you're talking about a civil war or at least a town-war shoot-out."

"I don't want it to come to that. Not good for the town, not good for all the people who wake up and find themselves dead. Hell of a shock."

"Speaking of dead, how do you plan on staying alive with a small fortune riding on your head?"

"First by staying here until it gets dark, then holing up in my favorite spot. I won't even tell you where it is."

"I don't want to know, in case I get tortured." He paused. "Can you set type, too?"

"A little rusty."

"Figures. Just some headlines with that twenty-four point. You should be able to find them. Here are half a dozen to start on."

Four hours later Spur cleaned the ink off his hands, then slipped into the darkness and made his way cautiously but quickly to the alley door.

The lock was open. He went inside then locked and bolted the door behind him.

Jodi stood at the stove working on dinner. Rebecca sat at the table. When she saw Spur she stood and smiled.

"Hope you like fried chicken," Jodi said. "That's what we're having. And some vegetables."

"Sounds fine. Hi, Rebecca."

She blushed, waved and then hurried into her room.

"I don't know what's got into her. She's been primping and looking in the mirror ever since I got home. Then she said it was my turn to cook dinner." Jodi turned, hands on her hips. "You haven't been romancing that girl, have you, Spur?"

"No. I did touch her hand and her shoulder the other day when she asked me to. She seems to be coming out of her shell a little."

"A little! Christ, Spur! This is the most progress she's made in five years. It's amazing. Whatever it is, just do it again. Maybe some day she'll be back to normal."

After they had supper Rebecca shooed them out of the kitchen since it was her turn to wash the dishes. The only place for them to go was Jodi's bedroom.

As soon as the door closed, Jodi kissed Spur hard. "I almost went crazy just now waiting until I could get you alone. Let me lock the door. There is not a chance that I'm going to let you get out of here before you bounce me about three times on the bed, belly to belly!"

He caught her, picked her up and then dropped her on the bed. She giggled and began opening the top of her dress.

"No, no," Spur said, sitting beside her. "Don't do that, that is man's work. Besides, I enjoy tearing your clothes off that fantastic body."

"Good."

He opened the bodice of her dress and pushed his hand inside, finding one big breast and grabbing it. She smiled and kissed his lips.

"Faster, Spur, faster, I'm burning up."

He felt the heat coming from her whole body. It seared his hand on her breasts, pounded through her thighs to his, erupted from her crotch in a massive wave that warmed him through and through. He rolled on top of her and her hips began to pump upward against him.

"Sweetheart! Please, right now, please!"

He drew a pocket knife from his pants, opened a blade and knelt between her spread legs. Deftly he cut a slice through the crotch of her drawers. She yelped in sudden delight and jerked the buttons open on his fly.

A moment later she had pulled his hard penis out of its cloth jail and pushed it toward her heartland.

"Now, damnit, right now!"

Her hips were still gyrating. He nosed against her, her fingers helped position him and he slid into her slot, driving in hard and fast until his hips smashed against her pelvic bones and she moaned in total rapture and delight.

"Oh, god but that is good! I think I would have blown up if you hadn't come tonight. I was getting so horny I would have jumped the first bum to stagger down the alley. I just love you so much, Spur McCoy that I'm never going to let you go. You know that. Harder! Pound it into me harder! Each time you flick against my little clit down there and it sends me absolutely over the edge of the world!"

He slowed his pumping and then stopped, pushed a little lower and worked his face inside her partly opened dress and blew aside the chemise until he could pull one of her breasts into his mouth.

"Tits!" he said around his mouthful. "Best meal in the whole fucking world. Big tits, little tits, round ones, square ones, I don't care. I love tits! There, I said it!" He pushed his face between her breasts and flapped them back and forth hitting hard and chortling. "Beat to death by a pair of big tits."

"Shut up and fuck me," she said grinning.

"I am fucking you. What do you think this is? Making May Day baskets?"

"He's just laying there."

"Then you provide the action."

She tried humping against him, but he was too heavy for her to get much action. He growled and began again. She lifted her legs around his chest, then pushed them higher until they were at his arms. He nodded and moved so she could lift her legs on his shoulders. It lifted her hips higher and he drove in deeper still until she screeched in wonder.

"Christ, I've never tried this before!"

"I bet you will again."

"Oh, Jeez, oh jeez, oh jeez! OH JEEZ!!! I'M GOING TO EXPLODE!" Her face contorted, her whole body began to tremble and shake, jolting in one series of tremors after another. She cried out in the intense pain-pleasure of it a dozen times. Then she shattered in an earthquake spasm that left her sweating and moaning in ecstasy.

He felt his cock swelling inside her. As her spasm trailed off, his began. He drove hard so their pelvic bones grated and crashed, swept apart and ruptured into each other again.

His moaning matched hers in intensity, then he trailed off and shuddered one more time, driving his hips into her to plant his seed.

He let her legs slip over his arms to the bed. They lay that way for ten minutes before he pushed off her and lay by her side. Slowly, gently, they undressed each other. It took them ten minutes, a tender demonstration of feeling for each other.

"Now that was a good one," Jodi said reaching up and kissing his cheek. "Why is it always better with you, can you tell me that?"

"Anticipation always improves things," he said.

"Not this much, not a chance." She looked away, then leaned up on her side so she could see him better. She traced his chin with her finger. "You won't be around here long, I know that. You're no regular man, I understand that. You're here to get rid of our sheriff, one way or the other, and I just pray that it doesn't get you killed. But I know that after it's all over, you will be moving on, to somewhere else where there's trouble."

He leaned up and kissed her.

"No, let me finish. You probably have a girl in every town you stop in. I know I can't keep you here, and I'm damn sure that I can't go with you. So I want the rest of these days to be ones that you will remember all your life. I want to do anything, anything that you want to do. Just tell me, or show me. Anything!"

He kissed her. "Jodi, that was tender, and moving, and sincere, and I *will* remember it always." He kissed her again and she rolled against him, her hand reaching to his crotch, finding him and working slowly to bring him back to life.

Tenderly she brought him to his full erection, then moved Spur on his back, spread his legs and took him in her mouth.

"I want to make love to you every way I know how, and I want to do it all tonight. I'm glad we have an early start."

Then she worked on him, teased him until he could stand it no more and loosed his second load which she took and swallowed and licked him clean and then lay beside him as he rested.

"This is going to be the most remarkable and wonderful night that I've ever had," Jodi said. "I know damn well I'm going to remember it forever. And that's a gold-plated promise!"

CHAPTER THIRTEEN

Wendy Hardy waited until her husband fell asleep that evening. When she put the children to bed, she told them to be extremely quiet because their father was hurt and needed a long sleep. When they were quiet and sleeping, she checked the clock in the living room. Just after nine P.M. and dark outside.

She locked the house and walked quickly to the store, unlocked the back door and went to the Emporium gun case. She took out a Spencer repeater rifle. When they were first married, Hardy had taught her to shoot. He had upgraded her education every year or so, showing her the new rifles and pistols. She was good with guns. She loaded the tube with seven of the big .52 caliber rounds and slid it into place, then worked the lever on the bottom of the stock, loading a round in the chamber. It was ready to fire seven times.

The weapon was heavy, over ten pounds and was forty-seven inches long, but she could handle it. She went to the upstairs of the Emporium and worked her way to the front of the storage area. Some day they would make the whole upstairs into a retail area. She wanted all the women's things there, but that had to wait. None of the windows opened. She looked through one window and frowned. It was not right. She could not see the sheriff's office.

She knew his routine. Every night about ten the sheriff and his two deputies began checking doors and walking through the saloons. She wanted to greet Johnson the moment he walked out of the office, while he was still lighted by the lamp light from the windows.

But this wouldn't work. She went downstairs, put the rifle in a long cardboard box and went out the back door. She walked down the alley and into the alley behind the next block. This should work fine. The Hartford hotel was here and the unoccupied rooms would not be locked.

She went up the Hartford hotel's back stairway to the second floor when no one was watching, and found the room she wanted. It was open. She stepped inside, closed and locked the door, then pushed a chair under the door. She looked out the window.

Perfect! She could see the sheriff's office on the street that dead ended into the hotel and formed a "T." Quietly she lifted the window a foot and looked out. Yes. It would work. She sighed it over the sliding rear sight and the blade front sight nodded. Then she pulled another chair over, rested the barrel of the rifle on the window ledge and waited.

Once she dropped off to sleep, but she snapped awake quickly. She remembered what the beast, the non-human, had done to Hardy and she bristled with fury. She had not been shocked or angry with Johnson raping her. No, it hadn't been rape. It started out that way, but she allowed it, she even helped at that point. It meant nothing. Her body was certainly no holy temple that had been violated. One man's penis was the same as another's. The experience was distasteful but not earth shattering.

What she was furious about was the way Johnson had beaten her husband, had threatened her future and the safety and well being of her family, her children. She was a furious sow bear protecting her cubs, and no one, neither Sheriff Johnson nor anyone else, was going to threaten them.

Someone came out of the office and she tensed, but she could see it was not the sheriff. She would recognize his bulk and the high-crowned hat he wore. He insisted all of his deputies wear low-crowned hats with a badge pinned to the crown.

It was a type of uniform.

Then she admitted the other reason she wanted to kill the sheriff. He had confirmed what she had suspected for a long time, that Hardy had a mistress at the ranch. She had never been able to prove anything beyond her own intuition. He was always subtly different when he came back from the ranch. More tender, concerned. He thought more of her wants and needs for a day or two, almost as if in compensation. And now she could tell that it had been. He was making it up to her without her knowing it.

Dear sweet Hardy. The last man she would suspect of having another woman. It didn't bother her that the mistress was an Indian. She did not have the terror, the fear, the anger and hatred for the Indians most of the people in town did. They were people to her, like anyone else. Uneducated, with no advantages, but people nonetheless who had been pushed off their rightful property ever since the Pilgrims arrived in Jamestown in 1607.

She had not worked hard for fifteen years to have it all blown away in one morning! She would fight for her husband and her family in the only way that Tyler Johnson understood—force. She would return hurt for hurt! If only she could have remembered to cock the pistol with her thumb in the store that morning, the sheriff might be dead by now.

She firmed her resolve as someone else came out the door of the jail. It was Sheriff Johnson. She sighted down on him, his chest, the best target. She knew the first shot was most important. She would have more time. After that she would be working the lever to push a new shell in and have to re-aim and he would be running for cover.

Wendy Hardy watched her target stop and look down the street. The blade sight centered on his chest and she squeezed the trigger the way Hardy taught her. The sound of the rifle going off deafened her in the small room. She saw the sheriff grab at his shoulder.

Damn!

Furiously she levered in a new round and aimed again where he had been. The sheriff had jumped behind a post holding up the front overhang of the jail. She fired again. The round slammed into the post. Four more times she aimed and fired. Her target surged back inside the door of the jail and she sent the last two rounds into the door, then dropped the weapon and looked into the hallway. No one. She stepped out and walked down the hall to the back stairs, went down them and into the alley just as she heard shouts at the front of the hotel and footsteps pounding up the front stairs.

Wendy Hardy walked through the alley, and back to her house. She had hit him, in the shoulder she guessed. The rifle must have been off in its aim. She should have "sighted it in" as Hardy had explained. Any rifle has a tendency to fire to one side or the other or slightly up or down. To make a weapon totally accurate, the sights can be adjusted, or the shooter simply takes the variance into account when she shoots.

Besides she wasn't a marksman. She had missed.

As she walked, Wendy evaluated her thoughts. She felt little different than she had when she had been planning the attack. She was still tremendously angry at the sheriff. She was angry at the system which permitted him to run rough-shod over them for so long. But she did not consider herself an outlaw or a criminal because she had deliberately tried to kill a man. He had it coming, she was totally justified. The only difference now was the sadness that she had missed, and that she probably wouldn't have another chance.

She had been home only five minutes when someone knocked on the front door.

When she opened the door she saw Deputy Sheriff Eliason. He was a crude character she had met in the store a few times.

"Mrs. Hardy?"

"Yes Mr. Eliason. What do you want? Hasn't your office caused me and my husband enough pain and suffering for one day?"

"Pardon, Ma'am. I was just supposed to find out if you was home. You been here all evening?"

"Of course. I'm not the kind of woman who goes parading around at night. Especially in Elk Creek where a decent woman isn't safe on the streets after dark. I want the sheriff to do something about that!"

"Yes, Ma'am. I'll surely tell the sheriff."

He turned and went down the walk without another word. Wendy smiled as she closed the door. She had lied so easily! When you have a just cause lying was not that hard. So the sheriff had suspected her. It was a good thing she walked home quickly. He could never prove that she fired the weapon. And there were a number of Spencer repeating rifles in town. She was safe for the moment.

What she had to do was come up with some way to kill the sheriff. Wendy lifted her eyebrows in surprise. Here she was thinking about, and planning, how to kill someone. She shrugged. It was the maternal instinct. She was protecting her home and her family. That was power, a drive more powerful than anything the preacher ever said on Sunday morning.

Wendy went inside and checked on Hardy. He was sleeping soundly. For a moment she stared at his bandaged face. Poor dear! He would be months getting over the beating. And he had done it to protect her. She kissed the cheek that was not bandaged and he reached for her in his sleep. She caught his hands and put them by his side. Not yet, she thought, but soon. She had been forgetting to care for his needs. She knew that he needed to make love to her once a week. Maybe later tonight she would minister to him, start while he was sleeping and when he woke, she would tell him to lie still and she would do for him what he wanted. It was little enough for the pain he was in. In time she would learn to enjoy the feel of him in her mouth and even the taste. She put his hands down and went to look at her children.

All the while, Wendy Hardy was thinking of some way she could get another shot at the sheriff, how she could catch him unaware. She found the pistol Hardy kept in the drawer of his work bench. She loaded it, then unloaded it and practiced dry firing, thumbing back the hammer and sighting and firing quickly. When she was satisfied that she could do it accurately and quickly with both hands holding the heavy Remington, she loaded it, left an empty chamber under the hammer as Hardy had taught her, and slid the four-inch barrel .44 into her reticule. She would be ready now, if she had the chance.

CHAPTER FOURTEEN

The next morning Spur wrote a note, then edged into the alley and watched at the first side street until he saw a small boy running by. For a quarter the boy promised to deliver the note to the sheriff's office and forget what Spur looked like.

The note was to Deputy Sheriff Eliason, and said that he could earn fifty dollars quick and easy. He was not to tell the sheriff and to come to the corner of Main street and Wyoming Trail just as soon as he could. It would be easier if he came mounted.

Spur ran to the livery, rented a horse and

saddle, told the wrangler to forget he was there, and rode out of town and came back from the north approaching the meeting place just beyond a small creek and its green ribbon of narrow leafed cottonwood and trembling aspens. The Secret Service Agent stayed in the green cover until he made sure that the deputy rode out alone to the corner. There was only one house nearby, and Spur decided there had not been enough lead time for the deputy to plant a man there with a rifle.

Spur rode out with the Spencer rifle angled over the saddle at the deputy. When he saw Spur coming it was too late to draw.

"Just a little friendly protection," Spur said. He stared at Eliason, then nodded. "Wasn't sure if I recognized you or not, Eliason, but now I'm sure. We met in Dodge once and you were not a nice person at all."

"What the hell you talking about? I never been to Dodge." The deputy was nervous, his hands both on his saddle horn but his right itchy to draw.

"Got a poster in my gear that shows your face plain as day. It says dead or alive, friend. How you want it?"

"Ain't never been no wanteds out on me. Never! But I know who you are, and there is a wanted on you. A thousand dollars. That's worth my time to gun you down right here."

"You're forgetting the old Spencer here aimed right at your gut. I was disappointed in the reward they offered for you. Only three hundred.

Christ, you'd think a big man like you would be worth more than three hundred. It cost me half that to come to town and wait until I could identify you. But hell, every little bit counts."

"You ain't got me yet, McCoy, and what's more, you ain't got me hauled all the way back to Kansas. Don't spend your money too damn fast!"

"Just who the hell is there here to stop me? Your back shooting buddy turned up dead. You never were known as being fast with that six-gun even if you do tie it low, and me, I got seven .52 sweethearts in here just roaring to get out and punch holes in your three hundred dollar hide."

"Never make it. I told the sheriff I was coming out here."

"Shit! You lie worse than you rob banks, or whatever it was. Didn't say on the poster. You got a choice to make: you want to go to Kansas belly down across your saddle dead as a headless rattlesnake, or you want to ride head up? If you decide to go on breathing, you drop your iron over my side of that nag, and keep your hands back on the saddle horn . . ."

Eliason dove from his horse away from Spur. It was the move Spur expected and with the Spencer he fired by instinct. The round lanced through the vanishing shoulder, and Spur dug his heels into his mount, moving away from the area, and out of range of the Colt he knew the deputy had drawn.

Spur pulled up fifty yards away. He sent a rifle shot behind the sorrel which made the horse side step away from the deputy on the ground. One more shot moved the mount another ten yards and then she discovered some new grass at the edge of the trail and began feeding.

"No chance, Eliason. You got a slug in your shoulder, you want to try for one in your head?"

"Come get me."

"Not likely. I can sit out here and pick you to pieces, first your legs, then your arm. Maybe one round through your crotch just for fun. Sound interesting?"

There was a long silence. The deputy lay on the ground staring at Spur. The deputy had no cards in his hand to play with let alone a hand he could bluff.

"What do you really want, McCoy? You know damn well I'm not wanted anywhere. That don't work with me. I was going for you for the reward. That's four years pay for me."

"Not if you wind up dead. Make you a deal. You throw out the six-gun and I'll take you into town. We go in the back way and let the doctor dig out that slug, then I give you a sack of grub, your gun back and your horse. You ride like hell and I watch you out the first ten miles."

"What's to keep me from circling back and gunning you down for the reward?"

"Two things, Eliason. You sound like you could be a halfway honest lawman, if you had a chance. You're not too damn happy working for Johnson as it is. You know his charges against me and that damn reward are both a batch of lies. And if you come back and show your face in town, I'll blow your brains out."

There was another long silence, then Eliason stood, threw his six-gun on the ground. When it hit the ground it went off, the wild round zinging away from both men.

"Your play, McCoy. Somehow I was sure that Sheriff Johnson never would pay that reward money anyway. I get the feeling he's thinking about pulling up and getting out of town while he's still got his gold. He was telling me the other day he has over thirty thousand in the bank. I don't know whether to believe him or not."

Spur came up and searched the man quickly. He had a knife in his boot, but no other weapons.

On the ride to the doctor's office, Eliason told Spur about the attack on the sheriff the previous night.

"He took a rifle slug in the shoulder, but it went on through. He's furious. Doesn't know who shot him, but he's going to be accusing everyone. You're on top of his list. The doctor fixed him up, but he won't be charging around much for a day or two. Give me time to get well out of town."

"How many more deputies does the sheriff have?"

"Full time men was four, counting me. Now he's down to three, and one of them ain't too much count. You want to take over the office and jail, best time would be about six in the evening. Sheriff is at the hotel eating supper, and only one day deputy there. He's waiting to get off duty. Night men come on at seven. Be just two of them now and the sheriff."

"Thanks. I've got to take it sooner or later. Is

there a back door to the jail?"

"No, too hard to protect."

"Figures."

Doc Paulson lifted his brows when he saw another shoulder rifle wound, but said little. Spur talked with him as he waited for the bullet to come out. It had hit a bone and broken in half. Eliason's arm would have to be in a sling for a week.

"This is one gunshot wound I don't want you to report to the sheriff's office," Spur said. "Turned out to be an accident. You know how these things happen."

"Like happened to Hardy?"

"No, that was different. Going to cut down on those kind of accidents just as soon as possible. Eliason here is heading out of town for good."

"Happy trails," Doc said and stitched up the slice in Eliason's shoulder.

Spur spent another half hour getting a sack of food and supplies for Eliason from the Emporium. Then they rode out the back way. Eliason said he was heading for Sheridan. They rode east and when two hours had passed, Spur gave the man his six-gun and knife. He tossed him a box of shells.

"I want your word you'll keep on riding to Sheridan," Spur said. "I think you're a man of your word."

Eliason shrugged. "Hell, being on the move is better than waiting for somebody to gun down the whole sheriff's department back there in Elk Creek. Never have been too keen on getting myself shot. Hell, no! I won't be back. If I am it will be just as a traveler heading west." He tipped his hat, held the six-gun but didn't load it, and rode on east along the Greybull River and toward the Big Horn mountains.

Spur watched him for a few minutes, then rode back to town at a faster clip. He had business to get finished in Elk Creek before the sun went down.

The plan was *attrition*. Nick and scratch away at the sheriff's deputies until Johnson was alone, or nearly alone. Make him do his own dirty work and make him sweat and eventually flounder in his own blood. That was the plan.

Spur timed his ride back to town so he arrived at the livery stable ten minutes before six. He paid for his mount. Carrying the Spencer he moved slowly toward the sheriff's office and jail which were not in the courthouse with the other offices.

He paused in the alley across from the jail and waited. Sheriff Johnson came out and went up the street to the Hartford hotel for supper. Another deputy, Spur hadn't got a name for him yet, went the other way to a small eatery on the corner. Spur couldn't wait for darkness, sunset wouldn't come for at least two hours.

He walked out of the alley shadows, the Spencer in one hand in front of him, and strode casually to the jail, went a step past it, then returned and opened the door and stepped inside. When he closed the door he had his six-gun in hand and stared at Deputy Winslow who was eating his dinner.

"Hold it right there in mid-bite, Winslow, then come out from behind the counter and go flat on your face on the floor."

"What the hell? Hey, ain't you that wanted guy, McCoy?"

"Right and if you don't move in two seconds you're going to be dead!"

Winslow jumped up and did as he was told. Spur spotted some new manacles. They were steel wrist bands that snapped together and locked and held together with a chain six inches long. Spur used them on the deputy, cuffing his hands behind his back. Then Spur found what he was looking for, the stack of "wanted" posters on him. He made a small fire in metal trash basket and burned the sheets one at a time until they were all gone.

No one was in the jail cells. Spur prodded the deputy into the first cell and locked the door.

"Winslow, you look too bright to be hooked up with a loser like Johnson. Do you realize we have more than enough on him right now to hang him for murder? We do. And anybody on his team is going to come in for a whole bunch of hell. If we can prove that you pulled the trigger on any of those killings, you'll be wearing a necktie right beside Johnson on the gallows. Been a long time since this town has had a twin hanging. It will be an event!"

"Hey, I ain't never killed nobody. Pistol Pete was the executioner."

"Maybe so, but you knew about it. That makes

you an accomplice, and just as liable as Pete or the sheriff. You'll hang, no doubt about it."

"Unless what? What kind of a deal you got for me?"

"Deal? You trying to bribe me?"

"Shit yes! I know where the sheriff keeps a goodly sum of cash, his ride-out money he calls it. Must be six, maybe eight thousand dollars in there." Winslow was sounding worried, then scared.

"Look, they'll be back in a half hour. Let me out of here and let me ride out of town, and I'll show you that money. Is it a bargain?"

"How do I know you'll ride out?"

"Once that money is gone, the sheriff will suspect all us deputies. I better be gone or he'll kill me."

"You got a bargain," Spur said. He unlocked the jail cell, then the cuffs, and Winslow led Spur to the last of the four cells used for storage. He dug out a locked metal box at the bottom of the goods. He broke off the lock with a steel bar. Inside were sheafs of bank notes. Spur nodded and they headed for the front door.

As they did, Spur handed Winslow his six-gun. There were no rounds in it.

Winslow hesitated. "I ain't been paid for two months," he said.

Spur opened the metal box, took out five twenty dollar federal reserve notes and handed them to the ex-deputy. "That should hold you, now let's both get out of here."

At the door Spur saw a deputy. He pushed open

the door and came in, frowned at Spur as a flash of recognition came across his face.

Behind the deputy, Winslow raised his empty revolver and slammed the side of the heavy weapon down across the other man's skull. The struck man went down as if every muscle in his body had relaxed at the same time.

"Thanks," Spur said and the two men walked out of the jail, Spur carrying the metal box and his Spencer rifle. They both moved into the alley where Winslow got on his horse and headed for the Emporium for some traveling goods. Spur walked the other way and after some judicious waiting and stalling, found his chance and went through the door into the alley that opened on the girls' rooms.

Jodi and Rebecca were there. It seemed that they had put on fancy dresses and they looked good enough to eat for dessert.

He stopped at the door and whistled. "What a pair of beautiful ladies!" he said. "Now I know why I come back here so often." He went to Jodi and kissed her cheek, then turned to Rebecca and before she could move or speak he kissed her cheek. Walking across the room he put the metal box on the table. "Come see what I liberated from the jail," Spur said.

The girls followed him and when he opened the lid they both screeched in amazement.

"Is it real?" Jodi asked.

"It's real."

"Whose is it?" Rebecca asked.

"It should belong to all those people in town

Sheriff Johnson stole from. He's also got a bank account or two."

Jodi was stunned by the cash. "How much is there?"

They looked at it closer. Each bundle was tied with a string and each had a piece of paper with a total on it. The eight stacks of cash totaled seven thousand, three hundred and forty dollars.

"I never believed that much money existed!" Rebecca said, her eyes wide.

Spur put it back in the metal box and handed it to Rebecca. "Keep this for me. We'll turn it over to the county authorities when this little ruction is all over."

"Oh, I couldn't!"

"Of course you can. Just put it under your bed or in a corner someplace. Nobody is going to come in here looking for it. Now, what about some supper? I've got work to do tonight. Is this hotel dining room open or not?"

CHAPTER FIFTEEN

Two more deputies! Spur McCoy had to find them, the two remaining deputies and scare them out of town, chase them out of town or shoot them. The choices were coming down close to the vest now. None of the usual ploys had worked, so it was back to basics.

He would stay on the side streets with the hope that he could catch one of them making his rounds. The plan offered few prospects, but at this point it was all he had.

Dusk was falling and Spur worked out of the alley carefully the long way, and angled up the street. A clerk hurried by on his way home, loosening his string tie and taking off his hat as he began relaxing. A saddle maker set quietly at his bench cutting leather and trying it in place. He waved through the open door.

Spur came to the alley and stepped in beside a clapboard side of the building and paused. A few rigs went past on Main Street half a block ahead, but most of the mounted traffic was quiet. Two cowboys from a nearby ranch rode in. Neither wore guns. Most men didn't in town. Probably half the town people didn't own a gun and wouldn't know how to shoot it if they found one.

Two men walked down the dusty street toward the alley. Both wore guns. It was fast growing dark. The men didn't seem to be together. One walked faster than the other. He was twenty feet beyond Spur in the alley before the other approached the dark slot. Then both men whirled, guns out aimed at him from thirty feet.

"Don't move, McCoy or you're buzzard bait!" one called.

Spur never hesitated. With the first recognition of "don't move" he dove into the shadows of the alley, rolled and came up running hard through the gloom for the far end.

"Stop!" someone shouted frantically in front of him. Spur had drawn his .44 as he ran, and now sent three shots into the darkness ahead, aiming at the sound. As the roar of the shots faded he heard a piercing scream just ahead, and saw a man down on his back, both hands holding a bloody spot on his chest.

Spur faded into the thirty odd people who crowded around the man lying in the street, then walked away quickly into a side street. His hunting expedition had wound up with him turned into the rabbit instead of the hunter. It wasn't supposed to work that way. Jodi had been right. The bounty hunters were coming out of every street and alley in town. It would be worse tomorrow with daylight. By that time more men would have read about picking up a quick fortune for the cost of a .44 round.

Tomorrow he would send another note to the jail. Maybe he could coax one of the deputies out for a conference. No, he'd used that ploy and they would know what to expect. He needed some new plan. Maybe he could put something in the newspaper. But that would be too slow. Things were starting to come to a climax, Spur felt. However, he wasn't sure he had the right kind of control so that things would turn out the way he wanted.

Johnson was down and hurt, but not dead by a long shot. There had to be one final blow that would drive him out of office and out of town. But just what it was going to be, Spur didn't know. He had taken his best shots and come up short. If the two deputies stayed under cover, he had no chance to force them out of town. From five deputies down to two would hurt the sheriff, but he still had many built-in defenses. It was like a tough chess match.

How could Spur get in there and checkmate the sheriff? Spur thought of all the tricks in his magic bag, but had trouble finding one that would work.

The sheriff had been shot from ambush and would be doubly careful now. He was keeping his deputies on a close rein. He wasn't giving an inch on his legal right to enforce the laws of the land.

For just a moment Spur wished the bushwhacker could have nailed the sheriff through the heart. The trouble would be over and the town could get back to normal. He knew that wasn't the ideal way to solve a community law problem, but damn effective. The more he thought about it, the more he was resigned to the fact that eventually it would come down to a contest between himself and the sheriff. He could have done that the first day he hit town. No, he couldn't have. Spur McCoy was a lawman, not a hired assassin. He had to play it by the book of laws right up to the last possible moment. Then if nothing else worked, the standoff and showdown might be the only way, the last resort.

He was walking down a dark street when he heard footsteps behind him. He slowed and the other steps hurried forward. With a quickness that took the person behind him totally by surprise, Spur drew his weapon, whirled around and dropped to one knee, the big .44 aimed straight at the oncoming figure.

"Hold it!" Spur hissed.

"God, but you're good!" a thin teenage girl's voice said. "Don't worry, I won't hurt you, Spur McCoy. It's me, Violet, remember? I'm the little lady with the big tits."

He swore silently, put the weapon away and stood as she walked up to him. She took his arm and pulled it against her side, touching her breast as she urged him to walk forward.

"I've been looking for you. You've been busy, I know. Come in for a cup of coffee or some whiskey?"

"No."

She frowned up at him. "What's the matter? Scared? Afraid you can't handle all this woman?"

Spur chuckled. She was persistent. He stopped and caught both her shoulders.

"Miss Violet. I told you before, I don't get familiar with little girls. I don't like little girls, I like big girls. In two years you'll be a big girl."

"Aren't these big enough for you?" she said cupping her breasts through her blouse and lifting them.

"Plenty, it's upstairs in the brains department that isn't developed enough yet. Do you think it's all sex? Christ, you have a lot to learn."

"So start teaching me." She was rubbing his crotch with both her hands. He had to let go and step away.

"When you grow up a little more."

"Shit."

"Don't say that. Ladies don't talk that way."

"Goddamn."

"Don't swear."

"I could undress right here and scream and yell and accuse you of touching me, trying to rape me."

"True, you could do that. Which would put me in jail for five or ten years and you never would get to see me undressed."

"Christ, you and your logic. I know, don't swear. You can at least kiss me on the cheek as we say goodbye."

"Agreed." He bent to kiss her cheek, but she caught his head, turned it and she kissed him on the mouth, her tongue hard against his lips which he didn't open. At last he pulled away.

"Nice, huh?" she asked.

Spur grinned. "You little vixen. I should paddle you and send you home."

"Please paddle me!"

Spur laughed again, stepped back from her and walked quickly down the street before she tried something else. He wanted to see what Les Van Dyke was up to at the newspaper office. Maybe together they could work out some strategy to blast Sheriff Johnson right out of office!

CHAPTER SIXTEEN

The front door of the newspaper office was locked but Spur McCoy saw lights in back, so he went around to the alley and in through the unlocked back door. Les Van Dyke was busy at the type setting case and jumped a foot off his stool when Spur said hello. He even reached for a six-gun lying on top of the case.

"Christ, don't sneak up on me that way, McCoy. I'm nervous enough as it is. Take a look at the front of the place."

"Don't see why you're nervous. Nobody has been shooting at you." Spur went through the curtain to the front of the office. All the windows had been boarded up from the inside as well as the one big one from the outside. The door was barricaded with 2 x 4's which had been nailed across it. He saw two or three two-inch holes that had been bored in the boards. On the counter across the room lay two rifles, a shotgun and two pistols.

Spur went through the curtain and looked at the copy Van Dyke was setting.

"What the hell is going on? Looks like you're getting ready for a war."

"It will be, as soon as the paper hits the streets. If you'll help me we can have it out by early tomorrow morning."

"This isn't Wednesday night. Tomorrow isn't Thursday."

"So, this is a special edition. Already got the front page printed. Just two pages. Read it right over there."

Spur moved to the stack of printed sheets. He picked up the top one and looked at the two-inch high, double line of screaming headlines:

SHERIFF JOHNSON CHARGED WITH
GRAFT, MURDER, MALFEASANCE

The sub head covering three columns under it and leading into the news story said: *District Attorney Beaten Up When Papers Served on Johnson.*

Spur didn't need to read the rest. He shook his head and went over to Van Dyke.

"I thought you said you weren't going to do

anything stupid. This is stupid. This can get you killed."

"How? Johnson only has five deputies, no, four."

"Wrong, only two. Two of them decided to leave town today, with a little urging."

"Great, he'll probably only burn us out then."

"Us?"

"Sure, this is your operation. I'm just a newspaperman. If you shoot him it's all in the line of duty."

"You mean that arsenal up there is for me?"

"Told you, I'm a lousy shot."

"You set on doing this?"

"Right, I figure it's time. Better than ever if he only has two guns left. And him with a slug in his shoulder. I've got a story about him beating up on Hardy too. Not why, never really knew. But I cover Johnson's demand for $5,000 a week blackmail money."

"So you're lighting the fuse?"

"Damn right. That's why I wanted to deliver the copies in the morning. One will be on the porch of every house and business in town. There won't be a chance that the sheriff can pick up all the copies. Then if he comes after me, us, it will be in broad daylight for everyone to see."

"Just dandy. I'd one hell of a lot rather get shot in daylight than after dark."

"Hey, if he's just got two men, he might not even make a play. He might cut and run."

"Not without his mad money. One of the deputies showed me where he had stashed it."

"He's got his money in the bank."

"I'll have to see the banker tonight."

"What good will that do, Spur? Otto is a stickler for rules and procedures."

"Good—it will be easier for me to deal with him. I better see him before he goes to bed. Where does he live?"

Spur got directions and knocked on Otto Toller's door. The banker was small and round, with reddish fat cheeks and tufts of white hair. He was about sixty.

"Mr. Toller, my name is Spur McCoy. I need to talk to you about something if I could."

The banker beamed. "Heard you've been around town, and bothering our sheriff. Just who are you?"

Spur dug out his badge and showed it to the banker. "I'm with the United States Secret Service. As a banker you probably have heard of us. We worked for several years on nothing but counterfeiting, but now we deal with almost any crime local authorities can't handle."

"That answers a lot of my questions. What can I do for you?"

"I want you to put a federal freeze on any and all accounts that Tyler Johnson has access to. This includes all official and personal accounts."

"Usually it takes a federal judge to do that. Your badge helps, but I don't see how, legally, I could do that."

"Could you close tomorrow or the next day as an official bank holiday? Founders Day? That should do it."

"You're afraid that Tyler Johnson will plunder the county treasury and skip out of town?"

"I'd bet he will try within two days. The problem is the money he controls isn't his. He's been blackmailing and stealing it for years. You must know about all this."

The banker nodded. "Nobody could do anything about it. I've seen good friends of mine killed." He looked away, then back at Spur. "It didn't seem important enough to die over."

"Now it's different. The newspaper is going to come out with the facts, the bald truth. There could be a lot of trouble. You might want to close down the bank the day the paper comes out."

"Tomorrow?"

"I'm going to try to get Van Dyke to put it off one day."

"We always close down one day for accounting. When I see the paper come out with the story, I'll close the bank."

Spur shook his hand, put his badge away and went back to the newspaper.

"Why for God's sakes? I've just got up nerve enough to do it, now you want to hold off a day?" Les complained.

"A few things to clean up first. Things I want to get done before you blow the lid off this whole county. Might even save some lives if I can do what I want to."

"All right. One more day won't make that much difference. You get the bank to hold his cash?"

"Something like that. Now you won't need me

175

to help you print that other page."

"Coward."

"Work, my son, work. And don't forget to work out some way to barricade your back door."

Spur went out the back, watched others on the street, and got into the alley where the girls lived without attracting attention.

Jodi and Rebecca were sitting in rocking chairs sewing. Rebecca sat up and smiled.

"We heard there had been some shooting," she said. "Glad to see that you aren't dead."

Spur grinned. "Me too. The only dead I am is dead tired. I've got to get up early so I need to roll into bed early for a long sleep."

"Me too," Jodi said. "You understand, don't you, Rebecca?"

She nodded. "Yes. He's your man and you're going to make love. That's fine. I have more sewing to do." She looked at them and smiled.

Spur went into Jodi's bedroom and she followed.

"Amazing. My little sister is really developing. She's so much more grown up now, more realistic." She paused, frowned slightly, then put her arms around Spur. "We do have time for one or two quick ones, don't we?" She caught his hand and pushed it between their hips and between her legs.

Spur kissed her tenderly. "Jodi, for you I always have time for a quick one or two. Now get out of your clothes."

They made love softly, gently, and somehow she had a feeling this was how married love would

Spur ran past, out of the far end of the alley and angled out of town. He heard the men running behind him. It wasn't dark enough for him to lose them quickly. It was going to take some time. He sprinted past a house, cut through the side yard to the next block and down a street to a big cottonwood tree.

Silently he slid behind the cottonwood and waited. Both men pounded the ground after him, but when they came to this street with few houses and a dozen large trees, they stopped.

He could hear them whispering forty yards ahead of him. They decided on their strategy. One came straight down the street toward Spur and his tree. The other ran to the next block and Spur guessed he would also move in Spur's direction.

When Spur was sure the second man had run through to the next block, he watched the guy ahead of him. He had to be a bounty hunter. He moved from tree to tree, checking each one carefully.

Spur picked up a rock near the tree and waited. The hunter came slowly, watching all hiding places. When he was three feet from Spur's cottonwood, Spur threw the rock behind the man. He spun around and Spur stepped out silently and cocked his six-gun two feet from the man's head.

"You even flinch, cowboy, and you're a dead man!"

"Oh, shit!"

"Drop the iron, now!"

The gun hit the ground and Spur brought his

weapon down on the hunter's head. It made a soft thunking sound, and the gunman folded up on the ground. Spur dragged him behind the tree, used the hunter's kerchief to tie his hands behind his back, and his belt to cinch the man's ankles together. Then Spur left, heading back the way he had come, hoping the last of the three hunters had gone in the other direction.

He walked casually, heading toward Main Street, still looking for the deputies.

The shot came from behind him, digging up dirt at his feet. He whirled, saw the gunman out of range, but running forward. Spur turned and ran down a cross street heading back out of town. It was almost fully dark now, but Spur saw that a full moon was shining, and already was blunting the black effect of the darkness.

Spur was quickly past the corner, using a house to shield him from the gunman. He pounded hard down the block and turned to find only one house between him and the rolling high plateau. No cover. It was enough to put fear into the heart of an old infantryman. Spur found a small depression and rolled into it, clearing a spot where he could see through the waist high grass at the end of the street near the house. A soft wind blew toward him.

He relaxed. The hunter would have to come and find him. So he had the advantage. The hunter would make noise as he moved. Spur saw the flare of what he guessed was a match thirty yards away at the edge of the grass. The man was lighting a cigarette? Then Spur felt the grass. It was dry, dead already. A firetrap! Spur sent five shots from the six-gun at the tiny flame, but he knew he was too late. He reloaded and watched as the flame spread, then caught by the breeze it spewed toward him rapidly. It crackled and snapped in the silent, warm night air.

Spur stood and worked his way away from the fire, bending over as he ran straight into the prairie. Only after a half mile did he circle to the left and begin walking back into town. It was a fifty-fifty chance the hunter would move this way to wait for him. And if the moonlight wasn't any brighter, there was almost no chance that the hunter could spot Spur coming back in.

A half hour later Spur was in town without his hunting companion. He decided he was too recognizable. He took off his brown leather vest and his low-crowned, tan hat with the string of Mexican silver coins around it and put both behind a box in an alley near Main Street. He walked up to t' thoroughfare bare-headed. It might buy hin. little more freedom.

Spur walked the length of Main Street twice, searching for the men with tin stars on their hats. He saw neither one. The sheriff would be on light duty for a few days. So who was keeping the store? When Spur went past the jail the lamps were on, but he couldn't see anyone inside. He checked in two saloons, standing at the bat wings, looking in, but saw neither lawman.

Spur had about given up when he took one more trip up the main avenue. He was at the far end of the four block long string of businesses when someone shouted behind him. Spur ignored it. The second shout was closer.

"Spur McCoy! I don't want to back shoot you, so turn around slow." Spur didn't react. "You, bastard! You with the black shirt and no hat, Spur McCoy. Turn around!"

Instead Spur dove to his left, drew his six-gun with his right hand as he hit on his left side, rolled and came up with the weapon trained where he had heard the voice. A short man with a full beard stood there, his weapon in a double handed grip as he sighted in on his moving target.

Spur fired first. The round caught the man in the left thigh. Before Spur saw where the bullet hit he fired twice more, the rounds slamming into the man's chest. He jolted backward, the gun dropped from his hands as he screamed and grabbed at his chest.

Spur got up, still holding his gun and walked up to the man. He was bleeding bad, but the rounds had missed his heart. He would live for a while.

"Why?" Spur asked.

"Damn reward. I could use that thousand dollars."

"First you have to live to enjoy it," Spur said. He pointed his Remington at the nearest gawker. "You, run and bring Doc Paulson. This man can live if he gets treatment. Move it, you, now!" The man unfroze and rushed off toward Doctor Paulson's office.

Spur waved at a bystander. "You, get over here and hold his head out of the dirt. The man's hurt bad."

Spur faded into the thirty odd people who crowded around the man lying in the street, then walked away quickly into a side street. His hunting expedition had wound up with him turned into the rabbit instead of the hunter. It wasn't supposed to work that way. Jodi had been right. The bounty hunters were coming out of every street and alley in town. It would be worse tomorrow with daylight. By that time more men would have read about picking up a quick fortune for the cost of a .44 round.

Tomorrow he would send another note to the jail. Maybe he could coax one of the deputies out for a conference. No, he'd used that ploy and they would know what to expect. He needed some new plan. Maybe he could put something in the newspaper. But that would be too slow. Things were starting to come to a climax, Spur felt. However, he wasn't sure he had the right kind of control so that things would turn out the way he wanted.

Johnson was down and hurt, but not dead by a long shot. There had to be one final blow that would drive him out of office and out of town. But just what it was going to be, Spur didn't know. He had taken his best shots and come up short. If the two deputies stayed under cover, he had no chance to force them out of town. From five deputies down to two would hurt the sheriff, but he still had many built-in defenses. It was like a tough chess match.

How could Spur get in there and checkmate the sheriff? Spur thought of all the tricks in his magic bag, but had trouble finding one that would work.

The sheriff had been shot from ambush and would be doubly careful now. He was keeping his deputies on a close rein. He wasn't giving an inch on his legal right to enforce the laws of the land.

For just a moment Spur wished the bushwhacker could have nailed the sheriff through the heart. The trouble would be over and the town could get back to normal. He knew that wasn't the ideal way to solve a community law problem, but damn effective. The more he thought about it, the more he was resigned to the fact that eventually it would come down to a contest between himself and the sheriff. He could have done that the first day he hit town. No, he couldn't have. Spur McCoy was a lawman, not a hired assassin. He had to play it by the book of laws right up to the last possible moment. Then if nothing else worked, the standoff and showdown might be the only way, the last resort.

He was walking down a dark street when he heard footsteps behind him. He slowed and the other steps hurried forward. With a quickness that took the person behind him totally by surprise, Spur drew his weapon, whirled around and dropped to one knee, the big .44 aimed straight at the oncoming figure.

"Hold it!" Spur hissed.

"God, but you're good!" a thin teenage girl's voice said. "Don't worry, I won't hurt you, Spur McCoy. It's me, Violet, remember? I'm the little lady with the big tits."

He swore silently, put the weapon away and stood as she walked up to him. She took his arm

168

be, more taking it for granted, not mountain top peaks every time. But a real, a solid love relationship, where both partners knew every move the other would make, and loved it.

She relaxed and let his hands caress her body, then returned the favor and soon they built and moved into delightful low key lovemaking.

"Hey, I could get used to this," Jodi said. She hurried on. "But I know, I shouldn't because you aren't going to be around that long and all the rest. So just let me dream a little, and love a lot, and hold you tightly while you are here so I have wonderful memories when my bed is empty and cold again."

Spur kissed her gently.

The next morning Rebecca slept in late. She had heard Jodi and Spur get up and smelled breakfast, but stayed in her room. Jodi knocked on Rebecca's door to say she was leaving and that Spur was already gone.

"Are you all right, Becky?"

"Yes, fine. Just sleepy."

"I'm going to work. You have an interesting day."

"Yes, I will."

Rebecca sat up in bed when she heard the outside door lock. She stretched, then lifted off the light cotton nightgown she wore and sat there nude. She usually didn't like to be naked. It was because *he* used to make her walk around the house for hours at a time all naked. *He* could touch her easier that way. She shivered. It had been months since she had felt strong enough to think about what *he* used to do. Now she felt good. She had been kissed by a man. She had not hurt him. Yes!

She got out of bed and stood in the room naked, then turned and looked at the small mirror over the dresser. It had been years since she had really looked at her body. Her breasts were round and pink tipped. Not as large as Jodi's but much larger than many women she used to see. Her glance left the mirror and she looked down at her body, breasts, thin waist, with a dark furry patch between her legs. She shivered again.

Rebecca dressed quickly, put on a modest dress that did not show her figure, went to the kitchen drawer a moment and then decided she would go for a walk. She could go to the edge of town and walk along the open country. Yes! It would feel good. When she was a girl she did a lot of walking. There might even be some wildflowers to pick!

Before she went out Rebecca looked in the mirror and decided a sunbonnet would be helpful. She found one that Jodi wore, put it on and went out the alley door.

Rebecca walked quickly through the alley, not because she was frightened, but because it was not pretty. She went down the street and hesitated which way to go when she came to Main Street. She decided to go north and was looking forward to finding some wildflowers in the prairie, when she bumped into a man on the boardwalk.

"Oh, sorry," she said stepping back.

Sheriff Tyler Johnson reached and caught her so she wouldn't fall. He stared down at her soft eyes and pretty face and smiled.

"Well, now. I might be shot up some, but I still know a pretty girl when I see one. I haven't seen much of you around town. What's your name?"

She tensed, then beat down the old furies and looked up.

"My name is Rebecca."

"Well, that's a nice name. Sorry I bumped into you. Sure you're not hurt?"

"No, I'm quite fine, thank you." She pulled away from him and it twinged the pain in his shoulder.

"You watch where you're walking now," the sheriff said, his glance following her as she walked down the street. He enjoyed the way her small bottom twitched the back of that dress.

Tyler Johnson was feeling better. The rifle slug in his shoulder was out and the pain easing. He needed some goddamn entertainment. Yeah, just some quick fun!

He had eaten a late breakfast, and belched softly as he followed her down the street in back of the blue and white calico dress. "Becky," he said softly. He had seen her around town, but not often. She was a real loner.

Fifteen minutes later Becky stood in the unspoiled prairie. It had been like this for thousands of years. She saw some yellowcups and bent to pick them. No more than two of anything because they were so beautiful growing there. She wanted others to be able to see them as well.

She saw some daisy blossoms ahead and ran to them. Before she realized it she had wandered a quarter of a mile from the last town street and found some wild roses. She was also down a small ravine and out of sight of town.

Sheriff Johnson had followed her patiently. When she slipped out of sight he grinned. He ran and found her sitting beside the start of a stream picking more wild flowers. He sat down beside her.

"Oh!" Rebecca said. "I didn't see you coming. Why are you here?"

"Why, to strip that dress off you and see your lucious, young, fucking body." He caught his hand in the bodice of her dress and pulled, but the stitches were strong and held. The sheriff swore and pulled her toward him, bending her into his lap. With both hands he jerked the cloth apart, tearing off buttons and exposing her chemise. He growled deep in his throat and tore the chemise away to expose her breasts.

"Yeah, nice," he said, and bent and kissed them.

Rebecca wanted to cry, but she couldn't. Anger shone out of her eyes. Then they took on a wild fury. She struggled to sit up, and he helped her.

"Oh, yes, sitting up that way makes your tits look bigger, don't it?"

Rebecca moved her hand slowly, felt in her skirts, but the pocket was trapped under her legs. She couldn't reach it!

He rubbed her breasts, grinned at her and

rubbed his crotch, then opened his fly and laughed. "You want to reel out my big cock, sweetheart?"

She shook her head. She had to move off her skirt to free the pocket. He moved enough so she could ease away from him and get up on her knees. His big hand caught one breast and held it tightly.

"Now, you ain't trying to get away are you, darling? You sit still and I'll show you big cock here and introduce you proper."

He got to his knees and unbuttoned his fly, then pulled out his hard penis. She couldn't look at it. Now she could get her right hand in her dress pocket.

"Want to bite on old cock here, Rebecca? He's good tasting, half the women in town can tell you that. Hell, take a bite."

Johnson caught her hair and the back of her neck and forced her head downward toward his crotch. She resisted, but he was stronger and his penis soon rubbed her cheeks, and across her mouth.

Rebecca wanted to vomit, but she gritted her teeth. She almost had her hand in her pocket. Then her fingers closed around the knife and she slid it from the pocket. Her hand with the long knife was behind her thigh now and he couldn't see it.

"What's the matter, Becky? You got to open your mouth to suck it. Come on, taste me. Ain't no big thing. My cock is the big thing!" He roared with laughter, and loosened his grip.

"Hell, after I get you a little warmed up I'll make you suck cock, whether you want to or not. Let's get the rest of that dress off. You want me to rip it off or will you take it off nice and easy?"

"I'll . . . I'll take it off."

"Yeah? Good. No tricks now. I'm stronger than you are, remember." He let loose of her neck and leaned back. She moved upward and turned slightly. He rubbed his penis a moment, then his hands came away from it.

She moved so quickly he never saw the swinging knife. The twelve-inch knife blade swung out from her hip and lifted upward two feet in front of Tyler Johnson's eyes before it reversed directions and in a hundredth of a second slashed downward with all Rebecca's strength.

Her aim was perfect. The heavy butcher knife blade hit in the center of his penis, and came with such force that it slashed through his genital member, chopping it off the way a heavy knife will slice a tree twig, with almost no movement of the still attached part.

The severed section dropped to the ground, and already Rebecca had thrown herself backward, away from the man. She scrambled to her feet and ran as fast as she could back toward town.

Behind her, Tyler Johnson slumped to the ground, sitting on his heels, his hand holding his severed stump. He grabbed his kerchief from around his throat and wrapped it as tightly as he could around his penis, holding it with his hand as he stood, and with shaky steps began plodding toward Doctor Paulson's office. If the sawbones said a word about this he would kill him!

He was dazed, shocked, so surprised he had not uttered a sound. As he walked the pain drilled through every nerve in his body. He screamed. He fell to his knees and held his decapitated member tenderly. Then he screeched out his fury for five minutes. He finally stood and, holding the blood soaked kerchief, ran as fast as he could to the back door of Doctor Paulson's office. Nobody was ever going to find out about this. And the girl, Rebecca, would die. She was as good as dead now. He would find out where she lived. In two or three days he would take care of her himself. But first he could cut her to pieces, cut her tits off, ream out her cunt with a red hot branding iron. Yes! He would treat her as violently as she did him. Then she would die.

Doctor Paulson heard the noise in back of his place and unlocked the door. He saw the sheriff, the blood soaked cloth at his crotch, and guessed what had happened.

Neither man said a word. The sheriff did not have to warn Doc Paulson. The medic quickly tied a tight cord around the shrunken, limp cut off penis. He heated up an iron and gave the sheriff a bottle of whiskey.

"Drink it all if you can, Sheriff. You're gonna need it." When the iron was hot the sheriff looked away. He gulped down another mouthful of the raw whiskey.

Doctor Paulson knew the bleeding had to be

stopped. The cord was not doing it. There was only one other way. The Romans used it three thousand years ago. The Egyptians had used it five thousand years ago.

He took the bottle from the sheriff, told him to stare at the wall, then brought the red-hot end of the soldering iron across the limp, bloody end of the penis. Tissues sizzled, blood vessels curled and seared shut, smoke lifted.

Sheriff Tyler screamed and swept Doctor Paulson and his infernal tool over the bench he lay on and dumped both on the floor. The pain was so outrageous, so totally debilitating, that Sheriff Tyler Johnson had time only to bellow his frustration, his pain, and his terror for five seconds before he fainted.

Doctor Paulson sat up on the floor and moved the still hot iron off his pants where it had burned a hole. He stared at the unconscious sheriff.

"Welcome back to the human race, Johnson," he said softly. "But I really don't think that you've got long to enjoy it. I just hope some small woman with a big knife did this to you. It's one hell of a lot better than castrating you. Now you'll still want to get a woman, but you damned well won't be able to!"

Doctor Paulson smiled thinly as he cleaned up the blood, put the iron away, then bandaged the shriveled penis and pushed it back in the sheriff's trousers. He even buttoned up the fly. Then he went back to his sick patients.

Three blocks away, Rebecca hurried down the alley and into her door. She locked it and then went to the bedroom. She took off the torn dress, and put on another, then looked in the mirror.

I knew exactly what I was doing, she told the mirror. It was not a wild uncontrolled thing. I knew what the man was doing and I was defending myself. It wasn't at all like before. And it don't hurt. I don't hurt inside the way I used to when I used the knife. She smiled at the mirror and it smiled back at her. Yes, it was going to be all right.

Rebecca took the knife from the dress pocket and slowly, carefully ripped the pocket out of the skirt. She threw it away. Each day she would take another pocket from one of her skirts. She told herself the pockets were just to carry things, but she knew they were only for the knife.

Later she washed the butcher knife off carefully, scalded it to be sure it was clean, then put it back in the knife drawer.

Rebecca took the dress into the living room and sat in the rocking chair, patiently stitching up the damage, sewing on the ripped off buttons.

Yes, it was going to be just fine!

CHAPTER SEVENTEEN

Spur was up early that morning. He had breakfast with Jodi and hurried out of the alley just as it was getting light. He wanted to surprise the one deputy he figured would be on duty in the jail.

There was no one on the street as he came around the corner and walked in the dust of the street the half block down to the sheriff's office and jail. His boots would make no sound on the dirt but they would be heard on the boardwalk.

Spur went across the boards quietly to the jail door and tried the knob. Unlocked. He edged the door open slowly and peered inside. No one sat behind the desk. He eased inside the open door and stepped soundlessly across the board floor. The first jail cell was open. Two thin mattresses had been put on the bunk. A man Spur guessed was the deputy lay there sleeping soundly.

The Secret Service Agent moved inside the cell and lifted the six-gun from the man's holster that lay on the floor. He touched his shoulder.

Ira Lincoln came awake slowly, rubbed his eyes and sat up. Only then did he see Spur's six-gun aimed at his chest.

"Oh, damn, no!" Lincoln said.

"Afraid so. You a deputy sheriff?"

"I was. The sheriff said. What do you want?"

"Take a walk with me. I'll hold your six-gun. No, you can have it, soon as I take the stingers out of the cylinder." He removed the five rounds and pocketed them, then put the Colt in the deputy's holster. "Now, we take a walk."

They saw a rig driving into town, and two early risers moving toward an eatery. Otherwise no one was up yet in Elk Creek. Five minutes later they banged on the rear door of the newspaper office. It took another five minutes to wake up Les Van Dyke and get him to the door.

"You think this is a damned hotel or something, McCoy?" Van Dyke asked. Then he saw the other man. "That's one of Johnson's men."

"Was one of Johnson's men, mighty publisher of the truth. Now he's one of ours, or he's dead. Either way he wants to play it."

Lincoln looked up, curious. "What was all that?"

"You'll find out. You got those pages printed?"

"Yep, but no thanks to you."

"Good. We tie up Lincoln here and I'll help you spread the papers around town. We got Johnson down to one deputy, and Johnson himself beat up some. Don't think he'll get too nasty. What do you say?"

"Ink isn't dry yet. Didn't finish until almost five A.M. Then we got to fold them. Should be ready by noon if both of you help."

"We'll both be glad to help. Won't we, Lincoln?"

"Anything you say while you got the guns."

They were ready by noon. Spur tied Lincoln hand, foot and gagged him. Then they filled their arms with the two page paper. They split up, each beginning at opposite sides of town and working toward the center, putting a paper on every porch as well as in every store and shop.

As soon as Otto Toller saw the paper, he closed the bank and sent his two clerks home.

The deputy on duty at the sheriff's office closed and locked the front door and put out three loaded rifles, getting ready for any threat of mob action.

People began gathering in the street. Before three that afternoon more than half the four hundred people in town had gathered in front of the Emporium. Spur talked to them from the porch and called to get their attention.

"I hope you've read what Les Van Dyke had to say in the newspaper."

There were cheers and shouts and a gun shot or

two fired into the air.

"Most of the facts are there," Spur went on when he got them quieted down. "This county is going to have a legal sheriff's department, just as soon as we get rid of Johnson, and can hold an election. Is our district attorney here?"

There were some shouts in the crowd, and Clyde Oberholtzer came to the steps. He still wore two small bandages on his face, but his eyes were full of fire.

"Citizens of Elk Creek. We are about to root out his devil who grew in our midst. It was partly our own fault for not standing up to him before. I understand the sheriff has only one deputy left and he is barricaded in the jail. I don't know where the sheriff is, but let me warn you that this is no time for mob violence. We do not want a lynch mob here. If there is I will watch and arrest for murder every man who participates!

"We are through with law by force. We are going to have justice under the law, and that means a normal course of action. I have an arrest warrant for the sheriff, and I will serve it on him as soon as I can find him. If we have any specific charges against the two deputies still in town, they will be brought through normal legal channels.

"What I want now is for those of you with felony complaints against the sheriff or his deputies, to form a line over here and I'll listen to each of you. We need hard evidence, eye-witnesses to any crime. The more evidence we have, the better. Now line up over here and let me sharpen my pencil."

More than twenty people moved to one side, and the district attorney for River Bend County began taking down statements.

Spur got the crowd's attention again. "Does anyone know where the sheriff is right now?"

Doc Paulson spoke up. "He was in my office two hours ago for some minor surgery. My guess is he's in his rooms over the Golden Horseshoe saloon."

"Hold it!" Spur called. "Nobody is to go down there. That's my job. Now, do you have a mayor or a city council? I think they should say something, and they will need to talk to the county officials about getting a temporary sheriff appointed until an election can be held."

Someone stepped onto the porch. It was the saddle maker. He was the mayor of Elk Creek. As he talked Spur moved out of the crowd and toward the Golden Horseshoe. Two men with guns on their hips started to follow.

"Figured you might want some backup," one of them said.

"Can you use those hog legs?"

"Fair to middling," the other man said.

Spur waved them to follow him. He had picked up his Spencer earlier and twenty extra rounds. There were three rooms over the saloon. Access was up an outside stairway or through one built into the saloon. When Spur pushed open the door with the sheriff's name on it, he found a woman sitting on the bed, her dance call costume pulled down to the waist.

She looked up with tears streaming down her face. "He ain't here," she said. "He rode out almost an hour ago, right after he saw the paper. It's so awful, awful what they did to him. You should be ashamed of yourself, mutilating him that way!" She threw a pillow at Spur from the bed.

"Where was he heading, Miss?" Spur asked from just outside the door.

"I don't know. Wouldn't tell you if I did."

Spur and the two men went downstairs. There had been no horses tied outside the sheriff's office. That should mean they kept them at the livery.

Spur ran for the horse barns and found the wrangler.

"Did the sheriff ride out of here about an hour ago?"

"Yeah, he was still reading the paper. Did you read this thing?"

"Which way did he go?"

"Damned if I know. He was demanding five thousand dollars a month from old Hardy. Can you imagine that?"

"Yes. Get me a horse, a good one with some speed and lasting power. And a saddle. And rush it."

By the time Spur got mounted and rode away, he decided the sheriff would head for the biggest town. That would be Sheridan, two days' ride to the east. Cheyenne was ten days to the south and east.

McCoy rode east, found the trail and paused at a dusty spot to check the trail. A thin sprinkle the night before had settled the dust and wiped out previous wagon wheel and hoof prints in the dirt. Spur noticed the tracks of a heavily loaded horse galloping to the east. It was worth a try. He put the sorrel into a gentle canter and headed down the trail. The sheriff couldn't be more than an hour ahead of him. Sooner or later he would catch up.

By five that afternoon Spur hadn't caught him. A wagon loaded with freight from Sheridan came past and Spur asked the drivers about any riders ahead.

The redshirted teamster nodded. "Sure'n hell we seen somebody, but he sashayed off into the brush while we passed. Thought maybe he was a rawhider, but he looked too clean for that. Big guy on a dark gray dun."

"Thanks, neighbor."

Spur rode on. He pushed the horse now, riding at a hard gallop for a quarter mile, then letting her blow at a walk for a mile and hitting a six mile gait for a mile or so, then walking again.

McCoy came to a brush covered hill two miles farther on. The trail led straight down toward a river for five miles, without a turn or bend. He studied the trail dirt and saw the same hoof prints. Then far down a black blob moved forward. A horse and a rider.

The rider had to be Johnson. Spur did not want to spook the prey. He could get into the brush and hills and out of sight so Spur could never find him. As long as he stayed on the trail, he was a much better target. Far ahead Spur saw the trail swing to the right. It seemed to follow along the side of a ridge of hills and head toward a pass ten miles ahead. As Spur studied the landscape, he saw a thin trail of dust lift off a point where he thought the trail headed. It belonged to a wagon or a stagecoach. It was the main trail. Spur moved his horse into the trail, then cut to the right, following a stream. He would cut across the long arc to the left. He hoped to come out somewhere below the pass on the trail before Johnson got there.

Spur pushed the sorrel now. He made her work hard for an hour, figuring he was half way there. He put her into a gallop along an old trail that bordered the stream, and then cut across a small hill. A mile ahead he saw the slash of the trail through the trees. Again he pressed the sorrel and she responded. It would be dark in half an hour. He had to take Johnson before dusk or the sheriff could get away clean.

Twenty minutes later he was there. He tied the mare in a lush little glen of green grass and ran the last fifty yards to the trail. No single horse had been across here today. He checked for cover, picked out a big yellow pine near the trail to hide behind. The trembling aspen shaded the lower parts of the trail and kept Spur in the shadows.

He had a long drink from his canteen and waited for Tyler Johnson to come.

It was five minutes before he saw the dun plodding along up the trail. Johnson had his hat off, wiping his forehead. As he came closer Spur saw a curious thing. The sheriff sat on a pillow over the saddle. What was that all about?

Spur let him come forward. Spur brought up his Spencer seven shot repeating rifle, quietly chambered a round and waited.

There was little chance that Johnson would elect to go back to Elk Creek to stand trial. Prison would kill him. He would make a stand here. For a moment Spur wished he had picked a better spot for his ambush. The easy way would be to blow him out of the saddle without warning and straight into hell with a head shot from the Spencer. But that wasn't Spur McCoy's way. He had to give Johnson a chance to come in.

Spur sent the first shot from the Spencer just in front of the dun's head when the rider was thirty feet down the trail from Spur's big yellow pine.

Johnson did exactly what Spur would have done. He dove off the saddle away from the blue smoke of the shooter and rolled off the trail into a slight depression that half hid him. Spur had another shot but waited.

"There's no place to go, Johnson. I've got three men around you, one on your side of the trail almost in your hip pocket. Throw out your .44 and give it up. You'll get a fair trial back in Elk Creek."

"Fair trial?" Johnson roared. "You know damn well they'll hang me for everything that's happened in the county during the past three years."

"You deserve it, Johnson."

"Fuck you, McCoy. Come and get me." A six-gun blasted and the round hit the yellow pine.

"You're talking about one of us getting killed, Johnson. It sure as hell isn't going to be me. That just leaves you. You tired of the good life?"

"There isn't any good life on the end of a rope, McCoy, or in one of those frontier prisons." Another round smashed through leaves a foot over Spur's head. He ducked. When he looked again, Johnson was gone.

CHAPTER EIGHTEEN

Spur stared at the empty chunk of Wyoming wilderness. He had just spooked Johnson into the brush, it was only minutes away from darkness, and he didn't want to lose Johnson overnight. If so he might never find him again.

McCoy used the other man's horse as cover and darted across the narrow trail and dove into the woods. A pistol shot cracked ahead somewhere but the lead came nowhere near Spur. He stood behind a lodgepole pine almost big enough to hide him, and looked around it.

The faint blue haze of the .44 round's powder

charge smoke showed back down the trail. Johnson was hugging the trail so he wouldn't get lost, and would make a try for his horse again. Spur stood and keeping enough cover between him and the smoke, moved silently toward it. He stopped every six feet and listened. The third time he heard someone moving, then running ahead of him. Spur sprinted too, aiming at a large yellow pine ahead. He got there without getting shot, reached up on tip toes and looked around the tree.

Movement ahead.

It was there briefly and then gone. Spur resisted firing five shots at the spot hoping for a lucky hit. He tried to move when the sounds came ahead of him. Gradually he closed the distance between him and Johnson. The third time they moved and stopped he caught sight of Johnson sliding into some brush ahead, only twenty feet from the trail to their left.

There was no protection, no cover, for those twenty feet. Just a small clearing. Spur knew he couldn't wait. The sun was down, darkness would close in quickly. He pushed the six-gun ahead of him, blasted four shots as he charged across the opening. He had aimed into the spot he had seen Johnson disappear. Spur hoped for a lucky shot. He would take Johnson now anyway he could get him. Time was running out.

There was no answering rounds, but also no scream of pain. Missed. Spur had rolled behind a log near the far side of the clearing and now lifted himself over it. Ahead he saw another clearing past a dozen feet of brush. Johnson was running across it, but not really running, a kind of limp legged hopping motion.

Spur pulled up his Spencer and fired by instinct more than sighting and he saw Johnson go down as his left leg buckled under him and left him lying in the edge of the clearing. He dragged himself behind a log before Spur could get off another shot.

As quickly as possible, Spur pulled out the spent cartridges and pushed six new ones into his revolver. He had been moving through the brush, and now paused at the edge of the woods, still in the shadows and out of sight. There was more open space behind the log. Johnson was still there.

"Give it up, Johnson. I can patch you up, get you back to town."

A pistol cracked and heavy lead slanted through the brush near Spur. He darted behind a lodgepole pine and frowned.

"I won't execute you, Johnson. My job is to take you in alive. That's why I didn't heart shoot you. Talk to me."

"Go to hell."

"I've been there, it's no fun. Is that where you're heading?"

Another shot came from the ex-sheriff.

"That must be it!" Johnson said sounding more cheerful. "You're a goddamn bounty hunter. Hell, I'll pay you more than they will. How much do you want?"

"Eighty-five thousand dollars."

"Eighty-five . . . you're joking. I've got money in my saddlebags. Yours. All of it. Over five thousand in bills and gold, you can kill me and take it, but you're not the type. Too pure."

"I'm not a bounty hunter, Johnson. I'm a United States Government Secret Service Agent. I work for Washington, go anywhere in the west. We heard about you. You were out of control out here. Somebody had to do something."

"So what do you make working for Washington, eighty dollars a month and expenses? I can give you five thousand dollars! Cash. Right now. No questions asked. Just ride back and say I got away clean. You'll never hear from me again."

"I can't do that." Spur put a rifle bullet just over the top of the log, shredding half an inch of wood.

"If you don't want the money, what do you want, McCoy?"

"I want you to throw out your six-guns, both of them, and the rifle. Then to walk out in the open."

"Then what?"

"Then I tie you to your saddle and ride you back to Elk Creek where you will answer to charges brought against you in open court."

"That will never happen. We went through that."

"You can't win. I winged you in the leg, you had some kind of surgery, you've had two bullets in your shoulder within the last two days. You're about washed up, Johnson."

"Not while I breathe. In five minutes it'll be

dark, then I'll be away from you for good."

Spur left the pine and circled the small clearing. It was not more than twenty yards across, but it seemed forever for him to get around it. Another thirty feet and he would be able to see behind the log where Johnson lay. McCoy moved cautiously, then saw the log, and the first dullness of dusk settled over the woods.

Spur lifted the Spencer and called to Johnson.

"Don't move, Johnson, I've got your chest in my sights. Hold it! That's better. Now throw that revolver into the brush over the log."

Johnson did.

"Good, now the other one from your left holster."

"Gone, lost it on my run."

"Then stand up, slowly."

Johnson did. "Hit my arm with that first pistol round." The arm hung at his side. Too late Spur realized his mistake. Johnson's arm wasn't hurt, he had hidden the other six-gun behind his leg. The hand came up waist high and fired as Spur fired. The rifle slug drove into Johnson's chest, slashing through his left lung, spinning him backward, the .44 dropping from his hand.

Spur charged forward, his six-gun ready. Quickly he saw the man was badly wounded. He lay half over the log, blood pumped from his shirt and Spur saw the weapon out of reach. He knelt beside the ex-sheriff and used his kerchief to stop the blood. He wasn't sure if the round went out Johnson's back or not. The man's eyes blinked, and he tried to laugh, but couldn't. His breathing came in ragged gasps.

"Breathe slow and easy," Spur said. "You're hit in the lung and it will be hard. You're hurt bad, but not dead. I can still get you into town. Did you bring any camping gear with you on that nag?"

"Yes, but you won't get me to town. End it right here. This hurts too damn bad to move, let alone ride back to town."

"You'll make it fine." Spur picked up the two pistols, searched Johnson and found a derringer in his boot and a knife. Spur took both, then lifted Johnson down so he was leaning against the log. The half sitting position made it easier on his breathing.

"Don't go away, I'll be right back."

Spur jogged through the mountain air to his horse, rode it back to Johnson's mount, and led it down the trail, then into the brush fifty feet to where Johnson lay. Darkness swept in for the night as he got down from the horse and tied both to brush.

A half hour later he had blankets over Johnson, a camp fire made and had heated up baked beans and made coffee. There were hard rolls and some apple butter.

"You eat well when you travel, Johnson."

He ate, grudgingly, but began to think about some kind of a defense.

"Hell, I might beat all the charges yet. Pistol Pete did it all. It was his idea. Did you know that he held me a virtual prisoner? He was the brains behind it all."

"Right, Johnson. Sounds good. Now get some sleep so we can get an early start in the morning."

The next morning they were up with the sun and shook the chill out of their bones in the high country as Spur packed up the gear, then helped Johnson on board. He insisted on the pillow, and sat tenderly on the saddle.

Spur tied his hands to the saddle horn, but left his legs free. He put a lead rope on the dun's reins and moved out on the trail.

"I figure we will be there just after noon," Spur said.

Johnson stared at him silently.

They spent the next half hour on the trail. Spur had not ridden it and was surprised when the open woods turned thicker and the trail hugged the side of the bluff. It wasn't a wide wagon road, but with a lot of courage a teamster could make it past the narrow spots.

Spur held the lead rope as they came to the first narrow place in the trail. The side of the cliff had been cut away by someone. The other side of the bluff fell away a hundred feet almost straight down. That had been the brownish slash Spur had seen from across the valley when he made the short cut.

Johnson hadn't said much on the way, now he began chattering.

"Yes, I've decided I'm going to like going back, fight all the charges, get a good lawyer from Cheyenne. Prove that Pistol Pete did it all. Did you gun down Pete?"

Spur looked back. "Yes, we had a small conflict but we settled it with .44's."

"Thought so," Johnson said. Then he rode up beside Spur dangerously close to the dropoff.

"Spur McCoy, you can't win every time. Changed my mind, I'm not going back with you. You want to come along with me, you just keep holding onto that lead rope!"

Tyler Johnson, ex-sheriff of River Bend County Wyoming, drove his heels into the flanks on the dun he rode and jerked the reins suddenly to the left. The horse bolted, charged to the left without knowing where it led, trusting the rider, only to find out too late she had no solid ground under her feet.

Spur stared in surprise as the horse headed four feet away to the dropoff, then slanted over it. He let go of the lead at once and saw Johnson's horse and Johnson charge over the side and then drop. By the time Spur had his horse stopped, dismounted and crawled out to the edge of the bluff, he saw only a red smeared pulp of a body on a rock a hundred feet below. The horse had gone farther. It lay against a large boulder that had fallen from the cliff years ago. The dun had broken its back and died instantly. There was no movement.

McCoy sat there a moment staring down. He could not possibly bring up the body. It would take ropes and pulleys and a dozen men.

He would send out a team from the district attorney's office to prove to the county that Johnson was dead. It might be easier this way after all. The search party could also bring back the five thousand dollars from the saddlebags, if Johnson was telling the truth.

Spur relaxed, got back on his horse and munched on what was left of the hard biscuits he had put in his saddlebags. He also had evened up the supplies and put two cans of beans and a tin of canned beef in his bags as well. At least he wouldn't starve before he got to Elk Creek.

As he rode he began checking off things he had to do. The biggest part of his mission was completed. Now the wrap-up and the details. Some of the details might be most interesting.

CHAPTER NINETEEN

Day two dawned clear and warm in Elk Creek. Nehemiah Hardy was up early. His headaches were gone, his cheek was healing and the bullet hole in his leg was coming along fine according to Doc Paulson. The rest of his injuries were healing but would take time. After the kids had gone to bed last night he and Wendy had made love three times. They hadn't done that in five years. Between the lovemaking he had told her everything about Girl, how he met her and how their relationship had just developed naturally. She said she understood.

He had promised then to break off any romantic and sexual contact with Girl. Wendy said she was glad, and he promised to take her to the ranch so she could meet Girl, and be there when he said goodbye to her.

Now they were in a rented buggy, a stock of provisions for the ranch as usual in the small boot behind them and they were driving to the ranch. He had made the trip a thousand times, but none with the light heart, the clean spirit, the sense of right and truth that he felt his morning.

"I'm glad we're going," Hardy said.

Wendy looked up at him and those fifteen years of loving and depending on him spilled over. She blinked rapidly and couldn't speak as she put her arms around him and hugged him tightly. He looked down at her. He bent and kissed the top of her head.

"I love you so much, Hardy!" She said when she could speak. "I . . . I wish we could stop over there under the trees and make love in the grass."

Hardy grinned and swung the buggy into the grove. They were a mile out of town and no one was on the trail. He tied the reins and kissed his wife. Then he put his hands on her breasts and she murmured deep in her throat. He opened her dress right there in the buggy and petted her breasts which were warm already, the nipples lifting in anticipation.

"Darling Hardy, I have two requests. I . . . I want to be on top."

He was surprised. "Yes, sure."

"And then the second time, I want to gobble

you up." She paused and he frowned. "I want to take you in my mouth!"

Hardy couldn't believe his ears. She had always shied away from any oral contact. He nodded, and kissed both her breasts.

"Of course, sweetheart. Anything you want."

Then they got out of the buggy, spread a blanket but she folded it, undressed him, they lay in the grass and held out her arms to him.

Two hours later they arrived at his ranch. It had grown since he first began it as a form of employment and income for Girl and her relatives. Now it was a fine working ranch, with over three thousand head of cattle, a drive to the rail head every spring, and a crew of ten cowboys and a resident manager. The manager, who had also taken a squaw bride, was hard working and honest.

Hardy drove the buggy past the main ranch house to the Indian quarters. They had been improved over the years and now included four frame houses, a bunk house and a tribal meeting hall. There were over twenty Indians living there. All worked the ranch in summer and fall and wintered over for the spring work. In the winters the braves hunted, made bows and arrows, and the smarter ones learned English and the ways of the round eyes.

The largest of the frame houses was a five room affair. It contained a big kitchen with a fireplace and a big wood range that had a built on copper tank and copper coils that went over the firebox to heat the water. The sturdy oven door was

Hardy's favorite seat in the kitchen. It was a fine place to get your back warm on a winter day.

Girl came running from the house, but when she saw Wendy she slowed to a stop. Her plain face showed no emotion, but Hardy knew she was surprised and shocked. She had learned to speak English over the years, and had taught her children to speak English as well, but now her second language failed her and she greeted Hardy in an old dialect of the Sioux.

He waved to her, got out and helped Wendy down from the buggy. She had worn a plain print dress, high necked and long sleeves, a fashion that swept the dust with the skirt. She held Hardy's hand so tightly that it was painful, but he knew she was hurting inside more than he could imagine.

"Wendy, this is Girl," he said, as the two women looked at each other. It was totally unfair. Girl had known about Wendy and his other family for fourteen years. Yet she hadn't been warned that she would meet Wendy today. Wendy had known about Girl and Hardy's other family for only two days, and she knew and dreaded meeting Girl.

Wendy gave the briefest of nods.

Girl looked at Hardy quickly, then her glance came back to her rival and she nodded just as briefly. Wendy gave a big sigh and leaned forward. She took two steps and put her arms around Girl and hugged her. Tears glistened in Wendy's eyes.

"Girl, I'm glad to meet you. I don't hate you. I

hope you don't hate me."

The small Indian woman looked up at the roundeyed squaw in wonder. She thought this meeting would never take place. She had feared and dreaded it for fourteen years. But as each year slipped past, she believed more firmly that she and Mrs. Hardy would not meet.

Girl felt a strange moisture in her eyes.

"Welcome to my lodge, to my home," Girl said. She stepped back, looked at Wendy once more, then reached out and took her hand and led her rival into the neat, clean house. It was nearly eleven o'clock and Girl quickly provided coffee for Wendy and herself and a shot glass of whiskey for Hardy. She spoke in her basic English as she prepared food. Any visitor of rank must be fed in an Indian lodge. It was a custom that always had to be followed.

The conversation was strained at first. There was no one else in the house. As was the custom, both the children and the others who lived there, whoever they might be, left the moment they saw the white man arrive. They returned only at his or Girl's request. Hardy had no thought of bringing his two half-breed children out. It would be cruel to Wendy. Girl would not call them. He felt sure that Wendy would allow that part of his relationship to remain clouded.

Hardy hobbled to the buggy on his wounded leg and brought in the supplies. By the time he got back, he found Girl and Wendy looking over her sewing basket.

"There are so many new things you need,"

211

Wendy said. "I'll see that you have two new pair of scissors, and some better knives, and all the new threads. We have some packets of needles that can be used for almost anything, from silk to tough buffalo hide. Yes, and I'll send some patterns too, and a dozen kinds of cloth."

They talked about other things, cooking and housekeeping, and Wendy kept adding to her list: more cooking pots, silverware, dishes, bowls, a new washtub and two of the new washboards that made getting clothes clean so much easier.

For the noon meal, Girl took a pot of boiled chicken off the fire, laying out bread and soft cheese and jam and coffee.

"No potatoes," she said and frowned. "Hardy always likes meat and potatoes."

Hardy looked embarrassed. Wendy glanced at him, then laughed, and after that it was as if the two women were sisters more than rivals.

When Girl brought out cold milk for the meal, Wendy stared at it in surprise.

"How do you keep it so cold, Girl?"

"Ice in pit," she said.

Hardy nodded. "It's an old Indian custom that I'm going to move into town this winter. We dig an ice pond near the river, a flat place three feet deep and fill it with water from the river. After it freezes in the winter we move in with crosscut saws and cut the ice into blocks two feet square and two or three feet thick, however deep it freezes. Then we put it in a ten or twelve foot deep hole we dug earlier before the ground froze. The pit is lined with hay or straw. We place straw between each layer of the ice, and then cover it up with a whole straw stack. I'm thinking of putting a roof over it to insulate it from the rain and sun.

"Inside it stays cold and frozen, and we have ice that way here at the ranch all the way into July on most years. We can do the same thing in town, and sell the ice during half the summer at a good price."

"What a wonderful idea! Every woman in town will thank you for that, Hardy."

They stayed for another two hours. Hardy was getting nervous. He went out for a tour of the ranch, talked with the manager for an hour and arranged for the sale of some stock to a young man who wanted to get started in the cattle business. They got on board the buggy. Girl had brought a two foot square of ice from the ice house and wrapped it in a blanket for the trip back to town.

Wendy stood near the smaller, dark Indian girl. She was barely thirty years old, four years younger than Wendy. She stepped forward and hugged the Indian girl again and smiled.

"I hope we can be friends. You know Hardy will not sleep with you anymore."

Girl nodded. "I know. Many years of happiness. Now I . . ." She stopped. They both knew she was about to say that she had her children to take care of and to love and to hope for. But she didn't say it. She touched Hardy on the shoulder, then turned and walked into the house.

There were tears in Wendy's eyes as she got into the buggy. She leaned against Hardy as they drove back toward town. When they came to the woods by the river where they had stopped that morning, she pointed to the spot and asked him to stop.

She got out of the buggy and led him to the grass beside the stream and drew his hands to her breasts. Without a word they made love again, gently, slowly and with more deep affection and appreciation than ever before.

She did not need to say anything to him, but he knew what she was thinking. Now he was truly her husband, and hers alone. Never again would he stray, never again would she worry about it, and they both could be good friends with Girl and her life at the ranch.

They got back in the buggy and hurried home now before the ice melted. They wanted to show it to the neighbors and the children.

CHAPTER TWENTY

Spur McCoy slipped into town quietly, put his horse into the livery and talked to Jodi a minute, then went on to see the mayor. The county commissioners were in session to pick a new temporary sheriff until one could be elected. Spur told the mayor that Johnson was dead and the new sheriff would have to go out and confirm it.

Then Spur went back to the girls' place to get his gear. He could take a room at the hotel now and not be shot in his sleep. When he knocked on the alley door, it came open almost at once, as if Rebecca had been waiting for him.

It was a little after ten o'clock. Spur was hungry. Rebecca fixed him breakfast and sat watching him eat it. When the things were cleared off the table and put away, she looked at Spur.

"Could we talk a minute before you move out?" she asked.

He nodded and they both sat on the couch.

"I guess Jodi told you about me," Rebecca said, her eyes wide, her face showing almost no emotion.

"We talked. She said you had an unhappy childhood."

"Yes, unhappy. My father molested me, sexually. He made me walk around the house without any clothes on. He did things to me that were strange and terrible. So one day I killed him."

"Yes, I know."

"For a long time I've hated all men."

"That's understandable."

"What Jodi doesn't know is that every once in a while I get so angry I go out at night and tease a man and then stab him. I killed some of them, I know." She showed him the pocket in her dress. "I tore out the pockets in all of my dresses except this one. I wanted to show it to you."

"But if you can talk about it, you are much better now. Did you know that?"

"Good! I hoped so. I owe it all to you. You helped me. You let me see a man as a person, not somebody always trying to push his . . . his thing, inside me."

216

"I'm glad I could help, Becky. You're a beautiful girl. I hope someday you get married."

"I might, but I'll need you to help me again. Did you find the sheriff?"

"Yes. He's dead."

Her brows lifted. "Good. I'm glad. He was a bad man. He tried to rape me yesterday. I felt so good I went for a walk to find some wildflowers. He followed me and ripped my dress down and felt me and opened his pants." She laughed. "Then I fooled him. I cut his pecker in half with my knife. But I didn't kill him. That's why I'm better. I don't need to kill a man anymore if he touches me."

Spur smiled. "Becky, you used your knife and cut part of the sheriff's penis off?"

"Yes, and he screamed and yelled and swore at me. I ran away."

"No wonder he was riding with a pillow on his saddle."

"Now, I want you to help me again." She reached over and kissed Spur on the lips. He kissed her back. She let her lips come away, and smiled.

"I like that. Once more?" She kissed him again and her lips opened and her tongue touched his lips then pulled back. She was like an eager teenager, curious, wondering. It was if she had forgotten the rapes, the molestations, as if that was in a different time, before her emotions had been fully developed.

She smiled and kissed him again, pushing herself against him, then easing back. The next time

217

she opened her lips his opened too. She let him dart his tongue into her mouth, and she nodded through the kiss.

She moved her hands as they kissed and he saw she was opening the buttons on her dress. He closed his hand over hers, stopping her.

"Rebecca, I don't want you to get excited and carried away. You don't have to do anything more. Why not let your future husband show you all about this?"

Her voice was small and soft. She shook her head as she blinked back tears. "No. I don't want to learn to love someone and have him love me, only to find that I can't let him love my body. I have to know for sure. Is that wrong?"

"No, Becky, not wrong at all. I think you deserve that much assurance. Are you sure you want me to help you?"

"Oh, yes! I'd love to marry you, but I know you like Jodi, and you bed her. I just want to find out for sure."

She moved his hand, then pushed it inside her dress and there was no other garment under it. His hand closed around her tender breast and he felt it throbbing.

Becky shuddered, then nodded. "Yes, darling, I like it. Yes, please go on."

She kissed him then, and she moaned softly. He touched her breast, then opened the dress top to her waist and pushed it back so both her breasts showed. They were beautiful, larger than he had guessed and tipped with dark red nipples centered on deep red aerolas.

"Yes, that feels good," she said.

He massaged them and caressed them, and at last reached down and kissed each breast, chewing a moment on the upraised nipples. She nodded.

"Yes, I remember now. Daddy used to suck on my tiny little titties. That's what he called them. Not so tiny now."

He felt her breathing faster, felt her move beside him. She turned and lay down on the couch. He followed her, lifted himself up so she could move her legs on the softness, then he lay on top of her, his growing hardness pressing against her soft belly and the void below at her crotch.

"Oh, yes, that feels nice."

He kissed her again, kissed her breasts, then put his hand on her leg and worked it up slowly. She gasped but she gritted her teeth and when he touched the softness between her legs, she smiled and nodded.

"Let me get out of them," Becky said. She pulled up her skirt and pushed down the drawers so she could kick them off her bare feet. When she lay down she kept her skirt bunched around her waist.

Spur kissed her breasts again, then knelt on the floor beside the couch and brought one hand up her inner thigh.

She shivered, then smiled again.

"Good, I haven't even tried to hurt you. It feels good. It's strange, as if I should stop you, as if I know it's going to hurt the way it used to when I

219

was twelve when he pushed inside. Please, don't stop!"

His fingers brushed over her mound, then dove through the soft hair and touched the wetness and she jumped and screeched for just a moment.

"Oh, I remember now! It used to hurt like fire!"

"Maybe we should stop. You know it's going to be all right."

"No, he never could stop. I don't think that I could let you now. Please."

He opened his pants and worked his stiffness out. She looked at it and took a deep breath.

"Let me look."

He moved up so she could see his penis and scrotum. For a moment she experimented, played with him, then she nodded.

"I'm ready."

Spur lay beside her on the narrow cot. His hand found her heartland. His finger toyed with her a moment, then touched her clit and rubbed it six times. She climaxed, but it was over after one short surge of spasms. He touched her wet lips and rimmed them, then gently probed with one finger until he was deep inside her.

She blinked and looked at him, then she nodded. Spur sat up and went between her spread legs. He wet his throbbing penis with saliva and gently nudged toward her.

"No, no stop!" she said. Then she blinked back tears and shook her head. "You have to, I want you to. If you don't now I'll wither up and be an old maid all my life!"

220

He bent and kissed her tenderly. "You're sure?"

She nodded. "Yes, please, go ahead."

He touched his slippery tool to her wet lips and then pressed gently. There was some resistance, but not much, and he pressed in an inch, then slid past the guardian muscle which was still strong, and plunged deep inside her.

He could feel her relax.

"Oh, my! That is so easy, that feels so magnificent inside me. It's wonderful. It didn't hurt a bit!"

"It's not supposed to hurt. You're a grown woman now. A marvelously sexy, grown woman."

"Do I excite you?"

"As much as any woman I've ever made love to." He reached between them and found her love bud and twanged it again and again until she climaxed. This time she had relaxed and the tremors came one upon the other until she was moaning in pleasure. Her body shook as the climaxes built and built until she collapsed in a sweat.

"I've never . . . that was so . . . so . . . Oh, that was wonderful!"

Spur felt his own system peaking. He powered into her and felt her react. It was more benign then helpful as he thrust at her a dozen times before he shattered inside her and humped her into the couch until he was spent and drained. He fell on top of her, panting.

They lay quietly for five minutes. Then she squirmed and he moved away from her. She went and found a wet cloth and cleaned them both. They dressed and sat close to each other.

"Wonderful man, Spur McCoy. I know you came to town to get rid of our sheriff. But I am delighted that you found some time to help me while you were here. I'll always remember you. I'll never be the same again. I'm going to start going to church and going to socials and things. I won't be afraid to stay alone anymore. Maybe Jodi and I can find a little house somewhere in town so we won't have to live here in the alley. Then maybe I could help at the store. I know about housewares. If they do put in that new part, I'll talk to Jodi about it. Oh, I'll tell her what you did for me. She will understand. I didn't mean to come between you two. You still like her, don't you?"

"Yes, Becky. And I like you too."

"So we all can still be friends."

"We'll always be friends. Now, I think I better move into the hotel so anyone who wants to can find me. It's going to take a day or two more to get everything straightened out."

"I'll help you pack." She leaned in and kissed his cheek. "I'll always have you to thank for helping me. I'm not ready to get married tomorrow, but at least I know I will someday."

She helped him put everything in his carpet-bag.

"That knife case is for your kids," he said. "You can share the knives."

She looked at them for a minute, then nodded. "Yes, I can handle them now, too. A week ago, I couldn't have."

Spur pecked her on the lips at the door, said he would be back for a good dinner before he left, and walked quickly to the Hotel Hartford to register.

CHAPTER TWENTY-ONE

By noon Spur had registered in the hotel, talked to the mayor again and met a Mr. Ronkowski who said he was Chairman of the County Board of Supervisors. A new sheriff had been appointed to serve until the date of the next election, which had been set for two months away.

"Fred Denton is the new sheriff." Ronkowski said. "He doesn't know much about the law or being a lawman, but he's honest and a good church man. He'll do us fine for two months. He would like you to guide him to where Johnson jumped off the cliff."

"Be glad to. When?"

"He's ready to leave right now."

It turned out to be a little over ten miles to the death scene. They made it in two hours and Spur and the sheriff went down the cliff a half mile before they came to the dropoff. They could ride directly to the death scene this way. Tyler Johnson was little more than a mangled mass of bones and flesh. In the saddlebags still on the horse, they found the money. The sheriff carried it, and Spur tied Johnson's broken body on the pack horse they had brought along for the job. They rode back along the base of the cliff to the trail where the others met them and returned to town.

The job took a little over five hours, and the county came out nearly seven thousand dollars richer. Spur went back to Rebecca's rooms and took out the metal box of money.

"I had forgotten about it," Becky said. She touched Spur and smiled. "It's fun to be able to touch a man and not worry that I'm going to be hurt."

Spur fingered the cash. It was all there. He peeled off five hundred dollars and gave it to Becky. "I realize that an officer of the county assaulted, molested and attempted to rape you. If you'll accept this five hundred dollars, the county will deem the incident closed. That means you can't use the county to collect damages. Is that agreeable to you?"

Becky looked at the money and nodded. "Then we can buy a house in town somewhere!"

"Right, and have a lot left over."

Spur took the rest of the cash to the district attorney, who was working and trying to whistle past his bandages. Spur told him about finding the money in the jail, and that it must be county property. The district attorney smiled and made a record of the cash in the county books.

Over at the newspaper office, Spur saw Les Van Dyke taking the boards off all except the broken window. He was back in business.

"That deputy we had here," Van Dyke said. "I turned him over to the new sheriff who released him. Said there were no charges against him. Were some against the deputy who barricaded himself in the jail. He finally gave up and now is in a cell all his own."

Spur looked at the now famous newspaper that had triggered the outpouring of popular support. He grinned and pointed to the headlines.

"Did you know you spelled a word wrong in the headline?" Spur asked.

Van Dyke screeched. "Goddamnit, I didn't! Which one?"

Spur snorted. "You'll have to look it up. How are you going to learn to spell if somebody helps you all the time."

Spur left Van Dyke needlessly looking up each word in the headline, and headed for the sheriff office. Everything was under control.

The Secret Service Agent caught the banker just before he left for the night.

Otto Toller waved and waited.

"You need some banking business done, Mr. McCoy?"

"Not so you could notice. Just wondering how much cash our ex-sheriff had in his accounts?"

"District Attorney Oberholtzer was wondering that this morning. We checked every account with the Johnson name on it. He had four, and together there was just over twelve thousand dollars in them. We've put a hold on them and will use most of the money to repay any citizen who can substantiate a claim against the county because of the sheriff."

"Sounds like you'll run out of cash."

"We have set limits. We won't contest any claim for a thousand dollars for a misconduct death. Everything else is scaled down. Assault and battery as on the district attorney and Mr. Hardy would be medical expenses plus a hundred dollars. We're trying to be fair."

"Sounds reasonable. Well, looks like I've tied up all the loose ends. And I'm getting hungry. Mr. Toller, where is the best place in town to eat supper?"

The banker chuckled. "That's easy, Mr. McCoy. Best place in town is a cinch, no contest. It's at my table with Bessie cooking. Could I invite you to supper with us tonight?"

"Mr. Toller, your wife would kill you for bringing home company with no notice. I better try the hotel."

"No comparison. Besides, Mr. McCoy, I like your style, and the way you get things done. Now, it so happens I have a fine bank here, and my only kin is a pretty little daughter just old enough to get married. You care to come to supper to take a good look at her?''

Spur chuckled. "Mr. Toller, I'm honored. But I'm just not cut out to be a banker. Like to get out and move around. Plain hell on a woman. So I guess I must graciously refuse your kind invitation. Perhaps the next time I'm through town.''

The banker closed his door, checked the locks, then waved at Spur and they went in opposite directions.

A few steps down the street someone grabbed his arm and held on. Spur looked down to see Jodi smiling up at him.

"Jodi, fancy meeting you here. Maybe you know where the best restaurant in town is?''

She nodded. "Trust me, I know. Did you get moved out?''

"Yes, to the Hartford.''

"Good, that's where the best food in town is served, in your room. We order the steak for two and a whole baked pheasant, along with all the side dishes and it will cost you more than three dollars! It's a banquet. They've never served it before, but they will tonight. I get the idea your fiddle feet are itching again.''

"Well, I am a working man.''

She turned him into the Hartford, asked him to wait in the lobby while she gave the order at the dining room and came back a minute later.

"You're sure this is the best food in town?''

"That and a few nibbles on a certain delectable female, namely me.''

"Now we are reaching full agreement.''

A few minutes later, they lay side by side on the

229

bed in his room, both fully clothed as they talked. The food was due in half an hour.

"I had a long girl-to-girl conversation with Becky. She insists now that we call her Becky. She wants to get a job and that she is cured of whatever ailed her before. She also told me that you were there this afternoon and made love to her."

"True. It seemed like a good idea. A kind of therapy, a treatment. She has to learn that all men are not trying to hurt her. The whole thing was her idea. Do you think it helped?"

"Last time you kissed her and touched her breasts and she was practically cured. Now you fuck her once and she is an absolutely different person. I'd say you should go into being some kind of doctor for crazy people."

"You're not upset with me?"

"I am delighted with you. That's why tonight I am going to fuck your brains out."

Spur laughed. "Not until after we eat. I'm starved."

The food came complete with a fold-out special table and dishes steaming under two big covered trays. There was more food than Spur had seen in weeks, huge steaks, big baked potatoes, three vegetables, and the whole roasted pheasant on a platter with carving tools.

Spur saw Jodi open a bottle of wine and dug into the food as though he hadn't eaten in six days. He demolished the steak, tore off the pheasant drumstick and the breast and kept washing it down with wine. He had not enjoyed such a fine meal for years. He worked at stuffing himself until he could hardly move. They set the remains in the hall and locked the door.

Then both fell on the bed. Jodi kissed him.

"Not tonight, I have a stomache."

She laughed. "You should the way you ate, but I feel so sexy not I could go right on eating you."

She kissed him again.

"When are you leaving?"

"I missed the stage. Somebody said it went through yesterday. That means I ride to Sheridan tomorrow morning, or I wait here another week."

"Wait another week," she said unbuttoning his trousers.

"In another week I'd be worn down to a nub without the energy to lift my head."

"Which one?"

"Neither one."

"Shut up and make love to me."

"In my condition?"

"I'd rather have you seduce me," she said. "But in an emergency I can be terribly aggressive. Watch." She stripped his pants down, then took off his shirt. Soon he was naked.

"Your turn," he said. He lay there watching her strip and it brought a certain amount of desire. He sat up to watch better and soon she was sitting astride him lowering one breast after the other for him to kiss and chew on.

"Not bad, not bad," Jodi said. "Hey, you ever make love to sisters the same day before?"

"Not lately," he said and she pretended to hit him.

Things progressed rapidly. They made love and fell asleep in each other's arms. He woke up once and thought he heard something, then slept again.

When he woke up the next time, soft hands were playing with him. He turned in the dim light of the low lamp to tell Jodi to go back to sleep.

For a moment he stared in surprise. The naked girl beside him was not Jodi.

"Violet!" he whispered. "What are you doing here?"

"Just a friendly visit." She reached over and kissed him, pushing her bare breasts against his chest. When the kiss ended her hand had him hard and ready.

She pushed over on top of him and ground her hips against his hips and his stiff penis.

"I think you're ready, don't you?"

"Now wait a minute. Violet, I told you. You're too young."

"That's what you say." She lifted over him, aimed his lance at her hot sheath and lowered herself. "Really, do you think I'm that young?"

"You're not seventeen?"

"I used to say that. I'm nineteen."

Jodi laughed softly beside him. "True, this little cunt is nineteen and has been working the hotel for nearly two years. Some guys like to think they're poking a young girl."

"Jodi, I don't know where she came from, honest."

"Hey, I don't mind. I like to share things. Only you're mostly worn out. My turn isn't going to

232

come until after breakfast, I can tell you that."

"He's got plenty of action left," Violet said. "Just watch him."

Spur laced his fingers together and put them in back of his head. He lay there and listened, enjoying the two women arguing over him. It was going to be an interesting night, and most of tomorrow before he could get his gear together, hire a horse and ride to Sheridan.

Over him Violet began grinding with her hips and doing some strange things that brought him to life in a rush. Tomorrow, well, maybe he should lay over here for a day or two more and see if he could tire these two partners out. He should be able to outlast two little girls like these. If not, what a way to be beaten!

PORTLAND PUSSYCAT

CHAPTER ONE

Sunlight slanted in through the windows as Alain DuLac mixed the oils on his palette, looking for the right shade of red. It just wasn't the same. The rustic city of Portland, Oregon, wasn't Paris. He couldn't even buy the proper paints, the only ones that he could work with. Six months in this frontier town had depressed him.

DuLac shook his head and dabbed more white onto the smudge of dark red that bled onto his palette. He mixed the two hues with the brush and stared at the unfinished canvas on the easel. If only he could be back in Paris!

The old melancholy oozed through him. That was impossible, he knew. He could never again walk along the Seine, visit the bakery, see his family and friends. That part of his life was over forever.

The short, unkempt man snorted. "Chin up," he

said in his newly acquired English. "You should be happy you got out in time."

He remembered returning home from the bank, seeing the *gendarmes* surrounding his studio, hurling his possessions into the street. Unnoticed in the confusion, DuLac had gone back to the bank, withdrew every cent he had and caught the first ship to America.

It had been nearly a year ago.

Satisfied with the new shade he'd created, he started feathering in the highlights of the girl's hair. He wanted to capture the memory of the way the sun had glinted across Rebecca's tresses. DuLac became absorbed by the image. It was nearly perfect, so real that those lips seemed to be trembling, so vivid that he expected the breasts he'd created with paint to be soft and warm.

He added each strand of hair singly and soon had to turn up the lamps in his studio/apartment. As he bent toward the window to close the shades, he looked out at the shabby buildings and the dark bulks of the ships bobbing at the wharves.

Soon enough he'd be out of this neighborhood. Soon the people of Portland would recognize his talent and flock to buy his paintings. Soon he'd be able to stop his other business and become an honest man.

And perhaps, someday. . . .

The pudgy man pulled at the ends of his moustache, his eyes misting and blurring the image on the canvas. Someday in the future, he might return to his beloved Paris.

Harsh pounding pulled him from his reverie. DuLac shook his head, set down his palette and brush and went to the door. Was it time already?

It was. He silently admitted the tall, distinguished looking man.

"So you did not change your mind, Cummings," DuLac said, bolting the door behind him.

The man's face was barely visible under his low hat and the high collar of his coat. "No. Of course not." Though the room wasn't cold, his visitor pulled his jacket tighter around his gaunt body.

The artist nodded and went to the table that lay next to the bedroom door. This was how he made most of his money, DuLac thought, but that didn't stop him from hating such interruptions.

"These are flawless. Absolutely flawless." He retrieved a small satchel which he'd hidden behind a stack of leather-bound art books that morning.

"Sure, friend. Sure," Cummings said.

DuLac walked toward the man holding the bundle. "The same price as before. Correct?" He held the package out of the man's reach.

Cummings smiled and produced ten one-dollar bills from his coat pocket. They were folded and fastened together with a gold money clip. "You haven't reconsidered my offer, have you, DuLac? We could work real good together—your talent and my brains."

DuLac bristled. Always the same talk. "No. I am in business by myself and for myself. I do not need or want a partner." Cummings never changed. "I am a busy man. Are you going to buy or not?"

"Yes. Of course. But not at that price." He extracted half of the ones. "Five should do."

DuLac fumed and returned to the table. "No. One on ten. That is the way it is and will be."

"Not as far as I'm concerned."

The artist faced the enemy. "You think I am an

ignorant immigrant? That you can take advantage of me?"

Cummings smiled and stuffed the money into his coat pocket. "I think this is getting too dangerous for me. People are noticing. It's getting harder to pass your shit."

"This is the best that you can find!" DuLac puffed out his chest.

"Shut up!" Cummings' voice was harsh. "I'll give you five dollars for a hundred. Take it or leave it. But if you turn me down, you'll have visitors here, DuLac. Visitors in blue uniforms who'll be very interested in this business of yours."

"You dare to threaten me?" He walked to his easel, furious. "You are just as guilty as I, Cummings. In as much danger."

"I only passed it, friend. I didn't print it. I'm not the counterfeiter."

DuLac's fingers clasped around the wooden handle. "I am an artist! Get out of my studio!"

He heard Cummings approaching him from behind.

"Not until I get what I came for."

Now, he thought. The Frenchman extracted the long-bladed knife he'd hidden behind the easel and spun. Cummings didn't flinch as he continued toward the table.

"You won't use that thing on me, DuLac! You're no murderer!" He sneered, walked past the artist and pushed away the stack of books.

"You underestimate me!"

DuLac moved to him. Cummings had turned his back. A stupid mistake, the artist thought. He gripped the handle and brought it down, sheathing the steel. Cummings cried out as DuLac opened up his back.

The doomed man thrashed and dropped to the table. It was hard going at first, working the blade through flesh and gristle and the bones of his spine. DuLac gasped. Acidic sweat dripped from his brow. The short man stabbed Cummings ten times, caught up in the rage and passion, ripping up his back.

He raised the knife again and stared down. Cummings slumped over the table, unmoving, his arms dangling over its side.

Dead. He was dead.

A sickening smell filled the air, blotting out the comforting sweetness of the oil paints. DuLac wiped his forehead and breathed deeply, glancing around to see that all the shades were, indeed, drawn.

They were. He wiped the knife on a paint-splattered rag and threw it into the fireplace. It would serve as kindling that night. Now what to do with the body?

DuLac sighed. Counterfeiting. It always led to the same thing, to this uncomfortable feeling of having something to get rid of. He gripped the face-down man's waist and tried to heave him from the table. The body moved sideways and spilled onto the floor.

The artist panted.

A door opened. DuLac spun around, fear coursing though him, and smiled when he saw her step out from the bedroom. The red-haired young girl yawned and stood on shaky legs.

"You woke me up," she said.

"Rebecca, I—will you—"

She noticed the motionless form on the floor and

sneered. "Oh, Alain! Again?" The girl shook her head and sighed. "I suppose you want me to clean up the mess."

DuLac's shoulder ached. He walked to her, arms outstretched. "Please, my love, will you help me?"

She sighed. "Alright. Just like before. I'll get my friends to come over and take *it* away." Rebecca pouted. "But this is the last time, Alain! I mean it! You can't go around killing every man who argues with you. It's—it's messy!"

"You don't know what he was doing."

She tossed her head. "I don't care what he was doing." The girl fixed her eyes on his. "But Alain, if I do this, promise that I won't have to model for you again."

"Rebecca!" DuLac shook his head. He didn't want to lose her. "Look at the easel! Look at the work of art I created with your face!"

She glanced at it. Her face, with cascading red hair, remained cool. "Sure, it's pretty, but I'm bored sitting for hours and hours every day when I could be sleeping, we could be pleasuring each other or I could be smoking opium. I'm so tired of it, Alain! I can't do it again!"

"Okay. Alright!" He threw up his hands, tempering his anger with relief. "Just get your friends in here. I will find another model."

"Fine." Rebecca yawned and stretched. Her lovely form appeared beneath the loose robe.

DuLac stared at the seventeen year-old girl. The danger of the last few minutes transmuted to lust. He stepped over the body. "Get your friends later, okay?"

Rebecca smirked at him. "Sure. But don't try to

pay them with those phony twenty dollar bills of yours. Alain, give them real money. Okay?"

"Yes." He unbuttoned his pants. "And I'll give you this."

CHAPTER TWO

"Git on your belly or you're dead!"

The voice blasted at him as Spur McCoy entered the Portland Home Bank.

"I said move!"

Three rifle-toting men aimed at him. Tense people lay strewn all over the polished marble floor—tellers, little old ladies, grown men. The air was thick with the smell of fear.

Spur sighed. He'd walked right into a bank robbery.

"Now!" one of the gunmen shouted.

"Okay. Okay! I'm unarmed!" he lied and dropped to the floor.

Spur laid his cheek against the tile and turned his head, keeping an eye on things. One man stood guard as the other two forced the bank president to open the old-fashioned iron safe. He couldn't hear their words over the sniffles of the women sprawled around him.

"It'll be okay," he said to the girl lying a few feet from him.

"Shut up! No talking!"

She hesitantly smiled, clutching the beaded purse with her white knuckles.

Great. Just what he needed. He was in Portland to investigate the flood of counterfeit money that had invaded the monetary system and he ended up in this.

Spur was at least 20 feet from the closest guard, 30 feet from the other men and the safe. These men were professionals. No quirky movements, no hesitations. They acted as if they'd done this kind of thing before.

A lot.

"Hurry up!"

McCoy heard a metallic click. The safe must have been opened. The nearest guard turned to look at it for a second. Spur slid his arm down to the holster hidden under his coat tails.

He froze when the man wearing the kerchief snapped back, his full attention trained on his captives.

"Shit! That's all you got?"

The Secret Service agent bided his time, waiting for the right moment. A breeze swept in through the open windows. It slid over oak filing cabinets and bannisters and the tellers' windows, spreading fine dust throughout the bank.

"Come on! Empty it out!"

The guard scratched his nose. He raised his head.

"Uh. Uh. Uhhh!"

Spur drew his weapon, the action hidden from the guard by his leg. He slipped the revolver onto the cold floor, fingers tensed around its handle.

Wouldn't he ever sneeze?

"Uh. Oh hell!" the guard said, waving his own weapon through the dust-laden air.

He snorted. His nose exploded.

In that blinding second Spur slid to his knees and blasted hot lead into the guard's chest.

Without even checking to see if his ammunition had hit its mark, he dove for cover into the office cubicle that lay behind him.

"What in hell!" a voice said as the explosion echoed through the room.

Women screamed.

Spur waited.

"Damn! Andy's dead!"

"Who the hell did that!" It was the leader again. "Who the hell did it?"

Spur's muscles tensed as he crouched, kissing the wood with his shoulder. The walls were six feet high, tall enough to keep most men from looking over it. Because it was walled in on three sides, he'd have a clean shot at anyone who investigated.

"Didn't anyone see anything?"

"No!" the hostages chanted. A girl screamed and somewhere a baby cried.

Spur sweated.

"Then we'll just start killing you off one at a time until you remember! Who'll go first. You, sweetheart?"

They'd do it, Spur thought. They were professional thieves. He tightened his grip, his trigger finger itching to pull, to drive those bastards into the dirt.

He couldn't see. He had no idea what was happening. Time to take a chance.

Spur moved over to the edge of the wall. He

removed his hat with his left hand, peered into the lobby and whipped back to safety.

The image crystallized in his brain. A gunman held a woman by her throat. She knelt, looking pleadingly up at the man as he aimed at her.

The other thief walked among the people, throwing up coats, looking for weapons. They must have forgotten about him.

"Say goodbye, girl!"

Spur lunged past the wall and peeled off a shot, instantly lining up his first target. The second man turned as his partner reeled. Spur's hogleg sounded again.

Both men went down as he paused, staring at them. Blue smoke filled the air and the echoes of the twin explosions bounced around in the big building for several seconds. Neither gunman moved.

Spur McCoy stood, stretched his legs and walked fully into the open. The hostages started to sit up.

"I'd stay down for a while if I were you," he warned them. "They might not be dead."

He cautiously approached the second gunman and kicked his foot. Nothing. Spur peeled the fingers from the man's revolver and moved to the third man.

The leader lay face up. His kerchief, whipped partially away, showed a lifeless face. No breath issued from his parted lips.

Lucky shots, Spur thought as he collected another revolver. He checked both men's pulses just to be sure. They'd never rob another bank.

"Okay. It's safe now."

Fifteen souls rose. Grown men and women ran outside without even looking at him. The young girl who'd been at the other end of a barrel smiled and pressed his hand as she made her way out.

In seconds he was alone with three bodies and the bank president, who was busily stuffing the currency into the safe.

"I don't know who the hell you are, but I'm glad you stopped by today."

Spur nodded.

Dan Norcross sighed as he slammed the safe's door shut and rotated the tumblers. A tight-faced young man, a teller, had the conscience to return.

"Mr. Norcross?" McCoy asked.

"Go get Commissioner Golden!"

"Yessir!"

"Look, Norcross, I came here to ask you about the counterfeit money."

"Counterfeit?" Norcross scratched his head, his eyes dazed. "Oh yeah! Lots of that. Some of it's turned up here. Don't have a clue who's doing it." The ruddy-complexioned man blew out his breath. "I'm sorry. It's a little hard talking about that after all that's happened here." He surveyed the dead men and shook his head.

Spur nodded. "I understand. I'll stop by later."

When Police Commissioner Golden arrived at the bank, Spur quickly cleared up his involvement in the incident. Unwilling to discuss his secret Service mission in public, Spur arranged to meet him that afternoon in his office.

Now, outside, he took long breaths and strode along the street, admiring Portland's crisp air and beautiful buildings. He hadn't been in the Northwest for some time.

Spur re-read the telegram that his boss, General Halleck, had sent him from Washington. Jessica Gerard was the woman's name. He went to the address—305 Hudson Drive.

It was a small, dark shop full of crates, completely unsuitable for a woman. But as Spur McCoy walked inside his nose was filled with the scent of flowers.

The figure bending over the counter raised its torso and Spur smiled at the woman.

"Yes?" she wiped her gloves on the leather apron that covered her gingham dress. "Can I help you?"

She was in her mid-thirties, pretty, with penetrating eyes and a full, sensuous mouth.

"You're Miss Gerard?"

The woman pleasantly shook her head. "Mrs. Gerard. I'm widowed. Inherited this business from my husband when he passed on two years ago."

Spur nodded and walked up to the counter where piles of red and white roses lay. She'd been stripping off their thorns and throwing them into a coffee can.

"Spur McCoy. I understand you got some counterfeit money recently."

Her nostrils flared at the word. "Darn tooting!" Jessica pulled off the leather gloves revealing white, flawless hands. "It was in payment for wedding flowers. Can you believe that?" She chuckled. "When I took my cash to the bank that afternoon they informed me that they couldn't accept counterfeit money. I was shocked!" She laid a hand on her breast. "But old Edward Bidwell knows me. He told me to talk to the Commissioner. That's about it." Jessica looked at him, eyebrows raised.

"Who gave you this money?"

She reached behind her back and tried to unfasten the apron. "Heck. Could you help me with this?" The woman turned around and looked at him over her shoulder.

"Of course." Spur untied the straps and she struggled out of it, letting the heavy garment drop to the leaf-strewn floor.

"Thanks." Mrs. Gerard smoothed down the bodice of her brown, well-fitting dress. "It was the McInallys. Two old Scottish people. Said they met here and decided to get married three days later. They're on their honeymoon now—Geneva, I think." Jessica shook her head. "So I'm out my $20."

"They didn't look like the type of folks who'd print up their own money, did they?"

"No. Just plain people in love." She made a face. "I don't even remember what it's like to be that much in love."

He nodded toward the pretty woman. "Is there anything else you can tell me? I'm working with Commissioner Golden on the matter of the counterfeit money."

"I see." She narrowed her eyes and thought. "I'm sorry. That about it."

Spur nodded. The scent of roses in the close room was overpowering. As much as he enjoyed looking at the healthy woman, he had to get some fresh air. "How do you stand it?"

"What?"

"Well, Mrs. Gerard, flowers are fine, but this place smells like—like—"

Jessica smiled, flashing perfect white teeth at him. "A cheap whore?"

"Ah, yeah!"

"I'm not cheap, and I'm certainly not a whore. Oh Mr. McCoy, I don't even notice it anymore. I've been around them too long, I guess."

"That makes sense. If you think of anything else,

I'm staying at the Riverside Hotel.''

"Fine."

"Good day, Mrs. Gerard.''

"Good day, Mr. McCoy.'' Her hand went to her breast. "I—I hope I'll be seeing you again.''

He hesitated before turning toward the door. Their eyes locked. "You can be counting on it.''

McCoy heard her humming as he walked outside.

A half hour later, after he'd eaten in the hotel dining room, Spur returned to the bank.

"Mr. McCoy!'' Dan Norcross said, rushing out of his chair to meet him. He took Spur's hand and pumped it up and down, squeezing his forearm. "I cannot tell you how happy I am that you dropped in earlier today.'' The bank president grinned at him.

"All in a day's work.'' He gently tried to take back his hand.

"Maybe for you, but not for me!'' Norcross vigorously shook Spur's hand. "It was a nightmare until you started shooting. They had me by the balls!''

"Ah, Mr. Norcross,'' Spur said.

"Huh?'' He looked down at their still-locked paws. "Oh. Sorry.'' The man released Spur's hand. "I'm just so—so grateful to you. We would have been ruined—not to mention what would have happened to the depositors and the poor, sweet girl who nearly got herself killed.'' He shuddered at the memories.

"Hey, relax, Norcross!'' Spur said, flexing his hand. "That's in the past. Now what can you tell me about this counterfeit money that's been coming into town?''

"Huh? Oh, yes. Have a seat, Mr. McCoy.'' He

motioned to the well-worn chair in front of his desk. "It's good. Damn good. Finest engraving work I've ever seen." Norcross shrugged. "Of course, it doesn't hold up under close inspection. The printing's off and the ink and paper just don't match the real thing."

"Do you have any idea how long it's been passed here in Portland?"

"Hard to say." The bank president sucked in his cheeks and mulled it over. "I don't know. It could have been floating around for weeks or months before we caught on."

"That's understandable. It's normal not to be too careful until the word has gotten out. Do you have any of the counterfeit money here that I could take a look at?"

"I hope to hell I don't" Norcross laughed. "Sorry, I hauled it all over to the police commissioner's office. On Golden's orders I had my boys go through our funds. Found maybe, oh, ten or eleven of them. Not too bad."

"And how many other banks are in town?"

The president hummed for a moment. "You're talking about my competition. There are two official ones. First Oregon over on Adams and Grayson's Family Bank down by the river."

"Thanks for your time, Norcross. I better head over to Commissioner Golden's office."

The man rose with Spur. "Hey, the pleasure's been all mine!" His face beamed.

Spur started to extend his hand and drew it back, smiling. "Yeah, right."

CHAPTER THREE

"Get that corpse outta here!" a male voice barked from inside the office.

"Golden?" Spur yelled into the office. He darted around the two policemen carrying a sheet-wrapped body out of the wood-panelled room.

No answer.

He walked in. "Commissioner Golden?"

"Yeah. You look familiar." The bearded man glanced at him and sat on the edge of his desk, biting off the end of a fat cigar. "Weren't you at that robbery this morning?"

Spur nodded. "McCoy's the name."

"Sure! I gotta wire about you." He turned around and surveyed his paper-strewn desktop. "Somewhere. You must be from the Secret Service, the man the government sent out here about that counterfeit money."

McCoy closed the door. "Hope you don't mind, but I have to take precautions."

"What? No. I understand. I just can't find my damned matches!"

Spur smiled. "Look under your butt."

"What'd you say to me?"

"You're sitting on them, Golden. I noticed them as I came in."

The man stood, turned around and grabbed the matches. "You've got a good eye, McCoy. And you do some pretty fancy shooting."

Thanks. But I'm not in town to catch the kind of men who rob banks." He walked toward the desk. "I'm here about the counterfeit money."

"I know, I know." He struck a lucifer and held it to the end of the leaf-wrapped cigar, puffing until the fire took hold and the tip glowed. "All this bad money. Just what I don't need."

The man wasn't being very helpful, Spur thought as he tapped his right boot toe. Golden seemed bored.

"Do you have any information for me? Any leads, suspicious characters, some guy who's done this kind of thing here before?"

He shook his head. "No."

"What about that dead man?" Spur asked.

Golden snorted and blew out blue smoke. "If he was the counterfeiter, he won't be giving us any more trouble."

The veins in Spur's neck tightened. "Do you think there could be a connection between that man's death and the counterfeit money?"

"How in hell should I know?" Golden took aim at a brass spitton and hit it dead center. "Goddamn it!"

"Found a lot of bodies lately?"

"Yeah. We're dragging up about one a week. More than average, even for a place of this size. Things weren't looking so dead until recently—very recently." He grinned at his own joke.

The man grated on him. "Would you say the murders started about the time the fake money showed up?"

Golden was silent. He puffed, smiled and exhaled. "Hard to say. Maybe."

"And all the victims were men?"

"Yup. Stabbed, most of them. One shot through the heart at close range. Found them floating in the river. Five so far, including that last joker. No papers, no clothes, nothing to identify them."

"What are your instincts?"

"My what?"

Spur made a fist and banged it against his right thigh. "What are your feelings? Could the murders themselves be connected? Were they all done by the same man?"

"How the hell should I know?" Golden huffed and walked to the window. "The mayor's breathing down my neck about this, and the phony twenty-dollar bills aren't helping any. Lots of stores are refusing to take anything except a one dollar bill— or gold. I'm just praying someone doesn't set up his own mint in this town."

"Yeah."

This wasn't getting him anywhere. Golden was obviously the kind of man who sat behind a desk and dictated letters. He obviously didn't like to get his hands dirty. "Heard anything about any new arrivals in town causing trouble? Artists, maybe?"

Golden scowled. "McCoy, I don't look at pictures.

I'd rather play a good game of chess or enjoy a fine cigar." He took several puffs. "Of course, there is one type of fine art I enjoy." He went to the front of his desk, slid open a drawer and showed Spur a small painting of a nude girl. "Mighty fine brushwork there, eh? I don't know anything about art, but that gal's talented." He guffawed.

"Sure." The quality of the image was excellent. So good, Spur figured he'd be able to recognize the woman on the street. "Is it by a local artist?"

"Who the hell knows?" He slapped the painting into the drawer and banged it shut. "I can't read the artist's signature. Friend of mine picked it up for me—actually, I won it in a poker game last week."

Spur made motions to leave. "I'll check back with you if I turn up anything important."

"Yeah, I guess so. And if you meet any more dead bodies in the hall, tell them not to come in here!"

He shook his head and walked outside.

Artists, McCoy thought as his heels clicked on the floor. Wasn't there an artists' colony of sorts in town? He vaguely remembered passing a row of studios not far from the police station.

Five minutes later he found them. The squat, ill-kept cottages were hard by a two-story structure. "Portland Museum of Fine Arts," the sign said.

He walked in past a snoring security guard. A matronly woman accepted his dollar 'donation' with a smile. The rooms were filled with smoke, large and small canvases hung lopsided on the walls.

Not many people roamed the aisles. Those who were present were mostly older, well-moneyed couples with plenty of free time and not much to do. Spur passed a Renoir, a sketch by da Vinci and a Rembrandt before finding a small room labelled "Local Artists."

It was dimly lit. He pretended to study the paintings but was actually memorizing the names of the various painters. Laleque. Feingold. Bohannan. Johnson. Douglas. DuLac. Frantz. Weinholtz. And Emily Curtis—the only woman represented. Not surprisingly, the subjects of her paintings all seemed to be male.

"Don't you just love her work?" a feminine voice said at close range.

He turned and smiled at the young woman. "Ah, I'm not familiar with it." He tipped his hat.

"I'm not either." She peered at the painting. "But there's something about that man's face, something that makes me. . . ." The brunette shook her head. "I don't know." She self-consciously patted her hair. "I hope you don't think I'm, well—well—"

"What is it?" Something about the woman got his curiosity.

She sighed and looked up. "I'm not wearing a bonnet!"

"So I noticed." Spur liked the woman. "You have lovely hair."

"That's not the point!" Her voice was violent. "You know there's only one kind of woman who goes out without wearing a hat."

"I'm sorry." Spur was perplexed. "Is there something I can help you with?"

She clasped her hands. "I don't know. I'm so confused. Oh, I forgot to introduce myself. I'm Clare Maxwell."

"Spur McCoy."

"Nice to meet you, though I wish it were under different circumstances." She frowned, marring her natural beauty. "I was nearly thrown in jail this morning—and not for what you may be thinking."

"I'm not thinking that."

"All I did was try to buy a new hat, and the sweet-faced lady grabbed my arms! She wouldn't let go and started screaming to her husband!"

"Let me guess. Did you try to pay with a twenty dollar bill?"

Clare widened her eyes and smiled. "Yes. How'd you know?"

He shrugged. "There's a lot of that going around. You must be new in town."

"That's right. Just got in two days ago from San Francisco."

"Where'd you get the bill?"

She looked away from him. "I'd—I'd rather not tell you that."

Over her shoulder Spur saw her left cheek redden. Spur smiled at her. The woman turned and started to speak, but he took her hand.

"I'm *not* thinking that, believe me! It's none of my business anyway."

Clare hung her head. "Alright. Go ahead. Call me a saloon girl, a tart like my mother used to say. But I'm not the whore of Babylon!"

"Fine." He'd never met a woman like her. Ever. She was obviously educated, well-fed, healthy and full of life. But she didn't have the money to buy a hat?

"I should be going. I have to earn some more—I mean, I—" Her blush deepened.

"Miss Maxwell, it's no concern of mine what you do. Honestly."

She shook her head. "Anyway, I really do like Emily Curtis's paintings."

The woman looked at him, flinched and ran off.

Spur watched the woman's hips swaying back and forth. He hoped her next customer would give her clean money produced by the United States Bureau of Engraving and Printing.

Until sundown, Spur poked through the artists' studios, gently asking questions, trying to root out any suspicious remarks from the motley assortment of individuals who did indeed fit the artistic temperament. He even visited Emily Curtis for a few moments. The artist turned out to be an eighty-year-old cigar-smoking gal who liked her male models more than selling her paintings.

Nothing.

A whore!
At least I have a bonnet for this outfit, Clare Maxwell thought as she struggled into the stiff black dress. She used her black handkerchief to scrape a layer of dust from the hotel room's cracked mirror and pinned the dark hat on her head. Lowering the veil to cover her face, she bent her torso forward, drooped her chin and grabbed the cane.

She looked perfect. No would suspect the woman inside the clothes was twenty-two years old.

Gleeful and excited as she always was, she pressed an ear to the door and listened. Footsteps and soft laughter in the hallway outside. She waited until all was silent and slipped out of her room.

As she slowly, slowly made her way to her favorite spot, Clare realized that she had to be careful. True, she didn't think she was in any danger of the police. Who would bother an old lady? Still, the counterfeit money she'd gotten yesterday had shaken her. What was the point if all she took home was pieces of paper that no bank or shopkeeper would accept?

An hour until sunset. She walked to the corner, pretending to measure every step she took, leaning heaveily on the cane, and started crying. At least, she hoped it sounded like crying.

Clare Maxwell finally paused in the middle of a block near the milliner's store where she'd been rebuffed earlier that day. A likely candidate walked toward her.

She put her act into overdrive, sobbing, reeling, pretending to lose her balance. She dropped the cane and wailed just as the young woman passed her.

"What is it?" the girl asked.

"No. No. No one cares about an old lady!" Clare glanced up at her, hunched over. From behind her veil the girl looked fresh-faced, well-dressed and just of marrying age.

"You poor dear. Come on, tell me!"

She panted. "Could—could I borrow a handkerchief?" she asked, sniffling.

"Of course." The girl opened her purse and handed her a lacey square of linen.

Clare took it and deepened the crackle in her voice. "Oh, I've dropped my cane." She stumbled forward.

"Here, let me get that for you."

Clare got into position as the girl bent over. In seconds flat she retrieved her cane, grabbed the purse and ran like hell down the street.

"Hey!"

Jubilant, Clare raced along the sidewalk, her black dress flying. She shoved the purse down her bodice, wedging it between her large breasts and laughing.

The girl had looked wealthy. If so, now Clare Maxwell was happy to have gotten a share of it.

She prayed that she didn't find any more counterfeit money.

CHAPTER FOUR

Spur spent much of the night curled up under a flowerbox across the street from the small artists' colony. Though it was spring, the air blowing off the Williamette River was chilled. He watched the small, squat cottages, waiting for something suspicious to happen, but had seen nothing more unusual than young women of questionable virtue (but obvious talent, as the police commissioner would say) slipping into the small structures.

If there was a counterfeiter among the artists, he certainly wasn't showing his hand. Spur chuckled into the collar of his coat as not one but two strapping men boldly walked into Emily Curtis's place. They didn't leave for nearly two hours. This was a little late to be painting, he thought with a wry smile, trying to picture the elderly woman tangled up with the bucks.

After sitting there half the night, wrapped in shadows, he returned to his hotel and tumbled into bed well after midnight.

McCoy didn't wake until eight. Walking to the windows to let in blinding sunlight, he wondered what his next moves would be. He had no leads whatsoever.

As he scraped off his whiskers with cold water and a semi-rusty blade, Spur realized that even if a working artist had gone into the money-printing business, he probably wouldn't have the operation set up in his studio. Naturally, not all the artists in Portland were located on that one street. A few of them must have made a fortune and had built fine homes.

He shook his head and splashed fresh water onto his face from the pitcher. What would he do? Track down every artist in town, break into their homes and search them?

Spur smiled at his misty reflection, wiped off his face and answered the urgent knock that suddenly issued from his hotel room door.

A bespectacled boy thrust a folded piece of paper to him and held out his hand. Still groggy, he handed the kid a quarter and slammed the door shut.

Another telegram from General Halleck. As always, Spur had wired his hotel and room number to his boss. What was it this time?

Bare chested, he sat on the bed and read. The man who'd transcribed the message wrote in a clean, neat hand, something which he hadn't encountered very often in the ruder towns of the west.

His boss had given him a new assignment while he was in the area. He was to investigate some sort of slavery operation located somewhere outside of Portland. A logging and sawmill business. The owners have been importing males from the Hawaiian Islands and forcing them to work sixteen hours a day under the most grueling conditions, felling trees and sawing lumber under armed guard.

The men are underfed, unpaid and unable to leave. Ankle chains. Beatings. Those who died were quickly replaced by fresh human stock. One man had managed to escape with a bullet in his stomach and told this to a passing sheriff before he'd died.

He'd been given the assignment because the slaves had been transported from Hawaii to the state of Oregon.

Spur frowned. He didn't need this diversion, but he'd be glad to crush it out of existence. The thought of men doing things like that to other human beings made his skin crawl. He carefully reread the telegram, deciphered its code, but it contained no indications of where the operation was located.

His mind raced. A sawmill? They had to sell lumber. Maybe excess logs. Who's buying, and did they know or care where the merchandise was coming from? Maybe the low prices that kind of labor could produce halted any questions.

It had to be located on the water to quickly move the lumber. A river, probably. It must be an armed, rigidly-run camp secreted somewhere in the woods. There wouldn't be open trails blazing toward it. On the water the men in charge could go to and from the camp by boat. It all seemed reasonable.

Spur pulled on his boots and dressed. He'd spend the rest of the day working on the counterfeiters and set out first thing in the morning to look for the outlaw logging operation.

He was getting tired of this city life, he thought, pushing the low-brimmed Stetson on his head. It'd feel good to get back on a horse again.

"Wake up!"

Groggy from his nap, DuLac growled as the young girl shook his shoulders. "Why? Are you going to spread your legs for me?" He lazily grabbed Rebecca's thigh.

"No! Not now!" Her hand brushed his away.

He rolled over. "Then let me sleep."

"Come on, Alain! We have to talk!"

The artist sighed and rubbed his face. "Why are you young girls so—so energetic all the time?"

"You never complained before."

DuLac sighed and sat up. "Alright." He kissed Rebecca Ledet's cheek. "What is it?"

She backed away from him, pouting. "I was robbed!"

DuLac regarded her with sleepy eyes. "I see."

"Robbed. Right on the street, during the day!"

"So. Did you have any real money in your purse?"

"Sure. fifteen dollars." The seventeen year-old girl smiled. "I managed to get change for one of your bills."

He waved a finger at her. "See? I keep telling you that I am a good engraver!"

Rebecca rolled her eyes. "Don't start that again! That's not the point. I mean, all I did was stop to help this old lady who was crying her eyes out. The next thing I knew she'd grabbed my purse and was flying down the sidewalk like—like some witch on a broomstick!"

"My dear, you exaggerate."

"No! Alain, I—"

"Please, Rebecca. I can replace whatever you lost. You know that. If this is your clever way to get more money from me, you do not have to be so elaborate."

"It's not that. Besides, Alain, it's getting harder and harder to find anyone in town who'll take a twenty dollar bill. Your *artwork* is worrying lots of people. And that worries me. What'll happen to us if we have to live on the sales of your paintings?"

The immigrant winced. "Please, girl. They will see my talent. Soon I will have a big exhibition in the museum. I can buy you anything you want with real money."

She snickered. "Not if you're locked up."

DuLac shook his head. "How would anyone find me? I am safe. We are safe."

Rebecca stroked his chest hairs. "I know, but I think you should stop—"

"No."

"—stop selling for a while."

"No!" He blinked. "Do not say that!"

He heard her gasp. "Alain, darling, I don't want to leave you."

DuLac frowned. Here it comes, he thought. His young model, the girl he'd shared his bed with for the last month, who'd spent all his money, was turning her back on him. He rubbed his eyes and took the girl's hands in his. "You forget where you were when I found you."

Rebecca looked stubbornly at the ceiling.

"You were common, a cheap whore, selling your virtue on the streets."

"I didn't sell my virtue. I sold myself. And I got a good price too!"

"Rebecca, listen to me. Everything is fine. I will stop printing as soon as I can afford to. Until then—take the money on the dresser."

She licked her lips. "How much?"

"Thirty dollars—real money."

"Oh, Alain!" Rebecca kissed his forehead. "You're such a dear man."

"Do not forget it," he said, grunting.

The girl snuggled up beside him. "How can I ever repay you?"

DuLac felt the old desires rising up in him.

The two men faced each other in the downtown alley. Brick walls rose up on either side; garbage festered around their feet.

"Hey, you trying to rob me?" the dealer said. "This is the best! Look at it! Better than before. The paper's better. The ink's closer to the real thing!"

"Keep your voice down, Jameson! The deal's off. I'd have to go outside of Portland to spend it, and I don't need that kind of trouble." He started walking away.

"A twenty for three dollars."

"No."

"Two!"

The departing figure stopped. "Well. . . ."

Jameson pulled four more bills from his pocket. "I'll make you a deal. Take the whole bunch--a hundred dollars worth--for seven dollars. Shit, with that much money you could afford to make a little trip to Astoria or some other town. Whaddya say, guy?"

"What do I say?" The man smiled and reached into his coat pocket. "You're under arrest, stupid!"

"What--" Jameson bolted.

Counterfeit money flew through the air. The criminal raced past the officer, cursing.

"Don't—"

He fired. That was all he could do. Jameson darted a few more feet and crumpled to the bare ground, filling a puddle with his body.

The policeman approached him. Damn! All that work and he'd blown it. They'd never find out where Brian Jameson had gotten the counterfeit money now. He stormed back, gathered up the bills that lay strewn in the alley, safely tucked them into his pocket and hauled the body to the police station.

Golden wouldn't be glad to see him. He started thinking about getting into another line of work.

"Competition? I have no competition, Mr. McCoy. As the only lady artist with a following in Portland, I stand alone." Emily Curtis smiled pleasantly at him.

"I understand. Then you wouldn't mind talking about your fellow artists?"

She laughed throatily. "Dabblers. No professionals among them. I could paint rings around their work any day!" Emily leaned toward him and lowered her voice. "They don't have the calling, you see?"

McCoy nodded. She smelled of lavender and, curiously, of tobacco. "Do you know if any of them might be involved in, ah, unsavory activities?"

The white-haired woman tilted her head. "What are you getting at?"

"Confidentially?"

She nodded, her eyes sparkling. "Yes, yes, I understand all that. You have no idea how many secrets I've had to keep about my models."

Spur grinned and remembered the two men he'd seen entering her studio last night. "Counterfeiting."

Emily Curtis set her jaw, straightened the lace collar of her white dress and turned. "What do you think of that?" she said, pointing a bony finger at a half-finished portrait of a young man.

"Very nice. Excellent. Finishing the eyes will bring it to life."

The artist suddenly turned, her skirts swishing with the movement. She stared hard at him, studying him, summing up the man. "Mr. McCoy, I've heard nothing about such doings among those gentlemen. But if I do, I shall certainly inform you. Where can you be reached?"

It was his turn to size up the woman. Her straight back and pungent personality didn't rile him. On the contrary, she seemed a woman of her word. "The Riverside Hotel. Room 305."

"Fine." She brushed her hands together. "Have a pleasant afternoon."

Spur walked outside, hoping that Emily Curtis just might learn of something that could help him. He walked above the Williamette River, admiring the broad, flat expanse of water and various craft surging up it or riding gently along the current.

He was surprised to see a Chinese junk—aptly named, Spur thought—sailing along, its massive, ill-shaped sails filling with the stiff springtime breezes.

Unfortunately, he didn't see whatever he bumped into.

"Oh!" It was a high voice.

Spur grabbed the woman's shoulders and stepped back. "I'm terribly sorry, Mrs. Gerard!" he said as the businesswoman spilled two dozen white roses onto the ground.

"No, it's my fault, Spur. Darn it! Now I'll have to start all over again." She looked down at the dirty roses, then up at him. "I was enjoying watching the river, not minding where I was going."

"So was I."

Jessica Gerard was so vibrant, so fresh when out of her storefront business. The woman's blonde hair spilled out of her simple hat. Her impressive breasts strained against the thin material of her dress, threatening to burst it. Jessica laughed and kicked at the roses.

"I don't care about them, but the Riverside Hotel does. I have to get them another two dozen as soon as possible."

"The Riverside? That's my hotel."

"What a curious coincidence, Spur." Jessica tucked in a lock of hair that had fallen over her forehead.

"May I accompany you?"

"Of course."

He took her arm. Soon she had prepared 24 more roses and dropped them off at the front desk, where the manager assured her they were right on time for the honeymoon couple on the fourth floor.

They went to the hotel's front door. "Having to do all that work again has just tuckered me out. Spur, do you think I could have a short rest—in your room?"

Their gazes locked together for a moment. "Of course, Mrs. Gerard."

The manager smiled at them as they ascended the stairs. The woman plainly wasn't tired, for she bounded up the stairs like a little girl eager for a treat. Once inside his room Spur locked the door and turned to her.

Jessica unpinned her hat and threw it away. Glowing yellow ringlets cascaded to her shoulders. The beautiful woman writhed like a cat, staring hungrily at him.

"I want you!" she said with undisguised lust.

"I thought you wanted to rest." Spur went to her, feeling tremendous desire pulsating through his body.

"Yes. After we finish." Jessica Gerard motioned for him to hurry his steps, met him halfway and started fumbling with his belt.

"Hey! We're in no hurry, are we?" Spur asked, surprised at her eagerness.

"I am. Come on, Spur! It's been two years. Two long years since I had a man! You don't know what it's like." Her voice was breathy. "I think I'm entitled. Don't you?"

"No complaints from me!"

"Good." Her dextrous fingers managed to slip the end of the leather belt through the buckle. Jessica slid it from the loops around his pants.

Spur was surprised when the woman moved behind him. Her warm mouth pushed through the hair that hung over his neck, sought and found the tender flesh. He gasped as her warm tongue licked him.

"I like that."

She bit him, sending shivers up and down his spine. Spur reached for his fly but the woman's hands gently grabbed his wrists and urged them behind his back.

He sighed at the erotic contact, fidgeting, letting her do what she wanted. After all, she'd waited for this for such a long time.

Spur didn't lose his smile until he felt the woman tightening the belt around his wrists, fastening them together behind his back.

Tieing him up!

CHAPTER FIVE

"Hey!" Spur said, struggling against the wide leather belt that cut into his wrists.

"Now, now," Jessica Gerard said, tightening the loop.

In seconds, the woman had managed to bind his arms behind his back.

"Jessica, what are you doing? I thought we were going to—"

She laughed. "We are, big boy. Haven't you ever done it like this before?"

"No. Ah, no. And I don't feel very good about it right now."

She walked in front of him and gave him a tight-lipped smile. "You will."

"That belt's pretty tight. Did you used to be a policeman, too?"

Jessica laughed. "No. It's just that Horace—my

late husband—taught me to pleasure him the way he liked it." She unbuttoned her dress. "He was the only man who ever had me, so I don't know any other way. Doesn't every man and woman do this when they—do it?"

"Well, not really." Spur had to smile at her. "Come, on, Jessica untie me."

She stood demurely before him as she unfastened the last button and let her dress slip to the floor. Her luscious body was plainly visible under the silky chemise and single petticoat.

"You're beautiful, Jessica!" Spur said, stumbling toward the woman.

She backed away. "Uh-uh!"

"What?"

"No! Not until I say so."

Spur looked down at the bulge in his crotch. "*That* says so."

She followed his gaze and grinned as she ran her hands up her chest and cupped her breasts. "Do you want these?" Jessica asked, tilting her head back and staring at him from lowered eyes.

"Yes, God, yes!"

She gently pinched the hard nipples that stuck against her chemise. "How much do you want them?"

"Right now, more than anything else!" Spur struggled against the belt. The woman was driving him mad. The incredible beauty she was offering him, and his inability to enjoy it, infuriated him. The erection in his pants was painful.

Jessica smiled. "Do you want them more than having your arms free?"

"Yes. Jesus, Jessica, Yes!"

The young woman pressed her hands between her

legs, covering the triangle underneath her transparent petticoat. "And this? Is this what you want?"

"Come on, Jessica!" Spur said, gasping. Any second it would rip out the buttons in his fly.

She rubbed herself up and down, digging her fingers into the clinging material.

"You enjoy torturing me, don't you woman?"

Jessica sighed, shook her head and ran to him. "Hell, no!" In seconds she had his hands free.

He grabbed her shoulders, backed her to his bed and forced her to sit. "No more tricks, okay?"

She nodded.

Spur lifted his right boot. She expertly pulled it off and then freed his left foot. the Secret Service agent threw off his coat, shirt, pants and long underwear and gripped his erection.

"I don't have to ask you if you want this, right?"

The woman moaned, staring at it, biting her lower lip.

"Didn't think so." He slid off her chemise and tugged the petticoat from her lower body.

"Ahhhhh yes. Yes indeed, ma'am!"

Jessica put her arms around him. "Do it. Do anything you want, Spur!" she hissed. Jessica raised her feet to the edge of the bed, spreading her legs, opening herself to him.

He stroked his penis and briefly glanced at the belt. No. He wouldn't use it. "Okay."

He knelt. Jessica gasped as he licked her left nipple, flicking his tongue back and forth over the hard, pink mass of flesh. She was delicious, warm and sweet with a whisper of rose petals.

Spur switched and stuffed most of the other mound into his mouth. He nursed on her breast and gently teethed it. Low moans issued from Jessica's throat.

He was more than ready but he decided to slow things down—for him, that is. He let her breast slip out of his mouth and kissed the soft skin between them, then pecked and bit her flesh, moving his head downward, toward the blonde mystery that lay between her thighs.

As he neared it Jessica arched her back. Trembling hands gripped his ears as Spur pushed into her crotch. It was moist and hot. He licked the outer lips, savoring the healthy taste of the woman, teasing her as he inhaled her sex-musk. Jessica bucked and moved his head. The woman gasped and went into convulsions as he locked his teeth around her clitoris and sucked.

"Mmmmmm."

"Oh. What are you doing to me?" she said between gasps.

He made love to her with his mouth and tongue, flicking back and forth, sending her into spasms of pleasure. Spur was enjoying himself immensely but the firm flesh between his legs demanded attention.

"No!"

The word escaped from her as he lifted his head, but Jessica sighed as he rose. He pushed her onto her back and fit his body between her legs.

"Yes!"

Jessica's face was flushed and shiny. He was perfectly positioned. Everything was lined up.

Spur waited, rubbing the head of his penis along her opening, feeling the jolts of fire that ran between their bodies at the intimate contact. Jessica groaned, clasped her hands around his torso and pushed her hips forward.

Spur sighed. The hot, liquid contact increased as he slid into her an inch at a time, prolonging his penetration. He pushed his tongue into the woman's mouth. Their hips locked together; his scrotum pressed against her soft buttocks.

She felt so good, so warm and tight and willing. McCoy kissed her savagely and she took his tongue, gasping as their lips slammed together and he thrust into her mouth.

Slowly, slowly, he withdrew. The simple motion made her shudder. Jessica's hands trailed down his back and fastened onto his hips.

"Come on, Spur," she said, her voice dreamy and low with lust. "Come on! It's been so long!"

"Okay." He pushed into her full-length. Jessica smiled up at him, eyes wide, nostrils flaring.

He did it again. Her breasts bounced.

Again. Faster.

Spur pumped between the woman's legs, driving into her, connecting their bodies with his erection. Jessica laid back. She gazed up at him in innocent awe, her throat tightening with each thrust.

"Yes. Oh God, yes!"

He jabbed into her body with deep, manly strokes. Spur raised himself on his hands and rode her higher, ensuring that he stimulated the woman to even greater peaks of pleasure. Their bodies furiously rubbed together, shooting off sparks, heating them.

Spur's movements became faster, harder. She dug her fingernails into his hips and forced him even deeper into herself. Their bodies slapped together at the waist. Jessica's moans quickly matched Spur's and then trembled in intensity, rising as the woman slithered underneath him, mouth open, eyes widening until she shook and whimpered and gasped through the ultimate peak of pure, sexual sensation.

The woman's climax encouraged Spur. He kissed her again and slammed into her body, driving himself right up to the edge but not caring, blindly thrusting and bucking until the fantastic release washed through him. Every muscle in his sinewy body contracted. He plunged full-length into her, spasming and orgasming and spurting his seed into her body, grunting as the awesome sensations swept her up again. They clutched each other, fingers digging into flesh as pure pleasure exploded deep inside them.

Ecstasy flooded through him. Spur sighed and gently kissed her lips, slowly pumping, gasping around her tongue. Jessica softened her grip on his buttocks and sighed as their hearts raced in unison.

He plunged into her one last time and lifted his head, looking in amazement at the woman below him. Her eyes were misty, filled with all the things a woman felt at times like that.

It was too much. He collapsed on top of her and they rested, lying connected over the edge of the bed, satisfied, sated.

Later, hours later it seemed to him, Spur was aware that he was crushing the woman. He started to move, withdrawing his still swollen penis from her, but Jessica grabbed his waist to keep him on top of her.

"What do you think you're doing?"

"Aren't I too heavy for you?"

She laughed. "No. It feels good."

He pecked her chin and took her head in his hands.

"I—I can't believe it. I'd forgotten what it's like. Two years, Spur!" Her eyes sparkled.

"You sure haven't forgotten what to do."

"Just hold me, you big brute!"

Spur did.

Model wanted the sign in the window said. Clare Maxwell thought about it as she stood outside the artist's studio and shrugged. Her short career at larceny hadn't been too successful. All those counterfeit bills showing up. She'd seen so many, she could get a job at a bank spotting them.

The young woman sighed and shook her head. "Why not?" she asked herself and went in.

A short, pudgy, moustached man looked up at her.

"Yes?" he said. "You come here to buy paintings?"

"No." Something about his European accent comforted her. Such men were more—well, cultured. "I'm here about your sign in the window."

The artist squinted at her. "Huh? Oh, yes. You have come to model for me!"

"Right. If you'll take me."

"Hmmm." He set down his brush. "Move into the light. Come along, my dear. Nothing to be afraid of."

"I'm not afraid." Clare walked confidently to the postion he'd indicated, before the floor-to-ceiling windows that opened up to a walled-in garden.

"Turn around, please?"

She slowly swirled, remembering every poise lesson her mother had given her all those years ago.

"Yes. You will do nicely. You do realize that this is nude modeling, don't you, my dear?"

Clare smiled. "I figured as much."

"Does the thought of taking off your clothes in front of me bother you?"

She studied the man. The more she looked at him, the more he could be her father. "For modeling? No. Of course not."

"Splendid!"

"How much?"

"I beg your pardon?" He went to her.

Clare felt him analyze her form with his eyes. "How much will you pay me to model for you?"

The artist smiled. "Ten or twenty dollars, depending on how long you are willing to pose at one time. But it will never be longer than an hour."

Twenty dollars! Clare smiled. "Mister, you just got yourself a model!"

"Fine. Splendid!"

She allowed the funny man to take her hand and kiss it, European fashion. "When do we start? Right now?"

"Ah, no. I do not have time for a full session this afternoon." He mused, putting his paint-smeared hand on his chin. "Maybe a quick sketch, to see if we can work together?"

"Okay. What should I do?"

The artist smiled and tugged at his shirt sleeves. "Undress, please."

Clare sighed and did as she was told. At least it was better than trying to earn a living robbing women's purses. And safer too. Clare had no desire to spend a few years locked away in a jail cell.

She reached for the buttons on her dress. The artist thoughtfully turned his back on her, searching for a suitable sheet of art paper, rifling through the bottles of brushes. Clare swallowed hard and removed her clothing. After all, this was art, wasn't it? Art isn't a sin.

"The door," Clare suddenly said, glancing at it. "What if someone comes in?"

"Ah! Of course. I am used to working with another model who did not care. Forgive me."

He didn't even glance at her as he crossed the cluttered studio, locked the door, and began lowering all the shades save for those on the garden windows.

Clare giggled as she removed her petticoats. Now stark naked, firmly resolved to give up her life of crime, she felt strangely free. Smiling, she arched her back and pointed a toe. "Like this?"

The artist turned toward her. His face lit up with a smile. "Yes. Perfect! Your form is ideal." He grabbed a charcoal pencil and started sketching.

As he worked Clare relaxed and thought about her future, completely unconcerned by the man's presence in the room and her vulnerable condition. That artist wouldn't hurt a fly.

A door to her left—not the front door—suddenly banged open.

"Darling, can't you—oh, I'm sorry, dear!"

Clare smiled at the young woman who appeared in the studio. If it had been a man she would have covered herself, but faced with a member of the same sex, she just relaxed. After all, she was going to be immortalized—and get paid for it!

"Can you not see that I am working?" the artist shouted with sudden ferocity.

She winced. "It can wait." The young woman sneered at Clare and disappeared.

"Where was I?" the man said, pulling on the ends

of his straggly moustache.

Clare's smile froze as the girl's face impressed itself on her mind. She'd seen it before.

Of course there was no way the girl would recognize her. She'd worn the black old woman's outfit when she'd robbed her, and not long afterward had thrown the expensive purse into the river. But the unexpected sight of that face chilled her. She was thankful she'd stopped that dangerous hobby.

"Please. Clare, is it? Please relax. You are tensing up all over the place!"

"I'm sorry. I've never done this before."

"You will grow accustomed to it."

She pushed her shoulders back just enough and repositioned her right toe in front of her. Clare made a conscious effort to keep her arms loosely dangling at her sides as she thought. That girl must live with him. His daughter? No. Like most artists, he'd probably taken an unlawful lover.

Clare sighed, remembering how she'd returned to her hotel room and locked the door. She'd gleefully looked over the treasures she'd just obtained, only to find a counterfeit twenty dollar bill. At least the fifteen dollars in real money, plus a small silver dollar, had made up for her work.

"There. Done!" the artist said.

The man's words broke her reverie. "I can get dressed?"

"Yes. Please."

She hurried into her clothing. Once again the artist didn't look at her. He gave her complete privacy as if he wasn't interested in her as a woman. That suited her fine, Clare thought, buttoning up her dress.

When she was finished the man surprised her by pressing two dollar bills into her hand.

"What's this for?" she asked, fingering the money. It seemed to be genuine but she just couldn't trust anyone these days.

He smiled. "To ensure that you come back. Same time tomorrow afternoon?"

She nodded. "Yes. Fine."

He unlocked the front door for her. "Good day, Miss Maxwell."

Her skin was crawling as she stepped out of the studio. The door banged shut and she heard the click of the lock. Clare hadn't minded posing for him, and indeed it was kind of an honor to think she was worthy of being painted. But the close call with the girl had been scary.

She shook her head and blinked, allowing her eyes to adjust to the harsh sunlight. Well, wasn't that an experience, Clare thought. And she'd go back, even face the young girl, if it meant steady money coming in. Besides, she wanted to see herself in a painting.

Maybe he'd transform her into Diana, queen of the heavens, or Juno, or that sweet, tragic, Helen of Troy.

Clare realized that she didn't even know the artist's name. She looked up at the sign in the window: "A. DuLac, European Portrait Artist."

CHAPTER SIX

Spur McCoy's trip into the countryside the next morning led him through lush valleys, past sparkling streams and atop small hills. His rented horse was sure-footed and wasn't easily exhausted. McCoy didn't work the mare too hard, regularly stopping to allow the beast to forage and suck the sweet water that seemed to flow everywhere through this area outside of Portland.

After a few hours, Spur realized he wasn't going to just happen upon the illegal logging operation. He never expected to, but it sure would be a nice surprise.

McCoy searched for rivers large enough to float trees, for rude trails that might lead to the camp, or some hint that he might be near the place. But nothing showed itself.

He returned to the city in the early afternoon. Spur visited the Bar B Lumberyard, found the owner, and asked the hard-faced man where he bought his wood.

"Johnson's Mill and Steele's Timber," he said with hesitation. "They got offices right in town," the man with the handlebar moustache said. "Best prices around, too."

"Thanks."

Spur visited both cramped, dirty offices and talked with their representatives. They seemed perfectly legitimate. Another dead end.

He walked his horse back to the wharf. A medium sized ship was off-loading freshly sawed boards from its hold. Spur secured his horse and approached a bearded, shabbily-dressed man who stood with his arms crossed on his chest. He was apparently overseeing the operation.

"New wood?" Spur asked him.

"That's a fact." The man spat a brown glop of saliva onto the wooden flooring.

"I'm gonna put up five stores on Hudson Street," Spur said, spinning his tale. "Need lots of lumber. You know where I might buy me some cheap wood? I mean—below normal cost?"

The captain's left eyelid twitched as he sized up McCoy. "Why?"

"Want to save money."

"Don't we all!" He mused. "I won't ask you if I can trust you because no man's worthy of that." He stuffed another plug of tobacco into his jaw and sucked it. "Fact of the matter is, I do know."

Spur tempered his show of interest. "Where?"

"Damnit! Watch that load!" The captain motioned to his hired hands. "What was I saying? Oh yeah. Can't tell you much, but I can tell you this. Bend of a river that has no name." He grunted and chewed.

"What river? Where is it?"

"Jesus!" he shouted. "You men wanna be paid?" The captain shook his head, sending his black hair flying. "All I can tell you. I found it by accident one day when my navigator took a wrong turn from the Williamette. Good luck." He walked off for closer supervision.

Spur shrugged. A river with no name. One that fed the Williamette. It was a start. He rode to the public library and got a map of the outlying area.

It showed dozens of streams and rivers, most of which emptied into the great body of water that had made the city of Portland what it was.

All of them were named. He put down the map and sighed. How many more were there running through the wilderness? And where was the one that he needed?

He ate, slept soundly that night and rose with the sun. This time he'd ride east and hope he got lucky.

Two hours later, Spur stopped in a shaded glen splashed with the blooms of rhododendrons and Scotch broom. His mare had let him know that she was thirsty. He dismounted, patted its mane and looked around on foot.

Tough, rugged country lay up ahead. The trees seem to bunch together in the distance, just before the land rose up to form a mountain. Its crest was hidden among the pine trees.

No sound of water nearby. No signs of a permanent, wide stream. Nothing.

Damn!

Clare Maxwell's fears materialized as soon as she left DuLac's studio the next day and looked at the twenty dollar-bill in full sunlight. It didn't seem right. She hurried to her hotel room, fuming. Once safely there, the woman retrieved the two fake bills she'd lifted from women and compared them.

They were identical. The money the artist had just given her for her second posing session was counterfeit!

So much for an easy way to earn a living, Clare bitterly thought. She tucked the three bills under her stiff black dress and briefly considered resuming her career as a petty, elderly thief.

Then the face of the artist's girlfriend rose in her mind. She shook it away. No. Too risky. If an able-bodied citizen, or worse, a policeman, happened by and heard a woman screaming that her purse had been stolen by an old lady, they'd stop her, even if they believed that she was aged.

There were always saloons and bawdy houses, but that idea didn't settle well with her. It was too involving, too messy, too disgusting. All those greasy, ill-smelling men pawing her and spreading her legs. She shivered at the picture she'd conjured up.

No. Clare Maxwell sat on her bed and cleared her mind. The best thing to do would be to go back to the artist's studio for one more session. If he gave her another counterfeit bill she'd have to decide what to do.

Emily Curtis peered out of her studio window. After all, she'd promised the fine-looking young man that she'd keep an eye on her fellow artists. Though she was one herself, Emily had never trusted her own kind. The foreign ones were the worst, she thought, nodding as a man dressed in black walked up to Alain DuLac's studio. He went inside.

Nothing unusual about that, unless he was selling one of his paintings. That would be the day!

The white-haired woman checked the clock. An hour until her next appointment. Unless she had unexpected visitors, she had time to think and to remember. Emily Curtis locked the front door and put her hands on her hips. Who should it be today?

Ah, yes—Charles and Mark, her midnight visitors. The young brothers with their barrel chests and furry legs. The men with absolutely identical genitalia that she'd delighted in capturing on canvas.

Where was it? Emily searched for the nude painting, shuffling through the stacks of unfinished pictures that leaned against every available inch of space.

As she looked something stuck in her mind. Alain DuLac, and all those European artists, how did they survive? They might sell one painting every two or three months, but they were always there, working away, using their brushes to scratch together their pitiful ideas of art.

Family money, maybe? She shook her head. Only the most dedicated—or the least talented—stayed on in the artists' colony. But they didn't have an ounce of talent among them. How did an artist like DuLac make a living?

Emily finally found the painting she was looking for. As always, her abilities surprised even her. She gasped as she set the stretched canvas on the easel and settled into the chair she conveniently left in front of it.

The aged artist stared at the image she'd captured on canvas. She constantly scrutinized her work which was why she was so good.

But how does DuLac make his living?

Spur stopped at another stream, far too small to be used for transporting timber. He slid from his rented saddle, stooped and tasted the water. The last rivulet he'd tried was bitter with the tannic acid which the slow-moving water had leached from countless leaves.

His horse whickered as he cupped his hands and drank deeply, enjoying its wet coolness. "What is it, girl?" Spur asked, wiping his mouth on his sleeve. "You smell something? Huh?"

Then he did, too. Smoke. Somewhere nearby.

Wary, he tied the horse to a sturdy sapling and ventured into the brush. Stiff branches tugged at his pant legs. It was slow-going, this plowing through centuries of unchecked plant growth.

The woodsy scent grew stronger. Eventually, he saw a pool of bluish smoke gathering in the air several hundred yards away. He steadily approached it.

Spur moved more slowly, silently, like an Indian. He didn't know who had lit the campfire and he sure as hell didn't want to reveal himself too soon. Not before he had the chance to check everything out.

As he gained on the unseen campfire, Spur heard a faint hum in the distance. It grew less faint, rising until he'd identified it. A river. A big, sprawling river from the sound of it. Thousands of gallons of water boiling over half-submerged rocks.

The river with no name?

He gathered up more landmarks to ensure that he could find his horse again and pushed on. The river must lay directly ahead of him, somewhere behind the campfire.

Movement in the brush beside him startled Spur. He froze, waiting, holding his breath as he reached for his colt .45. A squirrel popped into view from behind a rhododendron, jumped onto a bent pine tree trunk and scampered up it, its claws providing a steady grip.

He moved slowly and as silently as possible, his boots making no more sound than a leaf would as it fell from an overhanging branch. A fallen tree trunk, its furrowed bark covered with moss and iridescent mushrooms, lay across the underbrush. As he stepped over it, Spur's boot broke one of the fantastic looking growths sending white seeds spurting into the air.

The smoke was much stronger now. It started filtering into the air overhead him. He heard a man whistling and the sound of him breaking sticks into firewood.

Spur rounded an ancient oak tree. A brown creature reared up on its hind legs and bellowed at him, paws flashing through the air, saliva drooling from its lower lip.

The bear crashed toward him.

CHAPTER SEVEN

Spur's right hand slashed down to his holster as he sidestepped the advancing brown bear. The animal roared in fury. A paw went up and knocked the Colt .45 from McCoy's grip, sending it hurtling through the air.

Hell!

Unarmed, he was no match for 200 pounds of hairy, enraged power. He dove for his weapon and searched the thick layer of leaves. The bear landed on all fours behind him. Spur felt sudden, intense pressure on his left pant leg and heard the claws tearing and shredding the stiff blue material, dragging him backward.

Shit!

He locked his hands around a thin tree trunk and pulled, forcing his body along the ground away from danger. The pressure on his pants leg released.

Spur instantly stood and shot a look behind him.

The bear panted, staring balefully up at him, sniffing the air. It sat back and raised its huge, wet nose, inhaling a new strange odor.

Food. Frying bacon.

Spur remembered the campfire he'd smelled. He glanced down at the leaves and spied the butt of his Colt.

The bear silently wandered off toward the evocative scent.

Relieved, he retrieved his weapon. A split second after it was firmly in hand, a deep howl of terror ripped through the quiet forest.

Damnit, McCoy thought. He crashed through the underbrush toward the sound.

The trees gave way. He saw a thin man backing from the bear as it poked at the pan set over a small, smoky fire.

"What—what—" he said, looking at Spur.

"Don't move. It doesn't want us anymore—just that." He motioned toward the pan with his revolver.

"Yeah. I guess!"

"Let's just wait!"

The curious bear's nostrils flared. Globules of fat exploded from the strips of meat frying in the pan. The beast pawed it, spilling the cast iron utensil from its perch on the fire. The flames, fed by the bacon grease, roared up as the bear thrust its paw into the fire.

It bellowed in agony, stood and lumbered toward the cringing man.

Spur fired, sending a slug through the animal's heart. It danced on its thick hind legs, turned around, pathetically grunted and slumped onto the fire. Its bulky form quickly smothered the flames.

"Jesus Christ! Is it dead?" the skinny man asked.

"Yeah. I'd figure as much. In any case, it's no threat to us." He slid his revolver into the holster strapped onto his right leg.

The fair-haired man pulled off his hat and slicked the sweat from his forehead. "I don't know what to say. I mean, Jesus! I left my rifle on my mount."

"Not a smart thing to do in this country."

"Yeah."

He was a young man, about 25, but his face was lined and burned by the wind and sun. An outdoors man.

"You should be more careful."

"You sound like my father. I don't know, I just wanted to get away for a while." He shook his head. "So. Who do I have to thank for saving my life?"

"Spur McCoy."

"I'm Jason Miller."

They briefly shook hands over the bear's body.

"I'd heard those things were around here," Jason said, staring down at it. "Never seen one afore."

"You have now."

"Look," Jason said, shaking his head. "Least I can do is get you a cup of coffee."

"Not on that fire you can't."

He smiled. "Right. You got a horse?"

Spur nodded.

"Then come on back to my place. I'll get you the best cup of coffee this side of the Mississippi."

"Is it far?"

"Nope." He shook his head.

"Wait a minute, I'll be right back."

McCoy quickly found his horse and led it through the difficult area. By the time he'd returned, Jason

Miller was mounted and ready to go.

"Come on. It's just a few miles."

They were off, riding through the fir forest. As he bucked in his saddle Spur wondered who the man was and what he was doing out there.

"You got a cabin nearby or something?" Spur yelled as eight hooves crashed through the small bushes and mounds of brown pine needles.

"Or something. You'll see soon enough."

Interesting. Spur realized they were following a rude, seldom-used trail. The smaller trees had been cut off at the ground and, at some time in the past, the bushes cleared away to allow for easier passage.

No single man living in the wilderness would go to that much trouble, Spur thought.

Ahead, through the towering firs, he saw glints of molten silver. Then he heard it again, the sound that had run through the background during his encounter with the brown bear.

They crashed through the trees onto a rocky ridge. Twenty feet below, a huge, flat river flowed along, snaking through the canyon it had carved.

Things were looking up, Spur thought. He smiled. "I don't know the local terrain," he said as Jason smiled over at him. "What river's that?"

"Who the hell knows? We call it the Miller River. Almost there. Come on!"

Jason's horse surged forward as he kicked its flanks. Spur pushed his mare to its limits and caught up with the young man.

The ridge gently lowered, nearing the level of the river. They rounded a bend and, just past the trees, Spur saw it.

Buildings dotted a natural valley right on the edge of the water. A rude dock extended into the deep, blue river. Several men moved around, working at various tasks. Lumber was piled up on the dock. Huge trees, stripped of their branches, lay in stacks beside the river.

A logging camp. A sawmill. It had to be!

Spur smiled as they rode into the camp and halted before a large, well-built house. They tied up their mounts and quickly brushed them down.

"I never would have guessed it," Spur said. "A big operation like this in the middle of nowhere."

Jason shrugged. "It's no problem with the river." He looked at the horses and threw down his brush. "I guess they'll live. Let's get some grub. My stomach feels like it's splitting in two."

"I know the feeling."

As they went to the door, a dark-skinned man straggled by. In spite of the chilly air his only garment was a pair of ragged jeans that hung halfway down his hips. Bizarre, geometric squares of black ink covered one side of his face. The worker paused, gave Spur a dead-eyed stare and wandered off.

They entered a huge kitchen. Three stoves sat side by side and a larder covered one whole wall. Chickens and rabbits hung by their feet from the ceiling. Piles of freshly-caught fish rested in baskets on a table beside a large collection of gleaming knives.

A huge pot bubbled on one of the stoves, sending the warming, stomach-churning scent of food through the air.

"Yep. Should be ready. Cookie always keeps something on the stove in case one of us gets the hungries," Jason said, pulling two huge pewter bowls and spoons from a cupboard.

He ladled the thick, beef-rich stew into the bowls and slapped them down on the table.

"Have a seat and stuff your face," Jason said with glee. "Hell, this meal's on me."

As he ate, Spur held back his questions. No reason to seem too interested just yet. He'd bide his time.

Emily Curtis shook her head. That man had been in Alain DuLac's studio for far too long. Besides, the elderly woman thought as she pushed her rocking chair toward the window, he was no art lover. No art lover would go near that man's place.

She sighed and settled into the quilt-strewn chair. Though she didn't spend all her time spying on her neighbors, she did like to keep up with the art colony's doings. Emily shook her head.

As a matter of fact, a lot of strange men had gone into DuLac's place lately. She'd noticed because she thought maybe he'd become popular or some other nonsense. But the woman couldn't remember seeing some of them come back out again.

Emily Curtis, she told herself, mind your own business. You've that Carter girl's portrait to finish by five o'clock. You have little time for this foolishness, she scolded herself.

She rose and felt the old pain flare up in her knees again. That handsome man she'd talked to would just have to find someone else to tell him the local gossip.

"How long has this place been running?" Spur asked before biting into a crusty slice of bread.

"Little over a year." Jason burped and pushed away his empty bowl.

"Doing well?"

"Yeah, I'd say we're doing fine. Lots of orders, lots of sales, little overhead."

"Some kind of foreigners working for you, right?" Spur washed down the bread with a sip of whiskey.

"Yep. They work for a lot less than men from around here would. That helps us cut our costs and lowers our prices. It's good business."

Though the man's words were calm and rational, Spur noticed Jason tightening his lips. A vein throbbed in the young man's neck. What was going on here?

He decided to throw out the bait. "You wouldn't be interested in an outside investor, would you?"

Miller smiled. "Shore! I'd have to talk to the old man about it, but it's nothing he hasn't said before." He wiped a brown splotch from his chin and gave a satisfying, open-mouthed burp. "I'll see if I can find him. Just help yourself to anything else if you're not full. Be right back."

Jason Miller disappeared through a door.

Well, McCoy thought as he spooned the last of the stew into his mouth, things were moving along better than he'd thought they would. He'd found the camp. The solitary worker he'd seen so far—the one with all those stains all over his face—sure wasn't an Indian. A Hawaiian?

Probably.

He took another shot of whiskey, remembering a book General Halleck had in his library back home. The leather-bound volume was the record of some sea captain's voyage to the Sandwich Islands, or Hawaii, as it was starting to be called.

If Jason Miller and his father were running a slavery operation here, it was time they were stopped. He set his muslin napkin on the table and rubbed his gut. He'd have to learn as much about the place as he could before shutting it down. So he'd stay put for a while, gathering as much information as he could.

The outer door banged open.

"What in tarnation—"

Spur just had time to duck under the table as a weapon spoke, peppering the kitchen walls with shot.

CHAPTER EIGHT

The explosions echoed through the logging camp kitchen. The unseen man's yells were just audible above the blasts that ricocheted around the large room.

Crouching under the plank table, Spur figured he wasn't in any real danger, but he drew just in case. He heard the sounds of the man re-loading his shotgun.

"What in Sam Hell's going on here?" the man demanded in an authoritative voice.

"Calm down!" Spur shouted.

"Calm down? Christ, I find a stranger sitting at my own goddamn table!"

"Jason Miller brought me her," Spur yelled.

"Bull!" he snorted.

"Ask him!"

"You gotta do better than that. My son'd never do something that dumbass. Stand up so I can kill you properly!"

"Your son just went looking for you," Spur told the elder Miller. He sighed and rose to his feet, armed and ready for a fight. "Talk to him before you go killing me!"

Miller sweetened his aim. "I don't gotta talk to him to know trouble!" The oily man grinned.

Spur threw his revolver onto the table. "Didn't your mother ever teach you any table manners?"

"No," a voice said from behind Spur. "And he didn't teach me none neither!"

The elder Miller slightly lowered his aim. "Jason! What the hell is this man doing here?"

"Put that thing away!" Jason strode up to Spur and laid his arm around McCoy's shoulder. "Unless you want to kill the man who just saved my life!"

"Don't talk to me like that, boy!" The short haired, beady eyed man advanced on the pair. "You expect me to believe that crap?"

Spur felt Jason tense beside him. "Drop your weapon or I walk outa here right now, old man! I mean it!"

Miller frowned. "You wouldn't!"

"Try me!"

He sputtered, grumbled and laid the shotgun on the table.

"That's better, pop!"

Spur shrugged off Jason's arm. "You got one hell of a way of greeting your guests, Miller."

"Is that true? What he just said?"

"Yeah. If I hadn't run into your son out in the woods some bear'd be burping him up right now." Spur shook his head. "You can thank me later—when you relax."

The middle-aged man scowled, deepening the creases in his crimson face. "How can I relax? Hell,

I got labor problems. Some of my men aren't working their fair share."

"Can you blame them?"

Miller shot his son a piercing glance.

Spur looked between the two men. "Thanks for the grub, Jason. See you later."

"No. Wait, McCoy!" Jason turned to his father. "You know how you're always talking about bringing in some new money? Getting a partner to expand our operation out here in this hell-hole?"

"Yeah." Miller's eyes were guarded. He switched his gaze from Spur to his son. "Go on."

"The man you almost killed—the one who saved my life—just might be interested."

Harry Miller raised his eyebrows and tried to smile. His face was so tight that he couldn't manage more than a lopsided grin. "Ah, well, hell! Can't blame a guy for tryin' to protect his business. No hard feelin's, right, McCoy?"

"Right." Spur nodded.

"How much would you be willing to invest?" Harry walked to a small table and poured himself a glass of whiskey.

"I don't know. I'd have to look around the place first. See what kind of operation you're running."

"About that—" Jason began.

"What my boy's trying to say is that this isn't your ordinary logging camp."

"I figured as much. Heard some tales about this place—nothing definite, just that you sell lumber cheaper than anyone in town. A real good buy."

Harry Miller stared at him. "So?"

Spur smiled. "So I'm interested. I don't care how you cut your costs, Miller. All I'm concerned about is getting my money's worth."

"Dad, we could get a new mill. Double our output of lumber in a few months!"

"Yeah. Yeah." He bolted down the whiskey and poured another drink.

"Hey, Miller, I'm not squeamish. You do what you gotta do to make a dollar. Right?"

He was silent.

"So I don't care about that." Spur spoke slowly. "I don't care about anything but money. Understand?"

Miller brightened. "Yeah. Yeah sure!"

Spur smiled. Time to draw them in. "Okay. Just to give you two something to chew over, how's, oh, $10,000 sound?"

The man spit up the liquor.

"Ten thousand?" Jason grinned at him. "That sounds fine to me. More than fine! How about it, old man?"

Harry Miller sat at the table and nodded. "Sounds good. I import the finest labor money can buy. Bring those god-forsaken pagans all the way across the ocean. Give them naked savages jobs, a place to bunk and something to eat."

"Barely," Jason threw in.

Spur watched the two men lock gazes, realizing just how deep the conflict ran between them.

"It sounds good to me." Miller peered up at Spur. "As long as you understand you're just a money man. Don't go trying to change the way I run things around here."

"You're getting ahead of yourself. I haven't said I'll invest yet," Spur pointed out. "I need to study your figures, look at the future of your operation, see if it's worth my while."

"Yeah. Yeah! You can stay here for a few days.

Isn't that right, father?"

"Of course. Hell, be glad to have you around."

Jason went to the elder Miller. "Just think of it! We could set up the new mill and hire more help. Maybe treat 'em better, not work 'em so hard, so they won't di—ah, I mean, quit on us so fast." He faintly smiled at Spur.

"Yeah. Okay. You look over the place, McCoy. Take Jason with you and ask him questions. I'd do it myself but I'm too busy. Always too damned busy." He coughed.

"Fine. I'll let you know before I leave."

Harry Miller rose and looked at his son. "Git your ass outa here!" he bellowed.

"Right, old man."

"And don't call me that!"

"You promised me this wouldn't happen again!" Rebecca Ledet said, pouting and crossing her arms.

"I—I could not help it."

"Sure." She rolled her eyes.

"Your friends—"

"It wouldn't do any good." The girl frowned.

"Why not? They helped you before?" Alain felt an unusual sensation flooding through his body. It was tight, harsh and made him queasy.

"They just won't take your money any more, Alain. I warned you but you wouldn't listen. It's time you dumped that printing press in the river and concentrate on your painting, on earning an honest living!"

"You sound like my dead wife." Alain rubbed his chest.

"How could you compare me to that ugly troll?" Rebecca held her chin high.

He winced. "In the meantime, what do we do with him?" He pointed to the lifeless form lying in the center of his studio, slowly oozing life onto the floor.

"He doesn't look very big," Rebecca said. "Can't you handle it yourself?"

"Myself. Myself!" Alain knocked over his easel. "Myself? Why do you think I have kept you around?"

Rebecca sucked in her breath and shook her head.

"I—I mean—"

She shrank away from him, backing toward the wall.

"You *bastard!* I thought you loved me!"

"I love your face, your body!" DuLac shook his head. "I cannot love a woman. Any woman! My wife destroyed that in me. I told you that!"

"You just keep me around to get to my friends. Right?" The hardened girl laughed. "You never cared about me. Ever!" She stormed off to the bedroom, her skirts swirling behind her.

"What are you doing?" Alain asked, stepping over the dead man's body.

Silks and crinolines flew from the closet onto the bed. "Packing. I'm going to Madame Burchard's. She said I could stay at her house any time I wanted."

"Rebecca. Please! The body!"

The beautiful girl spun toward him. "That's all you care about. Bodies! Well this body's leaving. I don't care what you do with the other one!"

"No. No!"

"Don't worry, Alain. I won't tell a soul what kind of man you are. Not a word! But if you ever try to touch me again, I'll—I'll—" Rebecca shook her head and stuffed her belongings into the leather bags.

"I bought you all those things!" Alain walked into the bedroom.

"Sure. And I earned them—on my back!"

She flipped the cases closed and pushed past him. "Really, Alain," Rebecca said as she unlocked the front door, "If you didn't kill every man who walked in here, we might still be together."

He locked the door as soon as she'd bounded outside and turned toward the dead man. What, oh what was he going to do?

"You don't seem to get along with your father," Spur said as he walked with Jason Miller.

The man's thin features darkened. "That's no secret. He's changed. As soon as he got the idea of starting this business, sold the house in Portland and set up camp here, something seemed to snap inside him. The way he treats those men—" He sighed. "That's why we need you, McCoy. Your money could turn this into a normal, legal operation." Jason stopped. "You don't know how many men have died."

"Accidents?"

"I wish! Overwork, mostly. The old man seems

to think that a bowl of soup and a cup of water every day is enough for the Hawaiians. Not when they're working from sunup to sundown."

"He really is a bastard, isn't he?"

"Yeah." Jason Miller scratched his side. "But you can change all that, McCoy. I hate what he's done here, what he's done to the men."

"Can't you do anything? Can't you talk some sense into the man?"

"No. Only other thing I could do is walk out of here. But he's got me so involved I can't leave. Besides, if I turned him in he'd accuse me of cooking up the whole scheme. I'd wind up on the end of a rope right alongside that bastard—if he didn't kill me first."

Spur was silent.

Jason sighed. "That's the mill over there, obviously. We use a vertical saw. Right now we've got fifty men working for us. Most of them are out cutting down trees. We go into places that aren't easily visible, that wouldn't attract attention. We float half the logs for sale to a landing downstream, but not all the way to the Williamette. The rest we cut right here, haul them down to our outpost and load them onto our customers' ships. That's only after we've got the cash in hand. We cut to order, whatever they want."

"I see."

Jason's voice was dull, even-toned. "My father sails into town once a week, taking orders. Everything's done on the sly, mostly at night. Our lumber goes all over the place." He turned to Spur. "Sometimes I wake up at night and hear the men screaming." He shivered.

Spur slapped Jason's shoulder. "I gotta feeling

all that's gonna change. Mighty soon."

Jason looked at him and smacked his lips. "So what are you saying? You'll invest?"

McCoy nodded. "Yeah. I'll invest."

CHAPTER NINE

As Spur walked around the logging operations, he flinched at the looks of outright hatred the indentured workers flashed at him whenever he came upon them. Jason Miller hadn't been exaggerating when he described his father's treatment of the men. Things were ripe for a revolution.

Male shouts issued from the saw mill. Jason grimaced and slapped Spur's shoulder.

"I'll go see what the trouble is," he said and ran off to the sturdily-built structure.

Spur walked behind the mill, unwilling to get involved in the matter, and studied the river with no name. It was broad, deep and flat. He could tell it was deep from the hue of the water that swiftly flowed through its center. A solitary boat bobbed at the dock.

They must have other boats out. He was surprised by the lack of horses but then again, too many of them around might tempt the workers.

McCoy frowned and stared at the water. The sound of boots rapidly approaching him made Spur look up. An elderly, haggard-faced man rushed up.

"Who the hell are you?" he asked, holding a small black bag.

McCoy raised his hands. "Don't start shooting. I'm with Jason Miller."

The white-hair harumphed. "Some damn fool musta got himself all cut up in there." Doc hurried by and disappeared into the saw mill.

A stiff wind swept through the clearing, sending the towering pines whispering far above where nature took over from the works of men. Spur pulled his coat more tightly around him. The chill in the air surprised him. It didn't snow in spring up here in Oregon, did it?

As Spur was wondereing about it, a brown-skinned man stumbled out from the mill. His face was nearly blocked by the huge armload of firewood that had been piled onto him.

The slave, the human merchandise that Harry Miller had purchased from overseas, shivered as the wind cut through the torn jeans that were his only clothing. Moving shakily across the uneven ground, the man's bare foot crashed down on a sharp rock.

The firewood spilled to the ground, revealing the tattoo-covered face of the worker he'd seen earlier.

"Damnit!"

The curse was heavily accented. The Hawaiian threw up his hands and stared down at the wood.

It was a good time to make a move, Spur thought

as he walked up to him. "Let me help you."

The slave turned violently toward him and shook his head.

"Come on! How often do you get a white man saying that to you?"

Nearing the slave, Spur was shocked at his appearance. He was pathetically thin. The ribs were clearly visible under his skin. How old was he? Eighteen? Nineteen?

He proudly shook his head again, shivering.

"Look, son. There's no way you can pile all that wood onto your arms without some help." Spur squatted and picked up four heavy, thick pieces of oak firewood. "Are you gonna cooperate with me?"

Silence. A tight-lipped, angry stare.

"What's your name?"

"What is yours?"

At least he hadn't had his tongue cut out. "Spur McCoy."

He looked down at the ground. "I'm Kimo. Here they call me Mike."

"Well, Kimo, will you take this or are you going to let me stand here and look like a fool?"

He lowered his eyes and grabbed the wood. "Thanks."

Another Hawaiian man rushed from the sawmill toward the main house. He stared curiously at Spur and Kimo as he passed.

"How'd you like to get out of here? Go back home?" Spur asked.

Kimo grunted. "Yes."

Spur smiled. "I thought so."

The front door of the main house banged open. Spur turned to see Harry Miller, his face blood-red, charging toward the sawmill.

Kimo flinched at the sight of his boss.

Do something, Spur told himself. "And don't let me catch you dropping this shit all over the place again!" he yelled in a voice loud enough for Harry to hear.

The man barely acknowledged McCoy's presence as he rushed to where he had been summoned.

Kimo looked up at the white man with blank eyes. He shrugged.

Spur laid his hand on the man's shoulder. Kimo's skin, used to the balmy sun of the tropics, was icy. "Look. I can help you get home."

"No. No one can help."

"*I* can. But I need you with me."

"I already have a death sentence. I don't want to hurry that." Kimo stooped to retrieve another piece of wood.

Spur took it out of his hands. He looked around and saw the stables. "Come on. Let's get rid of this firewood."

Between the two of them they carried it to the woodshed outside of the house. Kimo started to walk away but Spur grabbed his shoulder and ushered him into the stables.

A very pregnant mare regarded them with huge brown eyes as he led the slave into the relative warmth and comfort of the stinking building.

Spur sloughed off his jacket and held it out. When Kimo regarded it with suspicious eyes, Spur cursed and slipped it around the man's shoulders.

"Why are you doing this?" Kimo demanded in far too loud a voice. "You are a white men like all the others!"

"No. I'm not! Listen to me, Kimo. The government is very interested in Harry Miller. I'm here to shut him down, to take him to jail."

Kimo raised his eyebrows, animating the checkered pattern that extended from his left jawbone to his hairline. "And then I could return home?"

"Yes. Yes, of course!"

He stuffed his arms into the jacket and held it around his still shivering body. "Oh."

"What's been happening here?"

"Three of my friends are gone."

Spur shook his head. "Gone?"

"Died. My brother is dead. Fell a long way when topping a tree—that's what they said."

"How did you get here?"

Kimo sighed. "A white man came to Maui and said he was hiring strong men to work on the Mainland. I signed up with many of my friends. When we got here, they treated us like animals." He glanced at the mare. "Worse than that. Work all day. Chains at night." Kimo sat on the ground and rubbed his feet against the straw-covered dirt, allowing himself the luxury of trying to get warm. "They said I could send for my wife later. I can't," he spat, staring at the ground. "No women allowed. And I have not seen my baby since it was born."

Spur shook his head. "Then I can count on you for help? At any time?"

Kimo nodded. "Yes. Any time."

The mare whinneyed. She was going into labor.

"You'd, ah, better get back to work."

Kimo reluctantly stood, slipped the jacket from his shoulders and gave it back to his benefactor as he walked out of the stable. The man returning to work seemed to hold his shoulders a bit higher, Spur thought.

Spur blew onto his hands and went outside. That night he'd find out what sort of security arrangements Harry had. He assumed they'd be heavy.

Three hours later, he was again talking with Jason Miller. He'd found out much of what he wanted to know. The men were indeed kept in ankle chains at night as they slept in the huge, long barracks that were set up in the middle of the clearing. Four armed guards were stationed on each side of the rectangular building and two inside it. A pair of additional guards roamed the perimeter of the area through the trees on horseback, just in case any of the men managed to escape.

Eight men plus Harry Miller. How could he break the news to Jason, Spur wondered, looking at the young man.

Jason halted his endless conversation. "You got something on your mind, McCoy?"

"Ah, no. Just thinking about your workers."

"If you join us we can do something about them."

"I can't believe your father thought he could get away with this!"

Jason shook his head. "The old man moved into Alabama about ten years before the war. I grew up on a plantation surrounded by slaves. He lost everything, including his wife, during the war. As far as he's concerned, the Emancipation Proclamation only related to Africans. I don't think he believes the Hawaiians are human."

Spur stared at Jason.

A bell rang nearby. "Time for grub," Miller said.

That night Spur lay wide awake, fully dressed, in the simply furnished room. He peered out the window at the barracks where the fifty men were kept. The only guard he could see stood there, rifle slung over his shoulder, constantly vigilant. His back was toward Spur and remained that way for as long as he looked. The man wasn't concerned about anyone breaking in—just getting out.

During a short, post-food conference in Harry Miller's panelled office, one of the guards had walked in and handed Harry a large key ring. "They're locked up," the grizzled man had said as Miller stashed the keys in his drawer.

Another piece of the puzzle. Spur realized he could ride back into town in the morning, get as much help as Commissioner Golden could spare and charge up there, eventually freeing the men. But the cost in lives on both sides would be heavy. Too heavy.

No. He had to do something tonight. Now.

Spur remained in his room until the house had been quiet for hours. Alert, ready for action, he worked out his plan, trying to account for every contingency, drawing up alternatives to keep in reserve.

He walked to the small clock, wincing as the floorboards groaned under his weight. The thin black hands revealed the hour: 2.13. It was time.

Another quick look out the window showed the thin moon starting its slide down the western sky. Nothing had changed—the guards were all in place.

Spur slipped out of his room and silently padded down the stairs. He turned left at the landing, thankful for the thick carpets that cushioned his boots, and made his way to Harry Miller's office.

The door was ajar but the room was dark. He walked into the man's office. Thin light issuing from the four lowered flames allowed him to move around without bumping into things.

Spur went to the desk and tried the drawer. It opened, much to his surprise. Harry Miller must not worry about things like locks. After all, he kept his enemies shackled at night.

He reached inside the drawer. Dried pens, bottles of ink, envelopes and other business supplies passed under his hand. Spur quietly, quickly searched for his prize.

A soft clink halted his fingers. He grasped the cold iron ring and smiled. Spur stuffed the keys into his coat pocket and walked toward the door. Just as he touched it a dark figure burst inside, nearly knocking him over.

"What the hell are you doing here?" Harry Miller demanded, turning up the kerosene lamp and staring him down.

CHAPTER TEN

"Well?" Miller yelled, blocking the entrance to his office. "What the hell are you doing here?"

Spur straightened his back and stared directly into the man's eyes, challenging him. "I had some things to talk over with you. Figured you might still be up. That's all, Miller!"

"Yeah, well," the oily man said, frowning. "I'm here. Now, anyway."

"Look, Miller, don't be so damn suspicious of everything and everyone!"

He laughed. "That's my business, McCoy. To be suspicious. I can't help it."

"If you ran your business differently, you wouldn't have that problem."

Harry grunted and moved to his desk. "How true, how true. McCoy, no one's forcing you to buy into this dump," he said as he sat. "Hell, if I paid my workers anything like real wages, or got regular hire ons, I wouldn't clear enough money to make the whole damn thing worthwhile. You're a businessman; you know that."

"Lots of others get by."

"Yeah, well, I'm tired of getting by."

"What are you working toward?" Spur fell into a chair facing the man's desk. "You must be making plenty of money but I certainly don't see it around here."

Harry Miller smiled. "I'm salting it away in various banks in town. Keeping it for a rainy day."

Spur thought about the keys in his pocket. "So you'll eventually get out of here? Close the business, move into Portland and have a regular life?"

Miller shrugged. "Something like that, but I don't have to tell you—" He stopped and lightened his voice. "Sorry. Short-fused, that's me." He scratched his head. "I haven't decided yet, but I'm working for the future."

"The here and now seems more important to me."

Harry Miller frowned and reached for his desk drawer. "That's because you're young."

"Not much younger than you are," he pointed out.

"Your outlook sure as hell is." Miller pulled on the drawer.

High-pitched screams pierced the night. The man winced at the sound. "Damn. I'm going back to bed," he said, slamming the drawer shut.

"Aren't you going to find out what's going on? Sounds bad to me."

"You'll get used to that, McCoy." He smiled. "One of the boys acting up again, most likely. Happens all the time." He rose and left Spur sitting in the chair.

Seconds later he was out of the house and walking swiftly toward the barracks. The guard at the main door stiffened as he tapped on his shoulder.

"I'm going in," McCoy said, shouting above the screams that issued from the building.

The guard shrugged beneath his dirty hat and spat. "Saw you with Miller before. Okay."

Spur opened the door and walked inside.

Twenty lanterns blazed along the walls, lighting up the place as if it were day. It smelled of dirty clothes, filthy bedding and unwashed human bodies.

Thin cotton blankets lay on either side of a central aisle. Each one held a man. Rows of iron chains extended from one worker to another, fastened to the worker's ankles, binding them to their inhuman life at the mill. Most of the exhausted Hawaiians were sitting up on the miserable beds, staring in mute, accustomed horror at the sight.

One guard held down a young Hawaiian. Another stood over him. The thick leather strap cut into the man's bare back, bubbling it with welts. Each stroke sent him writhing and coiling on the bare, cold floor.

Another vicious slap of leather against skin brought blood seeping from the man's back.

"Don't you talk back to me, boy!" the man said as he whipped him. "Keep your mouth shut!"

"Beat him good, Felton!" the second guard said, grinning as he secured the man's arms.

The skin turned to bright red ribbons of torn flesh. The man blubbered and fell silent, his voice exhausted, his spirit broken by the brutal whipping.

"What is going on here?" Spur yelled, storming

up to the pair.

The shackled Hawaiians lining the walls stared at Spur in stunned silence. Felton let his raised belt hang in the air, dropping his jaw in surprise.

"Who the hell are you?" he demanded.

"Spur McCoy, part-owner of this business—your new boss."

Felton glanced uncertainly at the second white man. "That true, Davis?"

"Yeah, yeah. Heard Jason and the old man chewing it over today."

"Well, so?" Felton demanded.

"Sorry to interrupt your fun, but that stops. Now!" He grabbed the belt and wrestled it from the man's hand. "No more beatings!"

"Hey!"

"Don't talk back to me!" Spur warned him, shaking the belt. "You do and I'll see Miller takes care of you just like he takes care of these men!"

Felton stepped backward. "Hell, no one told me anything's changed. It ain't my fault!"

Spur looked down at the bleeding man, who'd slumped into unconsciousness. "You've been told!"

"Well, well, shit!"

"Come on, Felton," Davis said, rising from his squat. "Let's play cards."

The two men wandered over to a table and chairs strategically stationed beside a small wood-burning stove that let out just enough heat to warm them but kept the rest of the building chilly. They turned their backs on Spur and slapped the devil's pasteboards onto the table.

A hundred eyes stared at McCoy. Spur searched them until he found a familiar face. He looked hard at the man and smiled.

Kimo nodded.

"Davis, get the doc here. That man need medical attention or he'll die before morning."

"He'll die anyway."

Spur stormed to the man. He hauled up the chair and dumped Davis to the ground. "Move your butt!"

"Okay, okay!" he said.

"Miller always told us we weren't supposed to leave for nothing," Felton said as the second guard disappeared.

"I'm in charge now." Spur's voice was pointed.

"Well, what the hell." Felton returned to shuffling the cards.

Spur stepped five paces away and looked over his shoulder. The man showed him his back. He held a finger up to his lips, studying the Hawaiians, who nodded at his silent signal.

He drew his Colt and silently moved back to the table. Spur brought the butt end of his weapon down hard on the man's skull. Felton grunted and slumped forward.

The Hawaiians murmured.

One down, one out of the way for the moment, four outside. He threw the keys to Kimo. "Hurry. Get them all unlocked but lay there like you're still shackled. Understand?"

Kimo nodded and plunged the key into the iron bands surrounding his ankles.

"Hey!" Spur yelled toward the door. "I need some help in here!"

"That you, Felton?"

"Just get in here!"

The man appeared. Spur blasted him full of lead. Kimo, freed, hustled from man to man.

"Two of you men take him to the far corner,"

Spur said, pointing at the wounded slave, "where he won't get trampled. Then lie down like you're still chained."

The pair of newly freed men stared at each other and hauled the man away.

The Hawaiians whispered to each other as Kimo worked on them. He was fast. The two men returned to their pallets and laid the opened shackles around their ankles.

A few more minutes, Spur thought, and every worker would be free.

The elderly doctor walked in, his head toward the floor. "What's so important that I have to get up in the middle of the night?" He saw Felton slumped on the table, then the Hawaiian moving among his own.

"Hey!"

Spur patted him down. The man wore no weapons. "There's a Hawaiian bleeding to death in the corner, doc! If you wanna be breathing in the morning you go save his life. And do it quietly!"

The white-haired doc froze, then nodded. He walked towards the downed man.

Spur took up his position beside the door, his Colt drawn. The wooden rectangle opened and Davis burst inside along with one of the exterior guards.

"Something fishy goin' on—hey!"

"Drop your weapons!" Spur said.

They stared at him. McCoy fired before Davis's finger could pull the trigger. The second guard managed to peel of a wide shot before Spur silenced his revolver and the man himself.

"Hurry, Kimo! The whole place is gonna come crashing down on us in five seconds!"

"Okay, okay!"

Loud voices outside. Shouts. Spur slipped fresh rounds into the empty chambers. He thought he might need them.

Kimo unlocked the last pair of shackles and scurried over to him.

McCoy pocketed the keys and Kimo silently took his position on his pallet. The Hawaiians were excited, their eyes alert at the new feeling that help just might have found them.

"What the hell you talking about, Riley?"

He recognized the voice before Jason Miller walked in.

"Look, Jason," Spur said as the man faced him. "You've got a chance. Help me or you're dead."

"I—I—"

"No time for that!" Spur yelled. "Help me get your father or you'll hang too."

Jason Miller shrugged and drew his weapon. "Okay." He hardened his face.

Spur retrieved the revolvers from the dead guards and a still unconscious Felton. He handed them to Kimo, who quickly distributed the weapons to the men who sat on their side of him.

"Keep those firing irons out of sight. Use them only when I tell you to!"

"Right!'

"Sorry," the doctor said from the far side of the barracks. "He's cut up too badly. Nothing I can do for him."

"Try, goddamnit!" Spur shouted.

He turned toward the door, waiting, itching for the whole thing to start.

The outside guards weren't coming in.

"What the hell's going on in there?" Harry Miller asked.

Jason turned to Spur and nodded.

McCoy sighed. He'd never led a revolution before.

CHAPTER ELEVEN

"Miller, get in here!" Spur shouted out of the barracks.

"That you, McCoy?"

"Yeah, it's me."

"What the hell you think you're doing? Give me some answers, boy!"

"Come in and find out!"

Silence. Spur glanced around the room—at the doctor who looked up from the man who was bleeding to death, at Kimo and his friends who, against his orders, held the unfamiliar weapons he'd given them in shaky hands, at Jason Miller who stood solidly on the bare earthen floor, at the dead guards near his feet.

From the table, Felton grunted and lifted his head. Spur gave him another knock to the skull. He quieted as his chin hit the wooden surface.

"I'm waiting, Miller! Or don't you care what's happening in here?"

"No. You come out here!"

"I hold all the cards. You scared, Miller? Afraid to confront the monster you've created, the monster that's spitting up in your face?"

"Damn you! I got two men with me!"

Spur laughed. "And I've got your son!"

Again, silence. Jason started to speak but Spur held up his hand.

"You holding my boy against his will? By God, I'll kill you for that!"

"It never bothered you to work these men to death, treating them like slaves! Come on in and get him, Miller! Or aren't you man enough?"

Jason smiled.

The Hawaiians rustled. Spur turned and saw Kimo shrug off the hated shackles and stand. One by one the others rose and stretched.

"You got ten seconds, Miller. Get your fat ass in here or you'll be burying your son at dawn!"

Spur motioned with his weapon to the door. Tension flooded the air. Jason bent toward McCoy's ear.

"If you have to kill him, go ahead," he whispered, his thin features set, hard.

Spur nodded. "Your ten seconds are up, Miller!"

McCoy motioned to Kimo, raised his revolver in the air and pantomimed firing it. The Hawaiian shook his head, widened his eyes and nodded. He lifted the bulky Army revolver, tensed and pulled the trigger.

The resulting surge of energy exiting the barrel sent the man to the floor. The explosion echoed throughout the barracks. Miller's shouts outside were lost by the rush of a hundred feet. The gunshot had triggered the Hawaiians into full-scale revolt. Jason and Spur stood back as they poured from the barracks, whooping and yelling.

"Let's go!"

Spur pushed through them with Jason on his heels. Outside, they saw a figure retreating to the stables. Miller, Spur figured.

"Stay here!" Spur said to the Hawaiian men as he raced to the small building.

Jason ran up to him as McCoy saddled up the closest horse.

"No," he said. "Take Frankie. He's the fastest horse we have."

"Thanks." Spur transferred the saddle and cinched it up.

"I can't go with you. I can't do it."

"I understand, Jason. You'll stick around and keep an eye on things here?"

"Sure," he said. "Just go out and get that bastard!"

Spur mounted and rode into the night.

The horse balked at the new rider, fighting Spur, snorting and refusing to respond to his commands. Damnit, he thought, as he coaxed the beast. Come on!

Miller had ridden east, past the main house, into the virgin forest. Spur had no idea of his destination but it was clear that Miller hadn't wanted a confrontation. He couldn't blame the man—152 to 3 odds weren't very heartening.

He'd seen no signs of the two remaining guards. They'd probably fled as well.

The horse finally warmed to him. Spur kicked its flanks and the gelding bolted forward, crashing through the underbrush, veering to the left and right of the sturdy trees that rushed up on both sides.

The moon gave little light and half of that was blocked out by overhead branches. Spur saw the signs of the man's passing, though—broken saplings and trampled bushes. Phosphorescent fungus hanging from the pine tree limbs and festooning long-dead trunks lent its own eerie glow to his passage.

Fast. Faster.

Spur charged through the wilderness. He topped a small hill and started down the other side. In the distance he saw the glint of the nameless river where it bent on its way to the Williamette.

A rider approached him from the rear. Spur didn't have time to see who it was. Maybe Jason had changed his mind.

He broke through the trees into a recently cleared section of land. The tree tops bobbed up and down, hiding and revealing the crescent moon. He pushed his mount as hard as he could for as long as he could.

A copse of trees loomed up ahead. Just before they enveloped him Spur turned back. From 50 feet behind him the rider fired a shot.

One of the guards. Must have figured out I wasn't his employer, Spur thought, and lost himself in the trees. At the same time, Miller's faint trail vanished.

Spur slowed his horse, dismounted and drew his revolver. He peeled off a shot as the pursuing guard crashed by him. The man grunted and disappeared into the trees. A shoulder hit, McCoy thought, hurrying back into the saddle.

He held the reins with his left hand, his Colt with

the right, his eyes searching the forest up ahead.
This wasn't going well. True, he'd done his job by
freeing the men, but if he didn't have Harry Miller
locked up or put out of commission, the man'd just
do it all over again.

The trees grew thicker, with less space between
their trunks. The horse slowed as it sped through
the difficult terrain. Spur caught a glimpse of the
guard riding hard ahead of him. He gently eased the
horse to a faster gallop and carefully fired.

The guard slumped in the saddle. His torso
slipped to the right and slammed into a thick tree
trunk. The man fell to the ground, broken, dead.

Spur didn't glance down at him as he raced past.
Where the hell was Harry Miller?

An hour later, McCoy halted his horse to let it get
its breath at a moon-spangled stream. He
dismounted and walked the surrounding area. No
signs of the man's recent passage. No signs at all.

The forest was holding its secret.

Hell, he thought, staring at the horse's long
tongue lapping at the water. What could he do?

Two options. Return to the sawmill and wait for
the man's inevitable return to pick up the pieces,
or keep heading into the wilderness searching for
him.

Miller was smart. He knew the terrain. He
wouldn't make a fatal mistake like lighting a fire.
He might know of caves where he could hide, tree-
shrouded valleys invisible to anyone riding above
them. He might even have cabins that dotted the
terrain to be used during logging operations.

Spur went to his horse and rubbed its mane,
flicking the long, coarse hairs thorugh his fingers.

Then he smiled. What had Jason Miller told him?

They floated the unsawn logs to a second dock down river. Could the man be heading that way?

Harry Miller had been heading south as he rode out of the camp.

It was a chance. Not much of one, but a chance. Adrenaline surged through his veins as Spur mounted up. "Come on!" he urged his horse with his heels.

He angled the horse through the forest, searching for the river, using the moon as his compass. He found it.

An hour later, Spur had followed its meandering course for several miles, looking ahead for his destination. The scene up ahead made him slow his horse.

"There it is," he whispered.

A small building stood on the rock strewn beach. From it, a rude dock extended into the water. A storm must have blown through lately, for the dim moonlight bouncing off the surging water showed jagged, broken planks jutting from the dock's end. The wind-whipped river must have ripped it in half during the storm.

Light glowed in the cabin's window and smoke trailed up from the chimney. Spur walked the horse to within 20 feet of the place and tied it to a tree. He calmed himself and approached the building.

One horse stood at a trough. He cautiously approached it. It started in alarm but Spur grabbed its muzzle and held it, quieting the beast. Sweat foamed on its back. The horse had been ridden hard and brought here only minutes before.

McCoy smiled. He almost had him.

When he'd reassured the horse, he slipped past the window. The curtains were drawn, blocking a clear view, but the shadow of a fire moved between them and the lamp. Spur figured the direct approach would be the best.

He reloaded, moved past the corner of the small house and tried the doorknob. It silently turned— must have been recently oiled. Spur cracked it open an inch. The visible slice of the cabin's interior showed shelves holding dusty cans of food and loaves of bread. Firelight flickered against a wooden chair. Where was the man?

He shook his head and pushed hard on the door. It swung open.

Harry Miller stared down at him from behind his rifle, his finger on the trigger.

"Nice of you to join me, McCoy!"

CHAPTER TWELVE

"I knew you were trouble the first time I laid eyes on you!"

"You never laid anything on me," Spur said to the rifle-toting man.

"Don't get smart with me, McCoy! You thought you could come in and break up my little operation, right? Thought you could ruin my little utopia."

"More like your hell."

"Shut up!" He gestured with his left hand. "Give me your weapon."

Spur grunted. "If you kill me and ride back to your camp, you know what you'll find? Dead guards, at least one dead Hawaiian—and no one else."

"What about my son?"

"You mean Jason? He'd probably meet you with a rifle and splatter your worthless guts all over the trees." He paused. "I wasn't holding Jason against his will. He joined me because he hates the way you've run your camp. He hates you even more and told me to blast you into hell."

Miller laughed. "Nice try, McCoy. My son'd never turn on me."

"He did, because you turned on him. He never expected you to run that place like a pre-war plantation, working the poor bastards to death just to save a few bucks!"

"Shut up!" Miller sweated.

It was working. "You've got blood on your hands, Miller! The blood of innocent men! Oh, you may not have actually killed any of them, but you sentenced them to death in a strange country far from their homes. You're worse than a murderer. You're a slaver."

Miller's face tensed. "Shut the hell up and give me your revolver, goddamnit!"

"Why? So you can kill an unarmed man? So I won't blast a hole through your skull as I drop? No way, Miller! If I'm gonna go, I'll take you with me— to hell!"

Their gazes locked.

"You don't scare too easy," Miller said.

"You've got nothing to go back to."

"The banks! All my money! I don't give a shit about the mill or those damned bastards!"

"Jason'll be in town at dawn and draw out every penny you ever deposited."

"Not if I get their first!"

Hooves pounded outside.

Spur smiled. "That's him now, come to help me kill you, just like we'd planned."

The man faltered. 'No. No!"

Spur fired during the split second that Harry Miller glanced at the door. The big man groaned, blasted the roof and dropped his rifle. His hands went to his chest. Boots rustled outside.

"Harry?" a voice yelled.

"Yeah!" Spur affected the man's throaty voice, moving to the wall near the entrance.

Miller fell to his knees, his face reddening, the veins in his neck popping out. His hands went to his stomach, covering and protecting the wound. "Jesus Christ!"

The door banged open. "Thought you might've—"

Spur rushed the man, easily disarmed him and kicked the rifle across the room.

"You!" the guard said, flustered.

He was young, too young to be involved with the likes of Miller. Sweat gleamed on his youthful features. A moustache was just beginning to sprout on his upper lip.

"Yeah. Me. We're all going back. Give me any trouble, boy, and you'll lose your balls."

Harry Miller bellowed but rose to his feet. "I'll be damned if I'm going anywhere with you!"

"Pipe down." Spur smashed his boot against the man's legs, sending Miller crashing to the floor again. He howled even harder as fiery pain stabbed through him.

"What's your name?" McCoy asked the guard.

"Riley, sir."

"How old are you?"

"Eighteen." He swallowed. "Look, he'll be dead inside an hour. That's a gut-wound. One of the boys at the camp croaked from one of those."

"Who gave it to him?"

Riley nodded toward Miller and frowned.

The boy stiffened under Spur's gaze.

"Hey, look, it was just a job! My dad worked for him and he got me hired on. I didn't know what it was like until I was in up to my ears."

"Right."

"It's true!"

Harry Miller crawled across the floor. Spur watched as the bleeding man's hands clasped the rifle.

"Don't try it!"

"Damn you!"

He levelled the rifle and slammed a shot into the wall. Too close, Spur thought, as he sent another load of hot lead into the man's body. A clean shot. Right through the heart.

Harry Miller would never buy any more slaves.

The big man slumped onto his back, kicked, shuddered and slowly exhaled his way into the next world.

"Wow!" Riley said as he stared at the still man. "He could've killed you!"

"Or you," Spur pointed out.

"Right."

"You gonna cooperate with me?"

"Yessir!" came the ready response.

"Okay. Let's get this man on a horse and head back. Right now, before dawn."

Two hours later, under Riley's guidance, they rode into camp. The boy had fully cooperated with him—out of disgust for his dead boss or because he was out of a job. Either way, Spur was glad he'd happened along.

The place looked deserted, but every light in the two-story house blazed away. Dozens of, voices mixed with music issued from the structure. The two men looked at each other as they untied Miller's body and hauled him into the deserted barracks.

"No sense in breaking up the party with this," Spur said.

Riley smiled as they unceremoniously dumped the man onto the cold earth.

The young man sighed, took off his hat and slicked his forehead. "That's a relief."

"Come on."

They walked into the house. Kimo, fully dressed, met them with a revolver. He smiled as he recognized them.

"McCoy!" The Hawaiian glanced at Riley. "What's he doing here? With you?"

"He's okay. Really. Don't worry about him."

Kimo nodded. His tattooed face darkened. "What about Harry Miller?"

"Dead. We just threw his body in the barracks."

A high-pitched giggle sounded above the noise.·

Kimo smiled. "We found the things Miller took from us stashed in the house. Kalani even found his ukelele. We are celebrating."

"Great. Is Jason around?"

"Yeah. In there." Kimo raised his eyebrows. "He rode out and brought us some presents that had just arrived. It's not a pretty sight."

Spur looked quizzically at him and shrugged. "You find the other guards?"

"Yes. We killed them."

"Then there's no need for a lookout. Come on, Kimo; show us your party!"

The three men walked into the parlor. Spur wasn't surprised to see dozens of brown-skinned women frolicking with the men. The whole room was a sea of clothed and naked bodies writhing around, locked in the timeless choreography of love. Hips thrust. Mouths locked together. Hands clenched.

The smell of sex-musk hung in the air.

"Wow!" Riley said.

"What's wrong, kid?"

"They even took baths!"

Spur shook his head.

A few of the Hawaiians, already spent, stood back and watched, sucking up the once-forbidden liquor and smoking cigars. One strummed a ukelele and sung in a lyrical, pleasant language.

"McCoy!" a familiar voice called.

Spur laughed as Jason Miller stopped in mid-stroke, pulled out of the blonde woman he'd been lying on top of and walked over to them.

"Can you believe it?" he said, spreading out his hands, taking in the whole room with the gesture.

"Not likely."

Jason smiled. "These girls got suspicious so they took up a collection at their church on Maui. The missionaries even helped them out. Raised enough money to sail over here and get their men back."

Riley loudly swallowed. "They got 'em, alright!"

"I sailed into town to get Commissioner Golden, who told me about the girls. Brought 'em back here two hours after you left." His smile faded. "What about my father?"

"Don't worry about him."

He set his jaw and nodded. "I won't! Have to get

back to business."

Jason dove back into the sea of pumping, sweaty flesh.

A naked woman sprang past them and ran outside, her full breasts bouncing. She laughed as two Hawaiian men chased after her.

Spur turned to Riley. The expression on his face was priceless, he thought, flushed and excited and disbelieving. The sight could be overwhelming.

"Look, son, if you want to leave—" he started.

A bronzed beauty sat in a corner, her face sullen.

"No, that's okay. Excuse me, sir," Riley said. "I recognize that girl from a picture Kamuela once showed me. He really loved her." He walked to her.

Kimo's slap to his back distracted Spur for a moment. The smiling Hawaiian buck led a nude woman up the stairs to one of the bedrooms and some privacy.

McCoy stepped into the kitchen doorway, enjoying the spectacle of all that pent-up sexual energy being released at one time. It was amusing, and even erotic, but he wasn't in the mood for love-making. Celebrating, yes, but he had to catch his breath.

"Come on, Spur!" Jason yelled at him. "You gotta help me out. Missy here's not satisfied and I'm afraid I've run out of steam. Three times is my limit!"

"Yeah!" she said, sticking up her smiling face.

He smiled and shook his head.

CHAPTER THIRTEEN

At dawn, Spur woke in the bedroom he'd been assigned the night before he'd freed the Hawaiians. He yawned, splashed cold water on his face to fully rouse himself, and walked downstairs.

He stepped over snoring bodies and smiled at the exhausted remains of the all-out orgy. The men had mightily celebrated with their wives and sweethearts. They may not wake up for hours, but Spur had work to do.

He located Jason Miller and shook his bare shoulders.

"Hell, Missy, I can't do it again," he mumbled.

"Jason!"

Miller lifted his head and regarded Spur with sleepy eyes. "Huh?"

"You fully functional?"

He turned over and looked at his crotch. "I'm

swearing off women for at least a month, but other than that, yeah."

"Good. How much cash do you have here on hand?"

Jason scratched his stubbly chin and yawned. "I checked that last night. Found $2,000 in my father's safe. I remember him saying he was going to deposit it today."

"Think that'd be enough to get all these people back home?"

Another yawn. "Probably not."

"Then take that boat of yours, go into Portland and withdraw enough money to book passage for as many of the Hawaiians as want to go back, plus something for them to live on." Spur stooped, grabbed the man's hand and hauled him to his feet.

"Oh God!" Jason said, stumbling along behind him. He tripped over legs and feet.

In the kitchen, Spur sat the naked man in a chair and pumped water into the coffee pot. "How much are you willing to give the men for all the work they've done? How much to compensate them for their suffering?"

Jason Miller shrugged and yawned. "Hell, McCoy, I can't think straight now. Anyway, this chair's cold! Can't I just put on my britches?"

"No." Spur splashed him with water. "A cold butt'll wake you up. Whaddya say?"

"Uh, I don't know."

"Did your father ever tell you how much he'd made out here?"

Jason stifled a yawn. "No, but I looked at the ledger in his desk last night. Splash me again."

Spur dipped more water from the pot and sprinkled it over his shoulders.

"Shit, that's freezing. But it's working!" Jason shivered. "Okay. He had records of $20,000 in deposits."

Spur whistled. "Even if that's not all the money he made, that's enough." He did some rough calculations in his head as he set the coffee pot on the stove and opened the firebox. "Fifty into twenty-thousand," he mused, striking a match and setting the already-laid kindling alight. "Four-hundred dollars sounds about right."

"For each of them."

"Yeah."

"Including the widows?"

"Of course! And the bereaved sweethearts."

"Yeah. Fine with me." Jason violently shook his head and stared up at McCoy. "I don't want a cent of the money my father earned with human blood. I'll start all over, run this place like a real business. Advertise. All that shit."

Spur closed the stove door and turned back to the man.

"You were with Riley last night, weren't you?"

McCoy nodded.

"He didn't give you any trouble?"

"No. Seemed to hate your father as much as you did. He warmed up to my side of the story real fast."

Jason sighed and rubbed his bare thighs. "Lay it on the table, McCoy. What happens to me? You gonna send me to jail?"

Spur paused. "If you pay the men the money and see that they get back to their home, nothin'll happen to you. I'll see to that. But Jason, if you try to pull anything on me you'll be behind bars so fast you'll—"

"Aw, come on, McCoy!" Jason shook his head.

"Trust me. I'm not my father."

"You sure aren't."

Kimo walked proudly back to Spur from the booking office, waving the tickets in his hands.

"Now I will see my six-year-old son," he said, his eyes shining. "Thanks to you."

The Hawaiian woman lowered her head. "We both thank you."

McCoy shrugged off their gratitude.

"I don't know how to—" Kimo lost his words in his throat.

"Look, just get on that boat, sail home and have lots more babies. Okay?"

The Hawaiian woman laughed.

"Forget about this place, Kimo. Put it out of your mind. You've got a family to think about now."

"I will. Thanks."

They shook hands.

Spur walked them to the dock where a great ship bobbed on the water. The brigantine *Flying Wheel* was leaving in an hour for Astoria. In ten days or so, weather permitting, the men and women would be back in Hawaii.

McCoy sighed as he walked to his room. His assignment with Harry Miller—now officially concluded after his testimony to Commissioner Golden and the telegram he'd sent to General Halleck—had been a break in his work to find the counterfeiters, but that job wasn't finished.

Yet.

As he made his way to the Riverside Hotel he passed the collection of cottages. The sign that bore Emily Curtis's flourishing autograph brought back the memory of the woman.

He stepped into her studio.

"Interruptions. Always interruptions!" the white-haired woman said before turning to him, brush in hand. Her lined face relaxed as she saw him. "Oh, Mr. McCoy." Her face sweetened with a smile. "How nice of you to drop by. Ah, I am rather busy right now." She gestured behind her.

Spur saw the young guard from Miller's logging camp standing uncomfortably on the platform. The stark naked youth gave Spur a lopsided grin.

"Hi."

"Hello, Riley." Spur couldn't hold back a laugh. "Picking up some extra money?"

"Yeah."

"You two know each other?" Emily Curtis asked.

"Ah, yes. It's hard to explain."

"I see."

"Do you have anything to tell me?"

She looked quizzically at him.

"Remember our conversation?"

"Landsakes! Of course I do. What do you think I am, a doddering old woman?"

"Never. Never!"

The aged artist turned back to Riley. "Put on your pants, young man, and wait. I'll pay you extra for waiting. And you, McCoy; come with me!"

He nodded and glanced at the canvas she'd been working on. So far the woman had captured Riley's thighs and everything that hung between them.

With a grin at the ex-guard, Spur followed Emily into a rear room in her studio. The air was heavy with the exotic combination of cigar smoke and lavender.

"I've been keeping my eyes open but I don't know much," she said. "Still, some of the egotistical bastards around here who think they have talent do some strange things."

"Like what?"

"You know, entertaining unusual visitors. People staying long hours, never seeming to leave."

Spur smiled. He guessed the obvious. "Customers, maybe? People buying paintings?"

Emily laughed. "Not those artless canvasses!"

"Models, then?"

"I don't know. Artists—even those just pretending to be true artists—are a strange breed. You'd never know it to look at me though, would you?" The white-haired woman stared defiantly at him.

"Ah, no. No I wouldn't, Emily."

She chuckled and patted his shoulder. "I'll let you know. You stop by anytime, young man!"

"Right."

Emily Curtis ushered him into the studio. "Okay, kid, take 'em off!" she yelled at Riley.

The man blushed.

Clare Maxwell slapped the money on the table. "Counterfeit! Fake! I couldn't believe it!"

"Where'd you get this?" Spur asked as he crossed his hotel room to look at the bills.

"Oh, ah, different places." She looked away from him. "You know, here and there."

Her evasiveness surprised him. When the woman had run into him on the street and demanded that he take her to his hotel, Spur had figured the pretty brunette had other things on her mind. Now this.

He studied the money. It was counterfeit, alright. No mistaking the slightly off-color ink, the smeared lower edge, the too-thin paper.

"I'm really nervous, Spur!" Clare said as he bent

over the table.

"About what?"

Though it was still daylight, he turned up the lamp to more brightly illuminate the bills.

"I feel like I can't trust anyone or accept any money. Sure, banks are supposed to be safe now, but anywhere else I'm bound to—to get more of this!"

"Hmmmm."

"It's getting so a girl can't—can't—oh, Spur, what can I do?"

"About what?"

"You know, money! That's $60 I've been cheated of!"

"I know."

"There's no way I can turn it in for the real thing?"

"No. Sorry, but that's impossible."

Clare frowned. "I knew it. So there's nothing I can do."

"You could always get out of the business," he gently suggested.

The woman blushed. "What—what business?"

"The kind of business where pretty young women make money, Clare."

"No. You have me all wrong. I've been a lot of things, but I've never been one of *those*!"

The look in her eyes beamed honesty. "Okay. Besides, most madames can spot a fake twenty. And they'd never pass it onto their girls unless they were real horrors."

He went to her. "Where'd you get this money?"

Clare squirmed and lowered her eyes.

He gently grabbed her wrist.

"Why's that so important to you?"

"Come on, Clare. I have to know. If you didn't want to talk about it, why'd you ask to come to my room?"

She stopped struggling against his grip. "Because —because I didn't know where else to turn. I don't know anybody in this town." Clare pouted.

"Okay." He released her arm. "But I can't help you if you don't spill the beans." Spur sighed. "Is it something you're ashamed of?"

She lowered her head and nodded.

"And it doesn't have anything to do with sex?"

Her face colored and she stepped back. "No! Ah, not really."

Spur advanced to her. "So you didn't work in a house. You sold yourself on the street, right?"

"No!" Her voice was harsh.

"Then by god, Clare, what the hell did you do to get this money?"

"I—" She bit her tongue. "Oh Spur, I didn't know how I was going to live! I had to do something."

"What?"

"I dressed up like an old lady and went out on the streets."

"Go on." What was she driving at?

"I walked up to women and—and—" Again her voice faltered.

"And?"

"And robbed their purses." Clare looked away, seemingly very interested in the bevelled mirror that hung over the table holding a basin and pitcher.

He knew there was more. "That doesn't have anything to do with sex."

"I know." She bit her lower lip.

"What else, Clare? What else did you do to get all that counterfeit currency?"

"I—I—" She touched the left shoulder of her dress. "I took off my clothes."

Closer, he thought. "Why? I mean, was there someone else there?"

Clare nodded like a little girl who'd broken a dish. "Who?"

She lowered her eyebrows. "Wait a minute. Wait a minute! You're awfully interested in all this, aren't you?"

"Yes." Okay, he'd tell her. "I'm a federal agent here in Portland investigating the counterfeit money."

She gasped. "You're—you're a policeman?"

"No. Not really. I only look into interstate crimes, especially those dealing with American money."

"Oh. Thank goodness! After I'd told you about my thievery I thought you might lock me up."

"Don't worry about that. I won't. Let's get back to the subject. Where did you take off your clothes?"

Clare frowned. "I did some modeling work the last two days."

That was it, Spur thought. "Who was this artist?"

"Alain DuLac."

CHAPTER FOURTEEN

"Heavens, Spur!" Clare Maxwell said as she stood before the man. "I wouldn't blame you if you booted me out of your hotel room for what I just told you."

He laughed. "Just because you posed as an artists's model? That's—well, that's art. Perfectly acceptable under the right circumstances."

The blush slowly faded from Clare's cheeks. "So I'm not a fallen woman?"

"From doing that? No." McCoy briefly smiled at the woman and peered at the counterfeit bills again. "But I wouldn't go back to that artist again if he slipped you phony money." He fingered it. "How many times did you pose for this man?"

"Twice. The first time he gave me one of those, but the second time it was real."

"Hmmmm."

"And I won't be going back to see him again. I

wouldn't even if he hadn't left the city for a few days."

"You said his name was DuLac?"

She nodded, her full attention to him.

"I recognize the name from the exhibit at the museum. He's gone out of town?"

"That's right. He told me when I left his studio two days ago. It didn't crush me. I wasn't counting the hours until I could humiliate myself in front of him again." She bent her head toward the floor. "At first I liked it, but then it just got so—so dirty. Seedy."

Spur went to her. "Clare, there's nothing humiliating about showing your body. Especially when it's a beautiful body like yours."

The woman lifted her chin and stared at him from lowered eyelashes. "Really?"

"Yes." The image of her standing there, defenseless in front of some aged European artist, was rather pathetic. "Was he any good?"

Clare lifted her eyebrows.

"I mean, does he have talent? At painting?"

"Oh, I'm no judge, but the picture did look like me—all of me."

"Maybe I'll see it for myself." Spur smiled reassuringly at the young woman.

She unconsciously licked her upper lip. "You mean the painting, or . . . me?"

Spur took a step toward her. "My dear Clare, I could never take advantage of a poor girl like you at a time like this." He unbuckled his belt, staring at her. She had all the signs. Clare was waiting for him, the woman with the arching brows and shiny cheeks.

"I suppose not."

She didn't retreat as he advanced on her. "Lost in this big city, low on money, barely recovered from doing something you detested doing just to buy a few crumbs to eat."

"Yes."

Spur slipped off his coat and let it fall to the floor. She raised her hands as he neared her. Nimble white fingers quickly clasped his shirt front, ripping off the buttons.

"It would be unthinkable to me to make advances on you, woman." He knocked off his hat.

"Of course!"

Clare's hands traveled from his now opened shirt down to his pants. Her eyes widened as she unbuttoned his fly, rubbing against the hardening lump with one palm. She smiled with delight at what she felt there between his legs and explored it, tracing its impressive outline.

McCoy rustled out of his shirt. "Miss Maxwell, you're safe with me."

Clare fumbled with his fly, furiously ripping away the cloth. "Uh-huh."

Spur watched her with amusement as her pink tongue darted between her lips as she worked on the simple task. When the last metal button was free, the woman reached inside and grasped his erection.

"Oh. Oh!" Clare looked up at him with a wicked smile. "Sure you won't change your mind? I'd like to be taken advantage of. Right here. Right now. Long and hard, as hard as you want!"

"Compromise your virtue?"

"Come on, Spur!" Clare stepped back and quickly undressed. Practiced hands removed the simple sheath from her body, exposing her creamy white chemise and cotton bloomers.

Spur readjusted his crotch. His stiff penis popped out of his drawers and reached for the ceiling. "You're forcing me into a difficult situation," he said with a faint smile.

"Difficult?" Clare said as she slipped the chemise off her head and lowered her bloomers. "It's the easiest thing in the world!" She glanced between his legs for the first time and sucked in her breath. "Come on, Spur. No more games." She panted and slid a hand between her thighs.

Spur rustled out of his boots, pants and long underwear and closed the drapes. In the semi-darkness, lit only by the single kerosene flame, he went to the woman.

Clare melted against him, kissing his shoulder, moving her lips across his bicep, tasting, clutching at his body like a drowning woman to a life raft.

Spur gripped the woman's buttocks and rubbed the soft cheeks. "You feel good," he said, pressing his throbbing erection against her stomach.

"You taste good." She flicked her tongue against his nipple.

"Two can play that game," Spur said as her teeth gently closed around the hard nub on his chest.

Clare laughed as he grabbed her head, pushed it back and bent before her. The woman's breasts hung there in a dazzling display of feminine beauty. He licked around her left areola, the warm flesh searing his tongue. Spur joined his hands behind her and forced Clare to arch her back, giving him easier access to her.

"Mmmm." He pushed her breast into his mouth, marveling at its firmness and size. It fit perfectly. Spur suckled her.

"Oh, you can compromise my virtue any day of the week."

As he worked her over Spur felt a hand worming between their bodies, grasping and squeezing his penis. Erotic waves of sensation flooded through his body. He switched to her other breast and gave it the full treatment—sucking, tonguing, nibbling, worshipping.

"I never thought I could want it this much." Clare's voice was breathy, dripping with tension.

He pulled off her with a loud smack. "Me neither." Spur put his hand between her legs and felt the furry patch. He slipped a finger into it, tracing her lips, teasing her as she teased him.

Their eyes suddenly met. The depth of the woman's expression increased Spur's desire. He probed her.

"Oh."

He pushed deeper. His fingertip touched her clitoris.

"Spur!"

Spur rubbed her, his hand splayed against her thighs.

"Stop it." Clare's voice was a moan. "Stop it! Spur, please!"

She circled her hips and pumped them up and down. He mercilessly aroused her, supporting the arching woman's back with one hand and torturing her with the other.

She squeezed her eyes shut and gasped, her hips jerking, her beautiful form tensing and releasing and spasming against his relentless finger.

For those few seconds he possessed her body, playing it like an instrument. Clare shook her head and straightened up. She locked her thighs around his hand.

"Hey!" Spur said, retrieving it.

"You don't play fair!"

"Who said anything about fairness?"

Clare's breath puffed out between her red lips. "You slimy bastard!"

Spur laughed in surprised delight as she threw her weight against him, sending him toppling onto the bed. The four-poster creaked. She scrambled around on top of him, jabbing her fingernails into his ribs, playing with his testicles, plunging her tongue into his ear.

The woman was all over him.

"Clare! Come on!"

She ignored him and lowered her head to his crotch. Spur's resistance melted away at the warm, liquid feeling of her tongue. She licked, outlining the flaring head of his penis, coating it with saliva.

His groin boiled with sexual energy. Spur slapped his forehead and raised his hips but she backed away, never quite taking him into her mouth.

"Damnit!" he said.

"Isn't that fair?"

Lick. Tease. Lick.

"That's enough!" Spur grabbed Clare's shoulders and rolled her onto her back. He parted her legs with his knees. The woman stared up at him with aware, aroused eyes.

"Okay—alright. Compromise my virtue!"

He grinned and pushed it into position. She was moist and more than ready. Spur sunk the first inch into her. Clare's face blossomed. She inhaled and nodded.

Spur drove into her body, sheathing himself until his testicles bounced against her. Their connection was so tight, so right, that they simply stared at each other in surprise for ten seconds, unmoving, reveling in the incredible desire building up in them.

"The—the—"

He kissed her. "No time for talk!"

Clare nodded. She rolled back her head as Spur withdrew and snapped it forward on his thrust. Her eyes tightened and he felt her body tense around him.

"Does it hurt?"

She nodded. "Yes. A bit. The boys back home are nothing like you."

He slowly pumped her. "I'll be gentle."

"No!" She flung the word at him. "Don't be! Just do it to me. With me!"

"Whatever you say."

Ignoring the sexual tension pulsating through him, Spur started slowly, gently pushing into her, sliding out almost all the way until she lifted her hips and demanded another penetration.

At first it was all he could do to keep himself from orgasming, but the hypnotic movements eventually allowed him better control.

"Yes."

Spur increased his pace, thrusting harder into her, faster, relishing the velvet feeling surrounding his erection. Their bodies locked together at the crotch.

"Faster."

He pushed into Clare with short, deep jabs. The woman smiled up at him, opened her lips and sank her fingernails into his back. Spur's pumps were so hard that the woman's body slid back and forth on the slick sheet beneath her.

"Harder!" she practically screamed.

Their pelvic bones banged together. Clare's breasts crushed against his hairy chest. She writhed beneath his body, fully enjoying Spur's rhythmic thrusts.

He suddenly lifted himself onto his hands and toes, riding her higher, changing his angle so that he rubbed against her clitoris. Clare went out of her mind, tearing her hair, her face suffused with the throes of the ultimate pleasure as he pounded into her body.

The old bed banged against the wall in time with Spur's movements. He slapped back down on top of her and pumped faster and faster. His throat tightened. The pressure built between his legs. Every muscle in his body tightened as he raced toward his pleasure. Clare's face below him dissolved into a soft, warm visage of ecstasy that gasped and moaned.

Beyond any semblance of rational thought, beyond all control, Spur thrust blindly into her, jerking and shivering and grunting as he drained his seed into her body. His wet lips molded to Clare's. His buttocks spasmodically humped between her thighs.

Time stood still. The moment stretched to infinity. Pump. Spurt. Thrust. Release!

Their mouths burned together, sealing their moment of love as he collapsed on top of her. Every nerve in his body flexed and finally quieted in the soundless wind of absolute peace.

Spur turned his head aside to take a breath and laid his cheek on hers. They stayed that way, joined together, spent and exhausted.

Finally, McCoy fought the lethargy leadening him

and raised his torso from hers. He stared down at the woman. Their lovemaking seemed to have magnified Clare's beauty—if that was possible.

"What . . . what happened?" she asked, lowering her eyebrows.

He managed a short laugh. "Huh?"

Clare looked up at him in surprised delight. "I mean—that only happens when I'm alone."

"Not when I'm around." He tenderly kissed her cheek. "I guess you don't have enough slimy bastards in your life."

She laughed and drew him into her arms, forcing him down on top of her again.

He gave her the tongue she wanted.

CHAPTER FIFTEEN

Clare turned to him as Spur finished dressing, smiling. She stretched like a cat and throatily laughed, shaking her head back and forth.

"What's that for?" he asked, buckling his belt.

"For the man who turned my day around. I came here mad and I'm leaving happy!"

McCoy shrugged. "No charge, ma'am."

She smirked, walked to the window and opened the curtain. Sunlight spilled inside, temporarily blinding Spur who backed to the bed. He tugged on his shoes.

"So this artist's name was DuLac?"

"Uh-huh." Clare put a hand to her mouth. "Spur! I just realized—that was my first time."

"Come on, Clare! You may not be a saloon girl, but I don't believe that."

She grinned. "That's not what I mean. I mean that

was my first time with a government man." She sat beside him and stroked his left thigh.

"Just don't go spreading that information around." Spur tied the laces. "Okay? I don't want anyone to know who I really am and what I'm doing here."

"Of course. I'll keep my mouth shut."

He kissed her as his left, booted foot hit the floor. "I hate to say this but—"

Clare pressed two fingers to his lips. "I know. I know. You have to go to work."

"Right." He kissed her hand. "As much as I'd like to spend the rest of the day with you."

"That's okay. I guess I'll live." She faked a swoon, falling into his lap.

Spur laughed as she picked herself up. He turned down the kerosene lamp and walked Clare to the door.

"If I get anymore of those counterfeit bills I'll tell you, Spur." She turned.

He grabbed her hand as she clasped it around the doorknob. "What kind of a man do you think I am?" he asked. "Where I come from a gentleman has the decency to walk a woman home after he compromises her."

Clare laughed as they left his hotel room.

Ten minutes later, the taste of her lips still lingered on his. He'd safely seen the comely woman to her hotel—a run-down but comfortable establishment close to the water. Interesting girl, Spur thought. With interesting information.

Time to return to work. He walked to the waterfront colony and passed by each cottage until he found Alain DuLac's. It was easily identified by the huge sign that graced the front of the building.

The shades were closed. Spur walked onto the creaky porch and knocked. No answer. He tried the knob but it wouldn't move. The man had apparently left town just as he'd told Clare. He'd have to have a look around later that evening, when things were quiet.

Spur sighed as he walked around the side of DuLac's studio. All the windows were draped, blocking out prying eyes. He found one that was barely closed. He put his hands on his hips, bent forward and peered inside.

The sharp slap on his back made him spin around. "Mrs. Curtis!"

"I'm glad I found you." The white-haired artist smiled. "Come with me, young man. We can sit in my garden out back for a while."

"Why?"

"Just do it!"

Emily Curtis tugged on his coat sleeve so Spur gave in and followed her between the studios, walking past rhododendrons and azaleas just bursting into splashes of red and pink colors.

"I never could get just the right hue to capture those danged things," Emily said, pointing toward the flowers.

"You don't expect me to pose for you outside, do you?"

Emily laughed. "That's not what I want you for."

They entered a small, sparsely-planted garden.

"Please," the artist said, extending her hand to an iron chair.

Spur seated himself. The woman took up the chair beside it and gave him a wrinkled smile.

"Seen anything unusual?"

Emily Curtis leaned confidentially toward him.

"Yes. I mean, I have something unusual. Never trusted the man from the moment he walked into my shop. Putting on airs, talking up a storm."

"I'm sorry—" Spur began.

"*You're* sorry!" She coughed. "I'm out of cigar money for a whole month! That's what the man did to me!" Emily Curtis shook her head and slapped her thigh. "I knew it! Why don't I listen to myself? But I hadn't made a sale all day and the thought of making my rent overcame my better sense of judgment." She frowned. "I never should have taken it."

"Taken what?"

"Money. At least, I thought that's what it was, but it's not good for anything but cleaning off dirty brushes. A young fellow walked into my place yesterday afternoon and bought one of my paintings —a good rendition of Mount Hood in wintertime, with the sun gleaming on the snow pack." She frowned. "McCoy, I got cheated out of $60."

"I'm sorry, Emily." He reached for the woman's hand, but she pulled it back, stuffed it down her bodice and produced a slim cigar.

"You said you were wondering if any of these artists around here were into making this counterfeit stuff. Well, I don't know anything about that. And I'm sure I'll never see the man who gave it to me again."

"*If* he knew he was passing it to you, of course. But it seems there's quite a few folks in Portland who still don't look at their money."

"I know." She stuck the cigar into her mouth. "I guess I'm one of them."

Spur smiled at the comical sight of the elderly woman chewing on the stogie. "You don't still have this money, do you?"

Emily Curtis shook her head. "Nope. The bank took it from me."

He nodded. "Emily, your neighbor doesn't seem to be at home."

Her perfect white teeth clamped down on the end of the cigar, expertly severing it. She inelegantly spat it out. "That's right. Left yesterday afternoon."

"Did he say where he was going?"

"Nope." She examined the cigar. "But he sure seemed to be in a hurry. Only took one small bag with him. I heard through the grapevine that he's left Portland for a few days." She shook her head. "That's a strange one for you, that DuLac. Hey, Spur, got a light?"

Amused, Spur produced a match, struck it and held the flame to the tip of the cigar planted between Emily Curtis's lips. She puffed until it glowed.

"Thanks."

She worked it until it was steadily burning and blew out a mouthful of smoke. Spur thought. Alain DuLac had given Clare Maxwell a fake twenty, then left town. Maybe he'd gotten stuck with it and simply passed it on—knowingly or unknowingly—to the woman. Maybe DuLac was an uninvolved party in the transfer of the bill.

His leaving town seemed suspicious, but he'd invited Clare to come back for another session. It just didn't make sense.

Emily's loud exhalation brought Spur back to reality. "You really enjoy smoking?" Spur asked as a blue haze gathered around them in the garden.

She smiled broadly. "Sure. A woman can want a cigar just like a man, can't she?"

Spur nodded.

Emily puffed. "And they should have the right to do whatever they want to do. Period. My daddy taught me how to smoke when I was a little tyke. Course, that was after he'd caught me behind the barn, trying like mad to get the damned thing lit."

"I see." Spur rose and shook his head.

"I owe what I am today—this genteel, cultured, little old lady, to one man—my father." Emily winked at him, her head surrounded by a halo of smoke.

"Thanks for the talk, Emily."

"Sure. Any time!"

Spur watched the sunset, had dinner and walked to the Beacham Saloon. The drinking establishment was located just two blocks from the artists' studios. Might be good hunting grounds. He walked inside.

It was a dark, dirty place, smelling of smoke, liquor and cheap perfume. A smiling man plinked tunelessly on the piano. Soft-bodied, hard-eyed women paced up and down the place, offering their wares to a motley assortment of men.

Old-time sea captains tipped back glasses with fresh-faced sailors. Two bearded men exchanged short, volcanic bursts of dialogue in a foreign language, each banging on the table to make his point.

Many of the customers played cards. All of them drank.

"Try your luck?"

Spur looked down at the haggard man who shuffled cards on the table next to the entrance.

"Sorry, no."

"I'll guarantee you you'll win. I ain't never won fer as long as I've been playing." Nimble fingers fluttered the cards like a riverboat gambler.

"No money." Spur pushed through the tables and ordered a whiskey from the one-eyed bartender.

"What you starin' at?" the apron challenged him.

He hadn't been. "Nothing."

Sullenly, the barkeep exchanged the drink for Spur's money.

Every seat in the place was occupied so Spur moved to the rear and leaned against the wall. He slowly sipped the warm whiskey, staring, listening, learning.

Two men hunched over their cards on a nearby table. Their faces were hidden by their hats.

"Emily Curtis had three of 'em last night," one of them said.

"No shit!" His drinking partner whistled. "How the hell does she do it?"

"Beats me."

"Naw, that's what your wife does!"

Guffaws. A hand reached across the table and pushed the man's chest. "At least mine'll touch me, Sam!"

"With a ten foot pole."

"Just deal. You're drunk."

"Yeah. So're you."

The men fell silent and played poker. Spur turned away from them but looked back.

"Ole DuLac sure left in a hurry."

"Yeah, you hear about that?"

"Hear about what?"

"Come on, the dame! Seems his girl left him high and dry a few days ago."

"You mean that uppity slut?"

"Yeah. If she'd had any brains she would've stayed with him. He sure dressed her fine. Rebecca never had it so good on the street."

"Wonder why she ran off."

"From what I heard, seems she got tired of cleaning up after him. You know."

The speaker's head slanted upward, catching Spur's gaze. McCoy grunted and turned away. He sipped.

"Anyway, you know."

"Yeah."

Silence.

A pretty girl, about eighteen years old, waltzed through the tables to a silent tune, one hand held high, fluttering a lace handkerchief.

"Hey hey! A floor show and everything!" one of the men at the table said.

The man seated at the piano managed to find a genuine tune and stumbled through it.

The girl, her eyes dulled with alcohol and, probably, opium, grabbed the front of her dress and tugged on it.

"Hoowhee!"

"Yeah, Angel! Do it!"

The room burst with noise. Every man, including the bartender, turned toward the slowly circling girl, waiting, watching.

"Show us yer fine woman-flesh!"

Angel smirked and ripped her bodice.

Spur walked out of the bar. He wouldn't learn anything there that night.

The air was bitterly cold. Portland may be in for another taste of winter, he thought, buttoning up his coat. McCoy walked through the deserted streets until DuLac's studio was before him.

The windows were dark. Nothing seemed to have changed. Spur slipped to the back. The outline of a small door, painted a lighter hue of brown, showed faintly.

He opened his wallet and extracted the three master keys he'd received, compliments of the Secret Service. They were designed to open nearly every type of lock made and hadn't failed him yet.

The first one did it. Spur smiled and opened the door.

He banged his shins on something. He silently cursed and lit a match. The thin light showed that he'd entered a bedroom. He crossed it and went through another door into the studio itself.

Three easels were stacked like lumber against one wall. The match illuminated piles of canvases and stained boxes filled with tubes of paint. The flame singed his fingertips. He shook it out and lit another.

Spur moved silently through the large room. It was common knowledge that DuLac had left town so he couldn't risk lighting a lamp.

What was he looking for? Something. Anything that might pin the counterfeit money on the artist. It was all he had to go on so far.

Spur pushed into the studio, carefully avoiding the canvasses, the heavy furniture, the tables and chairs that littered the building like a maze.

He stopped to look at the painting that stood on a large easel, and was impressed by what he saw. DuLac was an accomplished artist despite Emily Curtis's harsh words. The half-finished bust showed wonderful talent.

It took him several seconds to realize that he recognized the woman. He bent toward it. It was

Clare Maxwell all right—from the waist up.

He buried the memories of their recent time together and turned from the painting. If I was a counterfeiter, McCoy thought, where would I hide the goods?

His boot came down on something that skittered across the floor. Spur bent, lowered the match and peered at it. Just a paintbrush.

It rested against the edge of a small rug that partly covered a dark stain on the floor. Spur shrugged, rose and put out the match before it burned him again.

He lit another and started to continue his search. For some reason, he returned to the spot, squatted and took a closer look.

He nudged the small rectangle of fabric away from the darkened area of the floorboards. The match didn't afford him much light so he held it directly against the stain, shielded his eyes from its glare and studied the spot.

The longer he looked, the more certain he was. The color was right. The reddish-brown stain wasn't paint—it was blood. Not more than a few days old.

Spur heard a cough as someone walked into the bedroom.

CHAPTER SIXTEEN

Spur dropped the match, suffocated it under his boot toe and silently walked to the front door. The unseen intruder moved into the studio.

"Alain! Are you in here? Why'd you leave the back door open?"

It was a woman.

"You always were touched in the head." She turned up the flame on a lamp. It revealed a pretty, very young woman wrapped in an overcoat. "You're not Alain!" Her eyes widened.

"No." Spur relaxed. "Who are you?"

"Rebecca Ledet. I used to live here." She looked around the studio. "You didn't do anything to Alain, did you?"

"No. I just got here. DuLac's out of town, from what I hear."

Rebecca shrugged. "Oh well, it's no business of

mine." She walked toward the bedroom. "I have to pick up a few things I left here the other day."

Spur followed the young woman. "You were DuLac's girlfriend?"

"Yes. What about it?" She turned up another flame and walked to the chest of drawers.

"You seem a little young."

Rebecca laughed and pulled open a drawer. "Young? Mister, I ain't been young since I was twelve—if you get my meaning." The girl rummaged through the drawer. "I know I left it here! It's my best."

"Did you know him long?"

"Who?" she asked with a sharp voice.

"Alain. Your last lover?"

"Long enough." Rebecca smiled and picked up a lacy petticoat. "Doesn't it just figure? Hidden beneath his long underwear. He always got mine mixed up with his." She folded the garment and looked at Spur. "You still haven't told me what you're doing here."

"No, I haven't." He leveled his gaze at the girl. Her face, free of makeup, was lovely.

"If you're planning to rob the place you'll be vastly disappointed." She smiled at her joke.

"That wasn't what I had in mind at all, but why say that? Alain DuLac is a fairly well known artist. I saw one of his paintings in the museum."

Rebecca's smile broadened. "That's called advertising. Alain figured it was worth the ten bucks it cost to have them hang one of his pieces of trash there. Don't you know anything about art?" She brightly blinked. "What else was I looking for? Oh, yes."

The girl knelt beside the bed, reached under the

quilts and tugged out a metal box. She flipped it open to reveal a mass of tangled chains, military medals, yellowing documents and a small leaden souvenir piece in the shape of Notre Dame. "I hate being back here, you know?" the girl asked him as she searched. "Even though he's not around I just hate it. Too many bad memories."

"You don't like him very much, I take it." Spur sat on the bed and stared down at her bonnet.

"I despise him!"

Maybe he could use it to his advantage. "I understand you helped Alain sometimes."

The girl grew still. She looked up at him. "What are you trying to say?"

"Did you?"

"You mean help him with love? Yeah, but he helped himself to that most of the time. That was just business between him and me."

"No, not that." Spur paused. "Come on."

Rebecca shook her head. "I don't know what you're talking about, mister." She continued pawing through DuLac's box of junk and memories. "Where is it? I know I put it in here for safe-keeping."

"Some boys down at Beacham's said you cleaned up after DuLac. I gathered they weren't talking about washing the supper dishes."

"Oh that," she said in a bored smile. "So?"

"Why don't you tell me about it, Miss Ledet? If that really is your last name."

She tilted her chin. "I'm of French extraction."

"Yeah, and I'm U.S. Grant! Don't change the subject, girl! What do you know about Alain DuLac?"

She sniffed. "You a policeman?"

Spur shook his head.

"Well, then . . . ah!" She lifted a glittering golden chain. A huge pendant, encrusted with rubies and diamonds, hung from it. "I got it!"

He tried a different approach. "What do you know about that stain out in the studio?"

"Oh, I don't know. Just a mess Alain made a few days back." She kissed the jewel, unfastened its clasp and hung it around her neck.

"You didn't do a very good job of cleaning it up," he observed.

Rebecca slipped the diadem into her dress.

Spur leaned toward the girl. "It's hard to get blood stains out when they have time to set."

"What makes you think I had anything to do with that?" She started to rise.

Spur grabbed her wrists and hauled her to her feet before him. "Look, girlie, I'm tired of this! Start answering questions."

"Get your filthy paws offa me!"

Rebecca struggled but she was no match for the brawny man. She gasped and twisted away from him, their arms interlaced over her head.

"Not until you cooperate!"

"Alright. Okay! Just let me go."

He released her. Rebecca Ledet stumbled away from him and rubbed her wrists.

"You sure don't know how to treat a lady."

"Show me one and I'll treat her. Come on. Who did he kill? And why?"

Rebecca shrank away from him. She started to speak, smiled and screamed shrilly.

A burly man raced into the room. "You let her alone!" the big-nosed thug said as he lunged at Spur.

He tried to side-step the man but a hand clasped his waist. Spur tumbled to the floor with him. He pounded his fist into the man's jaw once, twice, smashing it, sending him reeling back.

McCoy pushed the man off him, stood and drew his Colt. 45. A foot jabbed between his ankles and tangled up his legs. Before he could recover he was down again.

"Yeah, get him good, Ernie!" Rebecca shouted. "Kill the bastard!"

Spur's weapon slid across the wood. Furious, he laid a punch to the man's gut. The thug groaned and jabbed at Spur's face. A quick movement later and McCoy heard the satisfying crunch of the man's knuckles smashing into the floor.

He rolled out from under the man and looked around the room. Where was his revolver? Nowhere in sight. He glanced at Rebecca.

She smiled. "I'll never tell!"

Cursing, Spur stomped the kneeling man's chest, punching his torso backward. "I don't like the friends you keep," he said, shooting her a harsh look.

She crossed her arms. "Well, I don't like you. So we're even."

Blood oozed from Ernie's chin as he lumbered up. This was getting boring, Spur thought. The man ripped a long-bladed knife from his back pocket and slashed it through the air, daring Spur to come closer.

"Who's the big man now?" he said, and winced with pain.

The assailant slowly advanced on Spur, stalking, grinning. Spit oozed from his lips, turned pink on his chin and dripped onto the floor.

"Easy, easy boy. Don't wanna get that nice knife of yours all dirty, do you?" Spur asked.

"It'd be worth it," Ernie said.

Spur walked backwards. "Yeah. I'm sure Rebecca would clean it up for you." He bumped into something. A canvas crashed down. Spur moved past it and saw the glint of steel on the edge of the easel.

"Damnit!" Rebecca shouted.

Ernie's smile faded as Spur gripped the knife and swung it up. "Try it. Just try it!"

The big man spat. His face tensed. Spur ducked before the blade was out of Ernie's hand and heard it sailing over his head. The knife glanced off the rear wall.

Spur smiled as he rose. "You got a chance to make, Ernie. Die or get your ass outa here!"

"Damn you!"

"Is that trash wearing a dress worth it, Ernie? Are you really willing to give up your miserable life for that piece of filly meat?"

"Don't you call me that!" Rebecca said.

"Shut up, bitch!" he threw over his shoulder. "Your decision, Ernie. Your move."

He hesitated. His dumb face came alive—eyelids twitching, brows rising and falling, lips tightening into two white lines. He wiped the blood and drool from his chin and looked around the room.

The girl gasped. "Ernie, come on! Kill him!"

He stared at her. "I don't need you. Jesus, he's right! You're not worth it." The big man turned and walked out of the room.

"Come back and you'll get this buried in your chest!" Spur hurled the knife. Its blade dug into the wall and vibrated with a dull metallic sound.

"Well. You can't trust anyone!"

Spur strode over to the girl and shook her shoulders. "Talk. Now! Or I'll have you thrown in jail. Accessory to attempted murder."

Rebecca looked at him with dull eyes.

"You know what it's like in women's jails? Let me give you an idea. Four-hundred pound female guards with beards rule the roost. You'll be lapping between their legs on your first night!"

She recoiled from him. "Never!"

"Hey, after a coupla years, you'll get used to it."

"I'm only a little girl!" Rebecca shouted.

"Not since you were twelve."

She dropped her head.

"That's better. You have any more friends waiting outside for you to call them?"

Rebecca shook her head.

"Good. We're going to my place. And if you don't talk I'll drop you off at the police station. Come on!"

Rebecca didn't give him any trouble as they walked to the Riverside Hotel. After a few minutes she even started humming.

"What are you so happy about?" he asked, gripping her waist tighter to keep her from running off.

"I'm finally going to get back at Alain. If you can promise me I won't get into any trouble—"

"No promises," he said.

"Well, it's worth the risk. But I won't tell you here. How much farther is it? These shoes are killing my feet!"

"That's surprising. I figured you'd be used to walking the streets."

"Very funny."

She didn't give him any trouble on the way. Once inside his room, the door locked, the curtains drawn, Spur sat the girl in a chair.

"Okay!" Rebecca said. "So he killed a couple of men."

"How many?"

"I don't know. Two—three. Something like that. Maybe even four."

"How could you forget?"

"Wouldn't you try to forget about it?" She sighed. "I had some friends of mine—including Ernie—get rid of the bodies. Think they dumped them in the river."

That explains that, Spur thought, remembering his first visit with Commissioner Golden. "Why did he kill those men, Rebecca?"

"Oh, I don't know." She pushed a foot under her skirts and scratched her left ankle.

"What?"

She sighed. "Alain wasn't doing very well selling his paintings."

"Why did he kill them?"

The edge to Spur's voice made her sharply glance up at him.

"Tell me!"

Rebeccca fidgeted in the chair. She started to rise but Spur forced her back in her seat.

"So, because he wasn't making very much money with his artwork, he decided to go into a different business on the side."

"Counterfeiting?"

Rebecca looked up at him in surprise.

CHAPTER SEVENTEEN

"Counterfeiting? Heavens, what makes you say that?" Rebecca asked.

"It seems DuLac passed a phony twenty dollar bill to a friend of mine who did some modeling for him. I'm checking it out."

"So?" She shook her head. "That doesn't prove anything. Alain's so dumb he wouldn't know real money from the counterfeit stuff."

Spur just looked at the girl.

"But he thought he was smart enough to kill men for their wallets. That was his source of extra income." She faintly smiled. "Making fake money—that's beyond Alain's imagination. Or his talent."

Spur measured her. The girl sat comfortably on the chair, her face poised. Her breathing was regular and slow. Hell, he thought, she was such a cold turkey there's no way he could know if she was telling the truth. Her years on the street had taught her much.

"Look, I'm an agent of the federal government."

"So?" She glanced around the room, seemingly bored with the whole thing.

"Secret Service. I have the power to arrest and to kill in the line of duty. I'm here in town investigating the counterfeit money that's popping up all over Portland."

"Look, mister, I answered your stupid question. When are you gonna let me go?"

"What made Alain DuLac kill those men?"

"I told you," she said, her voice sharp. "He just wanted their money."

"What could drive him to kill for money?"

Rebecca shrugged. "I don't know. The man's crazy! He's out of his mind. All he ever talks about is Paris and how much he wants to go back there. I wouldn't mind going there to spit on his dead wife's grave. " She bit her lip. "That's all he used to talk about when I was still staying with him—Paris."

"So you didn't leave him out of shock when bodies started piling up in his studio. You left because you didn't like having to call your friends—like that perfect gentleman, Ernie—to dispose of the bodies. Right?"

Rebecca Ledet turned to him. "Mister, when you've been as down as I have for as long as I have, nothing shocks you anymore." Her face hardened. "I've sold myself more times than I can think. Smoked enough opium to put under ten Chinese men. I've lifted men's wallets to eat. I'm not happy with the way I've lived, but I'm still alive. When

Alain started killing every man who walked in here for who-knows-what-crazy-reason, I figured it was time to leave. So I did.''

She wasn't a little girl. Rebecca looked years older than her tender age. As she sat silently before him Spur saw the lines creasing the corners of her eyes, the sad, worldly expression contorting her otherwise youthful face. Her hands were cracked and dry, her painted fingernails broken.

"Any more questions?'' she asked.

He thought it over. Whether she knew anything or not, that was all he'd get from her. Might as well wait for the source, the man himself to return to town. Then he'd get at the bottom of this.

"You're quite a young woman, Rebecca—and I don't mean that as a compliment.''

"I know, I know.''

"Okay, Rebecca. Get back to whatever hole you crawled out of. But if you lied to me, sister, you will be behind bars. Got that?''

"Yeah,'' she said, tiredly nodding her head. "I got it.''

Alain DuLac halted his carriage before the non-descript warehouse near the wharf. It was night-time, as usual. He didn't risk going there during broad daylight. He didn't wish to be connected with it just in case someone stumbled onto what he was doing there.

He tied up the horse's reins behind the building, unlocked the door and went inside. He'd been surprised how easy it had been to rent the space from a man who didn't ask questions and didn't want to answer any. DuLac simply paid his rent on time and that was that.

Now he lit the lanterns hanging along the far wall. The windowless building wouldn't reveal his presence inside. The artist ripped the dusty canvas off the printing press and calmly folded it up. Beside the press lay wooden crates. He smiled as he thought of how he'd secreted the counterfeit bills in the bottom of the crates so that they wouldn't be easily found. He'd been so careful, so very careful.

But things weren't working out like he'd planned. His short trip to Astoria had been disastrous. As hard as he tried, with as many connections as he had, he couldn't sell any of his counterfeit money. A few of the bills had shown up in Astoria and the alert was on. No one was buying.

It was time to shut down his operation in Portland, to move it somewhere else where he could unload as many of them in as quick a time as possible. A large city with lots of eager buyers.

San Francisco!

Now that Rebecca had left him there was no reason for him to stay in Portland. And maybe, in that art-conscious city, he'd sell his paintings faster than he had in the town on the Williamette River.

DuLac knelt on the cold floor and, with a prybar, opened a crate marked 'Made In Formosa'. He grabbed up the rubber-faced dolls and threw them behind him, quickly revealing the false bottom of the crate. He pulled up the thin piece of wood.

There they were. Neatly wrapped thousand-dollar stacks of counterfeit twenty-dollar bills. This crate alone—of the seven he had stashed in the warehouse—held $20,000. In the fresh market he should be able to turn it over for two of three thousand dollars. Alain DuLac smiled as he thought of his fortune there—soon he'd be $15,000 richer.

The image of Rebecca's face rose up before him, taunting him. DuLac stuffed the extra bills he hadn't sold in Astoria into the crate and refilled it with the dolls. He wouldn't be stupid enough to give his real money to some big-titted tramp again. No woman would get under his skin, would take control of him the way Rebecca had.

No more seventeen year-old girls with expensive tastes and exquisite bodies!

On his third consecutive night watching Alain DuLac's studio, Spur shrank back into the shadows as a drunken sailor and a woman waltzed by him on shaky feet, her giggles and his lewd comments slurred with the effects of too much alcohol.

DuLac hadn't returned home. After his night with the artist's ex-girlfriend Spur had thoroughly searched the man's studio but had found nothing— no counterfeit money, no plates, no printing press— to connect him with the scheme. He couldn't even find engravings of any kind.

Something about the way the girl had looked at him when he'd mentioned counterfeiting to her in his hotel room stuck in his mind. Though she hadn't told him anything he had this gut feeling. Spur followed it, sleeping during the day, staying up all night, waiting for the man to return.

Now, as a skinny dog padded by sniffing for food on the ground, Spur sighed and fingered his revolver. The tiny beast halted, pricked up its ears and barked at some imaginary enemy before scurrying out of sight.

A carriage approached. Its driver halted the four-wheel buggy before duLac's studio. The man's features were subdued by the thin moonlight but it certainly could be the artist, Spur thought.

The driver stepped onto the ground, brushed his hands on his thighs and walked to the studio's front door.

Spur slipped across the road and hid behind the carriage. He heard the squeak of the knob and the studio's door swinging open. McCoy moved past the horse and looked. The man was entering the studio. The agent raced across the ground and stepped onto the porch as the door closed.

Before the man could lock it, Spur forced open the door and walked in, pushing the astounded man to the floor.

"DuLac?" he asked.

"Ah, yes. I am Alain DuLac."

The room was even darker than it was outside, but Spur saw the thin outlines of the man sitting on his butt, staring up at him, the key still extended in his right hand.

"Where you been? Out on a little trip?" He snarled down at him.

"I do not have to tell you anything!" DuLac picked himself from the floor. He strode to the closest lamp and brightened its flame. "Who are you?"

Spur smirked as the light revealed the short, pudgy man. He drew his weapon and trained it on the artist's chest. "Come on, DuLac. Where's the counterfeit money?"

"What are you talking about?" he protested, unbuttoning his coat. "I am just returned from an exhausting trip and you accuse me of—"

"Ernie said I could get some from you."

DuLac froze. "Ernie?"

He'd caught the man off-guard. Good. "Yeah.

Ernie's a good friend of mine. Said you were an ornery bastard but that you had some quality merchandise."

DuLac shook his head. "If you come here to buy you do not show your weapon!"

McCoy laughed. "Ernie also told me how dangerous you are—how you don't mind stabbing your potential customers in the back."

The artist stiffened. "Ernie would not say that! Not about me!"

"He did—he even took me here to find you, but you were gone."

"Yes. I have business trip to Astoria."

"Forget all that. I want to buy. I wanna buy a lot. Where is it?"

"Do not rush me!" DuLac hissed. "I am tired. Very tired. You come back in the morning. Okay?"

As DuLac glanced at his easel, Spur was happy he'd returned the room to its normal appearance after his altercation with the bull named Ernie.

"Why are you still here? Leave!"

"I'll buy all of it—every bill you have."

Greed gleamed in the short man's eyes. "You are serious? All?"

Spur nodded.

He broke out into a sweat. "Well, I guess I could—" DuLac shook his head. "No. Come back tomorrow."

"Now! I'll give you cash money, DuLac." He patted his coat pocket with his left hand. "I have $5,000 waiting for you. You can't turn that down and you know it. And it's either tonight or you'll never see me again."

DuLac sweated. The breath blasted from between his lips. He thought it over, rubbing his chin, peering at McCoy.

"Well?" Spur demanded.

The man fidgeted with his coattails. "Okay. It is not here. You come with me."

"Sounds dandy to me."

They made a short carriage trip to the wharf. Spur wasn't surprised when the man led him to a small warehouse. It was perfect for that kind of operation—no direct, obvious connection with the counterfeiter. His idea to use Ernie's name had worked out fine. Now all he needed was the tangible, physical proof.

Like most criminals, DuLac couldn't turn down that much real money. His greed had overtaken his natural caution.

The immigrant artist let him into the building. As DuLac busily lit lanterns, Spur looked around the place. It smelled of mildew and dust, but fresh foot-prints marked someone's recent passage into the small warehouse. Canvas-covered objects littered the ground.

"Come on, DuLac! Stop stalling!" Spur said, snarling. "Where's the stuff?"

"Plenty of light. So you can see it."

McCoy grabbed his hand from the fourth lantern and jerked it away. "That's enough. Get it."

DuLac wrestled out of his fist. "Okay. Okay!"

Spur watched with interest as he ripped back a square of canvas. The man opened a wooden crate.

"Dolls?" he thundered. "You're trying to sell me cheap dolls?"

DuLac turned to him from where he knelt. "No. No! Wait a minute."

He emptied the crate and removed a false bottom. The artist produced a small paper-wrapped package and handed it to Spur. "Check the quality."

McCoy grunted and ripped off the covering. Inside it lay the counterfeit money. Crisp twenty-dollar bills. That was it. He had him.

"You make this stuff yourself?"

"Yes. Very good work, no?" The artist smiled up at him from the crate.

Spur nodded. "Not bad. I've seen better. Back in Chicago. By a man who used to work for the government. He's molding in a grave by now, six feet under." He felt the bill.

DuLac drummed his fingers on the wooden box, impatient. "You've looked long enough," he said. "It is fine. Pay me the agreed price."

McCoy snapped his fingers. "Sorry, DuLac. I just remembered something. I forgot to go the bank today."

The artist rose. "What did you say?"

"I don't have a dime on me."

Alain DuLac shook with fury. The soft lantern light showed the red that boiled up in his face. "You lie to me! You say you have money! Five-thousand dollars!"

"Hey, anyone can make a mistake."

Mistake!"

Spur smiled at the raging man. "I'll see you in the morning." He turned and looked over his shoulder.

DuLac scrambled across the warehouse floor. He reached under a piece of canvas.

"What's wrong, DuLac?"

"You die!" He hefted the revolver and fired.

CHAPTER EIGHTEEN

The lantern behind him exploded. Spur's shoulder hit the stone floor. He rolled as flaming drops of liquid and glass shards rained onto him from the bullet-ridden lamp.

"I kill you!" DuLac screamed.

McCoy came to a stop on his back. The small blaze that ignited in his crotch shocked him into action. He flipped over, smothered the kerosene-fueled fire against the floor, cursed and moved behind the heavy, canvas-covered object that had halted his dive to safety.

The artist stood in the middle of the warehouse, his weapon drawn, searching the shadows for his target.

Spur peeled off a shot. Expertly aimed, the bullet pierced the string attaching the lamp to the ceiling. The force of the lantern's impact as it hit the floor caused a spectacular explosion which consumed every drop of fuel. The fire burned itself out.

The light was much dimmer now. Good. Just the way Spur liked it.

"Where are you? Show yourself!" the artist raged.

He grinned. "It's over, DuLac. Drop your weapon or you're a dead man."

The immigrant wildly fired a second shot and scurried behind a stack of crates. "No. Not until you pay me!"

"You don't understand, do you? But then you're not from around here. I'm not buying your counterfeit money—I'm confiscating it for the U.S. Government."

Silence.

"Rebecca told me all about it, how you started printing cash instead of painting."

Spur heard the sharp intake of breath from across the room.

"No! That bitch!"

"We had a long talk last night—me and your girl." McCoy settled into his squat. "Hey, tell me something, DuLac. Is it true that your dick's only an inch long rock hard?"

The artist spluttered.

"Come on, DuLac. You can tell me. Just between us guys."

Feet scurried. He caught a glimpse of the man moving between two huge crates. The guy was trying to circle around behind him.

Two could play the game. Spur silently crossed the warehouse floor and slipped into DuLac's original position, crouching behind the crates.

Gunfire revealed the man's whereabouts.

"You moved!" the artist wailed.

"Ah, gee, I'm sorry about that, dickless!"

"You are a bastard!"

"And you're a criminal. You're also under arrest. Throw out your weapon. Now, DuLac!"

He roared and pounded four consecutive shots into the ceiling. A thick column of red brick dust poured down from it.

That's one way of using up your ammunition, Spur thought. "Come on. The game's over."

"No. No!"

DuLac moved too fast for Spur to properly target. He disappeared behind the huge object draped with canvas. The covering fluttered in the thin light.

"You're out of tricks, DuLac!" he yelled.

Two knives flashed toward him. Spur ducked as they slammed into the crate.

Shit! He had to admit the man was well prepared. Most criminals were.

McCoy shifted his position and peered around the blade-studded wooden box. DuLac wasn't in sight. He darted over to the next set of crates.

The canvas moved again. The artist must be searching for something.

"Why is that you men with little pricks won't give up, DuLac?"

"Shut your mouth!"

Their voices echoed in the warehouse.

More rustling.

What would it be this time now? A cannon? Spur smiled at the absurd thought until he saw the glow of a match.

No. The artist wasn't that prepared!

But he was unwilling to take the chance. Spur used the man's earlier trick. Crouching, he powered around the perimeter of the building, reaching the far wall and halted. DuLac wasn't in sight. McCoy snapped his eyes toward the door. Not there either.

Under the canvas? Yes. He'd probably lit the match for light.

Spur took a deep breath and walked up to it. "That's it, DuLac. Come on out."

A three-foot sword pierced the heavy material and jabbed at Spur's arm. It slashed back and forth, ripping the canvas. The artist blasted out agonized grunts.

"You could hurt someone with that thing."

"Damn you!"

"Trapped in your den like a wounded bear." Spur shook his head and stepped back.

The sword disappeared.

A tomahawk spun out of the huge tear and whirled inches from his head.

"Alright. I'll make you come out!"

The man was getting to him. McCoy was tired of him, tired of Portland, tired of the assignment. He stepped behind the huge object, away from the hole. The canvas draped out onto the floor all around it. What the hell was it covering?

Spur touched it with his left hand. The hard surface under the material seemed to be metal. An upright of some kind. He followed it down. It broadened into a flat surface.

It sure was heavy, he thought, as he pressed against it. The object barely moved. Then he knew.

Alain DuLac sprang from his canvas cave. He cut off·his howl of delight—and removed his finger from the trigger—when he realized Spur wasn't in sight.

"Where are you?" he wailed.

Why not, he thought? It would do the job. DuLac stared stupidly away from him. Spur increased the pressure on the object, transferring its weight. It tilted.

The artist heard it and turned. "There you are!"

Spur groaned with the effort.

The Winchester's barrels went up.

The metal printing press tipped. Alain DuLac screamed as it toppled over. The tremendous weight pulverized him, smashing his body into a worthless pile of broken bones, flesh and tissue, crushing out his life.

The floor shook beneath Spur's boots for a second.

A gurgle. A sickening sigh. Then nothing.

Alain DuLac was dead.

Thomas Golden shook his head. "Not a pretty sight." He mopped his forehead with a handkerchief, stepped away from DuLac's lifeless body and looked at Spur.

"No, but don't complain. You won't find any more counterfeit money in your town."

The warehouse blazed with light. Policemen poked around. Some counted the money. Others were uncovering the astounding arsenal of weapons that the man had deposited throughout the small, mostly empty building.

The police commissioner shrugged. "I have to admit, I didn't think you had it in you, McCoy."

"Thanks for your vote of confidence in me, Golden."

"Hey, look this whole thing's been crawling up the back of my neck for weeks now. I wasn't thinking straight. Got all puffed up on myself."

"Guess so. Have your men crate up that counterfeit money. It's taking a train trip with me to Washington, D.C. The plates, too."

"Sure, sure, McCoy." He turned to chat with an officer.

Spur rubbed his neck. He was tired. DuLac's guts were starting to stink. "Get those men to move their asses, Golden!" he yelled.

The police commissioner smirked, stepped back and held out his hand. "After all, you're the highest authority here."

McCoy sighed. "Alright, you men! Move it! Get that money into those crates!" He walked among the uniformed officers who looked stonily at him.

"What the hell do you think this city's paying you for!" Spur bellowed. "Loafing? Hell no! I want those plates and every last bill of that counterfeit money at my feet in one minute! Move it!" The men hesitated, glanced at Golden and scrambled to fulfill Spur's order.

"Hey, not bad," the police commissioner said. "You ever thought about retiring from the Secret Service? This town could use a man like you."

Spur shook his head and walked into the sunlight.

"So I couldn't have done it without you, Clare."

Fresh from a bath and a shave, dressed in clean clothing, Spur felt like a new man. He sat in the restaurant across from the prettiest woman in San Francisco.

Clare pushed her hand onto his. "I'm flattered, but I didn't do anything!"

He gripped it. "Yes you did."

"Well, you did that too."

Spur smiled at her off-color joke. "Anyway, I'll

be leaving in an hour."

She sighed. "Sure. I know the kind. Love 'em and leave 'em. You men are all the same."

Then she smiled at him, the same smile he'd seen on DuLac's portrait. The smile of a confident, self-assured woman.

"Keep that up and you'll go far in this man's world, Clare Maxwell."

She tilted her chin. "Keep what up?"

"That. What you're doing just now." He squeezed her gloved hand.

Clare shook her head. "I've never been able to figure out what goes on in men's brains."

The waiter set two glasses of wine on the table.

"I take it you won't be posing anymore?" Spur asked after the man walked away.

Clare laughed. "I doubt it. That was my first and last adventure in that area. But I've been thinking. I'm already a fallen woman." She snickered. "So why don't I go all the way?"

"Now Clare, you don't have to do that! You've got so much going for you—you're intelligent, you're resourceful—"

"Honestly, Spur! Why are you always thinking I'm going to whoredom?"

Several other diners glanced their way. The noise level in the restaurant dropped considerably.

Clare smiled and lowered her voice. "No, no. I fooled people into thinking I was an old woman."

"Don't remind me."

She winced. "Sorry. Anyway, I heard about a theatre they have here. There's a new play opening up in a month."

"So?"

"So, I'm going to be an actress!" She lifted her

chin and gazed at the ceiling. The reflections of countless crystal lamps dazzled her eyes. "A great actress. I'll play the best female roles."

He touched her wrist, staring at her unbelievable beauty. "If anyone could do it, you could, Clare."

She lowered her eyes to his. "And I owe everything to you. My future's stretching in front of me like an empty stage. You've finally given me something to put on it!"

She bent toward him, kissed his cheek, moved back and raised her glass. "Know any good toasts, Spur?" Clare blinked her brimming eyes.

He nodded and clinked his goblet with hers. "To . . . art. Real art, not the counterfeit kind. May its world—the whole world—sing your praises, lovely lady."

They drank.